KILL ZONE

A TOM ROLLINS THRILLER

PAUL HEATLEY

INKUBATOR
BOOKS

Published by Inkubator Books
www.inkubatorbooks.com

Copyright © 2025 by Paul Heatley

Paul Heatley has asserted his right to be identified as the author of this work.

ISBN (eBook): 978-1-83756-620-4
ISBN (Paperback): 978-1-83756-621-1

KILL ZONE is a work of fiction. People, places, events, and situations are the product of the author's imagination. Any resemblance to actual persons, living or dead is entirely coincidental.

No part of this book may be reproduced, stored in any retrieval system, or transmitted by any means without the prior written permission of the publisher.

For Aidan

are not. It's a bright day, summer, and people are out enjoying it. No doubt many of them are heading to the beach that isn't far behind him.

Tom watches the people and the vehicles. Watches out for repeating faces, and license plates. There are people out there looking for him, he knows. People unknown to him. He's spotted a few of them. Three teams of two, walking up and down the block. The teams never acknowledge each other. There's also a minivan. It's supposed to be inconspicuous with its ichthys – Christian fish – and family stickers on the rear window, and its Virginia plates, but there's no family in the vehicle. Only the driver, and he's mid- to late-twenties. Fair enough, it's a weekday, the kids could be at school and the wife could be at work, but Tom still doesn't trust it. He trusts the way it circles the block, slowly, even less. The driver is careful in the way he searches; he doesn't turn his head and inspect every face on the sidewalk, but Tom has no doubt that behind his shades his eyes are regularly cutting left and right.

The people patrolling, looking for him, they're no doubt wearing earpieces. They'll have radios, too; tiny microphones pinned to the wrists of their jackets. They haven't used them yet. It's important for them to keep a low profile. They haven't seen anything so far that would necessitate them communicating with each other. They haven't seen any sign of him. Not yet.

They will soon.

Opposite Tom, there's a pizza place. Over the road from it is another hotel. The Atlantic Hotel. Its vacancy sign is lit up, above the store at its side selling T-shirts and other tourist-amenable goods. Directly in front of the store, next to the crosswalk, there is a trash can. Inside the trash can there

CHAPTER ONE

Tom Rollins is twenty-six years old. So far in his young life, he's been overseas; he's gone to war; he's been in pitched battles and minor skirmishes. He's saved lives, and he's taken lives. But that was all when he was in the Army.

He's not in the Army anymore. And if he fails today, he's not sure what comes next for him. Where he'll go. What he'll do.

And so, failure is not an option.

He's in Virginia Beach, but he's not here to enjoy the weather, despite the cloudless skies and the rising heat of the day. The sea is close. He can smell its salt faintly in the air. If the road wasn't so busy he'd probably be able to hear its waves, too, lapping at the shore.

Tom stands in the shadows, watching, waiting. There's a chill in the shade, without his jacket. He's in the open-air parking garage of the Fairfield Inn, pressed against a wall and concealing himself behind a bush. He glances over his shoulder, watching out for movement in the lot, but it's quiet. The road and the street outside of the Inn, however, is something Tom needs. The men on patrol are going to do their best to keep it from him.

Tom waits. He checks the time. Just two more minutes.

While he waits, he continues to watch. Tom has been in training for more than a year now. He's been trained for the field. He's been shown how to perform dead drops. How to gather information.

How to torture.

He's going to get his hands dirty, he knows. The Army made him into a weapon, and the Company has honed him. Sharpened him. And they're soon to direct him, like a bullet, or a missile. He's going to get his hands dirtier than they've ever been before, but he knew that's what he'd be signing up for when the CIA first approached.

"We were impressed by your actions in the field," Jack Reynolds told him. This was soon after he'd saved Adam Lineker and Lorne Henkel and carried them to safety from behind enemy lines. There'd been talk of a medal for him, not that Tom had much interest in anything like that. He hadn't done it for the glory. Regardless, talk of medals fell silent when Reynolds made his presence known. "We think we could put your skills to better use."

Reynolds could be somewhere nearby right now, observing. Checking in on his recruit.

Today, Tom isn't making a dead drop. He's intercepting one. And the plan is to do so without being picked up by any of the people out looking for him.

He's checked the rooftops and the windows of the buildings nearby. They're clear, so far as he can see, but there are so many hotels on this block it's hard to be sure. Anyone could have booked a room with a clear view of the trash can.

Tom watches the civilians. Sees men and women dressed

for the hot weather in shorts and tank tops, and in swimwear. He sees how they laugh while they walk, their spirits buoyed by the warmth. They have no idea what's happening so close to them. All they're thinking about is the sun, the sand, and the sea.

The two minutes have passed. Nothing happens. Tom allowed for this. He can't expect his new friend to be punctual.

There have not been any homeless people passing by. On a busy day like today, the cops are regularly patrolling, watching out for anyone who might be begging or panhandling. Anyone who might be hassling the tourists and the locals. They want to keep the area looking clean and vibrant. They want to keep the visitors comfortable.

They're not hard to find, though. Tom spotted an encampment earlier, off the boulevard, while he was checking the area out in the early hours, familiarizing himself with its layout. He's been here a long time. He saw the dead drop happen – a man in a suit who furtively glanced up and down the road before he dropped something wrapped in a newspaper into the trash, along with an empty coffee cup and the last few bites of a pastry. The trash can has filled up since then, but today isn't a collection day. Tom checked the schedule. Because of this, he can afford to be patient.

A homeless man comes into view from the direction of the beach. He waits at the crosswalk. He wears dirty, tattered jeans, and boots that are scuffed from days spent dragging himself through the city. Despite the heat, he also wears an overcoat a couple of sizes too big. This is as tattered as his jeans. Under the overcoat he wears a different, newer, cleaner jacket. Tom's jacket. The overcoat is open. Tom's jacket is exposed.

The homeless man, whose name is Jimmy, has short hair and a clean-shaven face. He wears a baseball cap pulled low to cover his features – this item is the most recently purchased on his person. The haircut and shave, too, were paid for courtesy of Tom. Prior to this, he had long hair and a beard, both matted and coated with a sprinkling of sand.

What happens next will go one of two ways. Jimmy will either rummage undisturbed through the trash can, find the newspaper, and bring it to Tom at their prearranged location. Or else, and more likely, the men looking for Tom are going to swoop in.

Tom is expecting the latter.

The crosswalk changes to walk and Jimmy makes his way toward the trash can. He looks around, left and right, though he has no idea what, or whom, he's looking for. When he's satisfied that the way is clear – or at least clear enough – he starts rummaging in the trash.

Tom sees movement close to Jimmy. A couple of the teams that he recognizes by now have spotted him. They're on their radios, speaking into their sleeves. The minivan comes speeding up to the crossing. It screeches to a halt right next to the trash can. One of the team of two hurries forward and grabs Jimmy from behind. Jimmy is clutching tightly to something he's found in the trash. Tom told him to make sure he had something in his hand when and if they grabbed him, but to make sure to leave the newspaper behind.

Jimmy is bundled into the minivan, accompanied by a couple of the teams who have been patrolling on foot, and the minivan speeds off. One team stays behind. The two men raise their arms to the concerned onlookers and indicate that everything is okay. They flash badges. Tom can't see what the badges show from where he is, and he wonders if local police have been brought in to help out.

When the remaining team are satisfied that the area is calm, that people are buying what they've said, they hurry around the corner, to where their own vehicle has been parked.

Tom waits. He continues to watch. He sees the two men in their car now, coming from around the corner, driving down the road in pursuit of the minivan.

Tom looks around. He doesn't see any familiar unfamiliar faces. This is his window. He doesn't have long. He leaves his hiding spot in the parking lot, hopping over the wall and making his way to the crosswalk and then to the trash can. He reaches down into the bottom of it, sifting through the trash that has been dumped on top of the newspaper since he first saw it deposited. He's kept an estimate in his head of how deep it'll be, but an estimate is nothing compared to the stark reality. He has to go deeper.

Eventually, he finds the newspaper and the object it's wrapped around. He pulls it from the trash can, wiping mustard off it on the side of the can. He opens the newspaper. Inside is a hard drive. He dumps the newspaper and pockets the hard drive, then crosses the road to the pizza place. He has a promise to keep.

While he waits for the pizza to bake, he keeps an eye outside, on the corner. It doesn't take long for the minivan to return. It pulls up to the side of the Atlantic Hotel. Soon after, the car with the team of two parks behind it. He can see the men inside both vehicles. None of them looks happy. One of them gets out of the minivan and hurries over to the trash can. He starts rummaging inside it. He spends a few minutes searching, and Tom can see from his body language how he's getting frustrated and desperate. Finally, he rises, slamming a hand on the rim of the trash can. Defeated, he returns to the minivan, wiping his hands on his jeans.

Jimmy is with them. They push him out of the minivan, but they don't let him go. They keep hold of his arm. Tom can see the way Jimmy grins. He was looking forward to getting one over on the hunters.

"Order up!"

Tom takes the pizza. Plain cheese. Tom had asked him, "You sure you don't want anything else? No meat? No vegetables?"

"Just plain, man," Jimmy said. "I like it plain."

Tom leaves the pizza place and crosses the road, holding the box in both hands. He stops at the back of the minivan and looks left and right. "Jesus," he says. "You guys look *pissed*."

The men spin on him, angry and annoyed, ready to dismiss him, but then they realize who he is.

"Son of a *bitch*," one of them says. "You got it?"

Tom pats his pocket, then hands the pizza to Jimmy. "You can let him go now," he says.

The man holding Jimmy grumbles and avoids looking at Tom, but he does as he's told. Jimmy is still grinning as he takes the pizza. Tom hands him a twenty, too. "How long'd it take them?" he asks.

"We got a few blocks thataway," Jimmy says. He laughs. "They were all excited because they thought they caught you. They didn't even look at me. I just kept the cap pulled low and let them think what they wanted."

Tom smiles back.

"Oh, hey," Jimmy says. "You need your jacket back."

"Keep it," Tom says. He catches the eye of one of the men who were searching for him. They're still annoyed. Tom grins. "You earned it."

Jimmy leaves them, looking pleased with his pizza and his twenty, with his new jacket and his new baseball cap, not to mention his shave and his haircut. He makes his way back toward the beach.

One of the men watches him go and spits. "God*damnit*."

"I suppose we should say congratulations," the driver of the minivan says to Tom, leaning out of the window. "I just don't really feel like it right now. Reynolds is ready to see you. He said to hop in the back."

"I'd like to hear that from him," Tom says.

The driver pulls out his earpiece and hands it over. Tom listens.

"Test's over, Rollins," Reynolds says. "Well done. Now, get in the van."

CHAPTER TWO

Reynolds is in his early fifties. He doesn't do field work anymore. His primary job for the Agency is recruitment and training. Despite this, he keeps himself firm. It's clear that although there's a little softening in his midsection, he still regularly hits the gym. His hair is still mostly dark on top, some greying at the sides and back, and his face is clean-shaven.

Right now, he sits and appraises Tom from behind his desk. It was less than an hour drive back to Langley from Virginia Beach. Tom sits up straight in the chair, and he waits for Reynolds to speak first.

"That was quite a show you put on," he finally says.

"Is that a compliment, sir?"

Reynolds grins.

"I thought you would've been close to the site, sir," Tom says.

Reynolds smiles at this. "I like to think if I'd been out there, instead of just listening in, I would've seen through your little ruse."

"I guess we'll never know."

Reynolds pauses, regarding him in silence. He leans back in his chair and tents his fingers. "If that had been in the field, if those men looking for you had been enemy combatants, would you have put the life of a bystander in danger like that?"

Tom is sure there's probably a right answer to this question.

"You had the security of knowing there would be no guns," Reynolds says. "That this was effectively a glorified game of tag. But if you were in the field, and you were intercepting a terrorist communique, would you make the sacrifice?"

"Not of an American, sir," Tom says. And while he's sure this is the right answer, he has to follow through with the truth, too. "And I'm not sure I'd feel comfortable with anyone else, either. Not an *innocent* bystander, anyway."

One of Reynolds' eyebrows arches a little. "Then as a hypothetical, let's say we remove your homeless friend from today from the equation. Let's say that guns *had* been involved, and this was a life-or-death situation. What would you have done?"

"If they were patrolling the area of a dead drop, I'd know it was a trap and whatever had been dropped in the trash was likely worthless."

"Not everything is a test, Rollins," Reynolds says. "This is a hypothetical. It doesn't have to make complete sense. What would you have done?"

"Well, I'd made the teams, and the minivan. I'm confident I would have been able to evade them without the use of a distraction."

Reynolds grunts. "Very well. But time won't always be

on your side. Sometime you might have to make a call like you did today, bring a bystander into the equation, and you'll have to decide if they can eat a bullet instead of you. Do you think you can do that?"

Tom looks straight back at Reynolds. They hold eyes. Reynolds said not everything is a test, but this certainly feels like one. "Yes," Tom says. "I can do that. If I have to. If it's that important."

Reynolds nods, just once. He's not smiling. It's unclear if he believes what Tom has said. "You've got promise, Rollins. You could go far. But do you know what concerns me?"

"Sir?"

"We live in a world of grey, and I think you see it a little too much in black and white. There's *us* and there's *them*, Rollins. That's the only black and white that exists. Everything else is grey."

Tom holds Reynolds' eyes. "I can assure you, sir, that all I see is grey."

"Mm." Reynolds watches him. "We've assigned you to a team," he says suddenly. "Captain Robert Dale will be your commanding officer going forward – and believe me, there's no one who sees the world for how it is more than him. You'll learn a lot under his guidance."

Tom blinks, taking in this tonal whiplash. "Yes, sir," he says.

Reynolds leans forward, pressing his hands flat on his desk like he's about to push himself up. "Do you want to go meet them?"

CHAPTER THREE

Tom walks with Reynolds through the building, following his lead toward the gym.

"I had confidence in you today, Rollins," Reynolds says. "That's why I called them in. They've been here a couple of hours now. I'm sure they're looking forward to meeting you."

Tom says nothing.

He's made it. He's part of the CIA, unofficially. Recruited to run black ops missions. To spend a lot of time behind enemy lines. To continue doing what he's good at – killing, and evading capture. Surviving in the wild. So far as anyone else is aware, he's still part of the military. Reynolds told him, during recruitment, that if he was successful, he wouldn't be able to talk with friends and family about what he's doing.

"You can tell immediate loved ones that you're part of the Agency," Reynolds said. "But you must never divulge the objectives of your missions. And believe me, Rollins, for the kind of work you're going to be doing, the fewer people who know about it the better."

Tom doesn't really have friends. There's no one from his childhood that he keeps in contact with. His father and stepmother are back in New Mexico. He'll probably talk with his father about his work eventually. He can trust him to keep it quiet, despite Jeffrey Rollins' feelings about the government. His brother, Anthony...well, he's not so sure if he'll tell him at all. They don't talk often. They're not exactly close. And outside of his family, Tom doesn't have any loved ones. No wife, no girlfriend.

He thinks, briefly, of Alejandra. He finds himself gritting his teeth. They're almost at the gym now. He stops thinking about her. It's easy enough to do right now.

There are other people present, working out. Lifting weights or on the various cardio machines. Reynolds leads him through the gym and toward four men in the far corner. Three of them are white. One of the men is Black. He's doing pull-ups while two others do bench press, one of them lifting the weight while the other spots. The fourth man stands to the side, arms folded, watching them. His hair is slicked back and there's sweat at his temple showing that he's been working out, too. He spots Reynolds and Rollins' approach. He turns his body toward them, looking Tom up and down. He smiles.

"Captain Dale," Reynolds says, holding out a hand.

Dale takes it and they shake. "Reynolds," he says, flashing his teeth. Captain Dale has a predator's smile. Like a shark. "Gather round, boys. Come and meet the new recruit."

The two men at the weight bench finish the set and then come and join Dale. The Black man drops from the pull-up bar and makes his way over. He's first to hold a hand out to Tom.

"Zeke Greene," he says. His smile is warmer. He doesn't look like he wants to eat Tom alive. "Pleased to meet you."

"Tom Rollins," Tom says, accepting the shake and the smile.

Captain Robert Dale makes the other introductions. The man who was lifting weights is Simon Collins. The man who was spotting him is Nathan Sapolsky. All four of the men have a deep pump. Their muscles bulge and flare with blood. Their veins are popping. Tom figures they had a lot of time to kill while they were waiting for him to arrive from Virginia Beach. At the same time, he wonders if this display of testosterone is them showing off, macho posturing for his benefit, showing him the kind of team he's joining.

"We hear good things," Captain Dale says, refolding his arms after everyone has shaken hands and become acquainted. "Jack here speaks highly of you. I hope you can live up to that praise."

"I'll do my best, sir," Tom says.

"We need better than your best, Rollins," Simon says. "This is no beta squad."

Nathan is nodding along. "Best of the best," he says. "It's a lifestyle and you have to be prepared to live it. We've got no time or space for people who can't step up."

Captain Dale is grinning. "He'll find out soon enough if he's got what it takes. We all will."

Tom notices how Zeke Greene rolls his eyes. He does it so the others don't see him.

"Murray was one of us, and he still died," Nathan says. "We just gotta let the fresh meat know the standard of excellence we expect him to hold himself to."

"Oscar Murray is, unfortunately, the man you're replacing," Reynolds says to Tom.

"I'm sorry to hear that," Tom says.

Captain Dale waves a hand. "He was a good man, but it was a long time ago now."

"Six months," Simon says.

"What happened?" Tom asks.

"Cartel caught up to him down Mexico way," Nathan says.

"Tried to pump him for info," Simon says.

"Tough son of a bitch didn't say a word," Nathan says. "And they went at him with hot pokers. Shoved them up his ass. Put them down his throat, and through his eyes."

Zeke's eyes narrow. His jaw clenches. He doesn't look happy about this kind of talk.

"We couldn't save him," Captain Dale says. "But we avenged him. Fuckers got what was coming to them, and then some."

Reynolds looks at Tom and raises his eyebrows. "And that's why you're unofficial."

Captain Dale, Simon, and Nathan all laugh. Zeke does not. He folds his arms and waits for the hazing to be over. Already, Tom can see the invisible division in the team. These four men are comrades, but they're not all friends. Zeke will no doubt have their backs, but it's clear he doesn't really like them. It's clear they don't impress him.

"You think you can stand up to some hot pokers and keep your mouth shut?" Nathan asks.

"I don't intend to find out, sir," Tom says.

Captain Dale chuckles at this. "That's a good answer, Rollins. Make sure the rest of us don't ever have to find out, either."

"He'll do his best, *sir*," Simon says, grinning.

"You've got a week of personal time," Reynolds says to Tom. "And then it's straight to work."

"I expect you to use that time well," Captain Dale says, eyeing the gym equipment. "Keep it sharp. I don't allow anyone to get soft or sloppy in my team."

"Yes, sir," Tom says. Captain Dale is a hard man to get a gauge on. He's not a likeable man, that's clear. His smile is menacing, and he's quick to flash it. Tom suspects that Dale knows it scares people. He probably doesn't like it that men like Rollins and Reynolds don't back down to it. And judging from his sycophants, Simon and Nathan, if that's the kind of company he keeps, then Tom doubts he wants anything to do with any of them outside of work hours. He can see which side of the divide he'll fall on.

Of course, this is work. It's business, not personal. There were plenty of people he didn't like in the Army, too. He'll look out for all of this team. He'll have their backs and keep them safe, and he'll expect the same from them. They don't have to go for beers together. They don't have to attend barbecues and birthday parties together. They just have to travel the world and eliminate threats. That's as far as their relationship extends, and that's all it ever needs to be.

"Good," Captain Dale says. "Then we'll see you in a week."

CHAPTER FOUR

Babak Rashidi has a favorite sound. It comes from the human body. He has a favorite musical instrument, too. That is also part of the human body.

Right now, his favorite instrument is silent on the gurney it's been wheeled in on. Of course, it makes *some* noise. The man's arms and legs strain against his shackles. He grunts and makes muffled cries through the gag covering his mouth.

Babak's favorite musical instrument is the human throat. His favorite sound is a human scream. It's all such sweet music to him.

Babak sits close to the gurney, a shelf of sharp and shining tools on a medical tray beside him. He watches the struggling captive, a slight smile playing across his lips.

The captive avoids meeting his gaze. He's scared. He struggles harder against his binds, but he isn't going anywhere. He no doubt has some kind of idea of what's coming. He's no doubt heard of Babak from across the border, and what he does.

Slowly, Babak rises to his feet. He twists his body side to

side, limbering up. He leans over the gurney, reaching for the gag. The captive closes his eyes tight and turns his head, his arms pulling with all of their strength. The veins bulge in his neck. His face turns red. Tears stream from the corners of his eyes. Babak removes the gag. The captive screams.

Sweet music.

But it's not right. Not quite. Not yet.

No, the real music begins when Babak starts to work. When he brings out his tools. When he sets about making art upon his favorite canvas – the human body.

Babak allows the captive man to scream. To scream and to struggle and to wear himself out. He can't escape. He's not going anywhere. This is all futile. Babak sits back down and he waits, the small smile always there.

The screaming stops. Temporarily. The captive looks at Babak, finally meeting his eyes.

"I can see that I don't need to introduce myself," Babak says. He pauses, watching the man's face, making sure he understands. Babak is speaking in Persian. The man is Afghan. They speak the same language, separated only by dialect. Babak speaks Persian. The man speaks Dari. The man can understand him well enough, and vice versa.

The man says nothing.

Babak lights a cigarette. He holds up the pack. "Smoke?"

The man hesitates, considers his predicament, and then nods. Babak puts a cigarette between his lips and lights it.

"Take a deep breath, my friend," Babak says. "There, that's good. Fill your lungs. Enjoy it." He removes the cigarette and drops it on the ground, stubbing it out under his heel. "I hope you enjoyed that."

The captive still doesn't speak.

Babak remains standing. He leans over the gurney,

resting his forearms on its railing. "I have a very straightforward question for you, my friend. Just one question, and when you answer it, we'll be done here. Now, of course, I can't send you home. But you won't get hurt. Right now that might not seem like such a great deal, but soon it will feel like the most important thing in the world. Unless you answer my question. Do you understand?"

The captive swallows. It's acknowledgement enough.

"That's good," Babak says. "Are you ready? Good. Where is Bill Irving?"

The captive stares up at him, eyes wide. He swallows. Babak hears how his throat dryly clicks.

"No?" Babak says. "Oh well. I'd say that's disappointing, but frankly, it's exactly the answer I was hoping for." Babak circles the gurney, returning to his tools. He interlocks his fingers and pushes them outward, popping his knuckles. He runs his fingertips over his tools, trailing them over the scalpels, the scissors, the surgical clamps. They gleam. They call out to him. Next to them are bandages and wipes, to prolong his fun. He picks up a scalpel first. He always does.

The captive speaks. "I don't know," he says. "I don't know where Bill Irving is. Nobody does."

Babak says nothing. He goes to the man's legs. He cuts away his right trouser leg, exposing the bare skin below.

The captive grows frantic. "I don't know!" he says again. "I don't know where Bill Irving is! I've never met him – I don't even know what he looks like!"

Babak looks up at him. "Okay," he says. "But I'm going to make sure." He presses the tip of the scalpel to the man's shin, just below his kneecap. He doesn't press down hard, but already a drop of blood appears. When the captive begins to twist and tremble, Babak clamps a hand down on his ankle, holding his leg in place. "You shouldn't thrash like this," he says. "You could make things so much worse."

"Fuck you!" the man cries, spurred by the pain, and by the knowledge of what's coming. "Fuck you! You betrayed us! Bill Irving will find *you*!"

Babak snorts. "I betrayed no one. I was always loyal to my own government, to my own country. You cannot say the same. You are subservient to another." He straightens, removing the scalpel from the shin. The spot of blood runs down the side of the leg, soaking into the gurney's sheet. Babak returns to the head, closer to the man's face. "You know what I'm going to do to you, don't you?"

The man is pale. He's sweating. He struggles to swallow.

Babak nods. "That's right. I'm going to peel pieces from you, inch by inch. I'm going to strip the flesh from your body. I'm going to flay you." He points with the scalpel, down toward the man's legs. "I like to start at the bottom. I like to work my way up. The legs, they're easiest to control. By the time I reach the hands and the arms, the fight has always gone out of my interviewees. They can't struggle against me as much as they would if I started at the top. And people, they always think they'll grow accustomed to the pain. They never do. I like to surprise them with that."

The man is shaking his head. "Please," he says. "I do not know where Bill Irving is."

Babak stands in silence, tapping the bloodless handle of the scalpel against his chin. He stares at the man's throat. His favorite instrument. His favorite sound. It's time for him to make music.

"I believe you," Babak says. He smiles into the man's face. "But I'm sure there's plenty more you can think to tell me." He returns to the base of the bed. To the legs.

The man pleads. Babak doesn't hear it. He grips the right leg by the ankle. He returns the scalpel to its previous position. He presses it in a little deeper this time, to cut through the dermis, down to the muscle. Babak looks up at the man. He's screaming. It's almost sweet enough, but not quite.

Babak cuts.

CHAPTER FIVE

Babak spent the day with his captive. He took his time. He heard enough of his favorite sound to satiate him for a while.

When the work was done, he was bloody. He left the interrogation room and summoned his men to spray it down and dispose of the body. Babak stripped off his soiled clothes and walked barefoot and naked to his quarters. He took a long shower, rinsing the blood and bits of the captive's severed flesh from his body.

The captive, as he'd promised, did not know the whereabouts of Bill Irving. Babak made sure of that. Unfortunately, he didn't know much of anything else worthwhile, either. Nothing that Babak was not already aware of, anyway.

Still, it wasn't a complete bust. He'd enjoyed their time together. It had been a good cut, and the captive had held on until the very end. Babak had not allowed him to bleed out. He never does. When he was finally done, he'd pulled out his PC-9 and shot the captive through the head, putting him out of his misery.

It was late when Babak had finished showering. Almost midnight. He went straight to bed. He had an appointment the next morning.

He wakes early and dresses, and goes through notes and reports until one of his men knocks upon his door. Babak tells him to come in.

"Farhad Gorji is here to see you."

Babak nods. He smiles. "I'll be right out."

Babak finishes what he's doing and then leaves his quarters. Farhad Gorji is waiting for him in a room at the front of the building. He never likes to come too deep into The Abattoir. Few people do. They understand its importance, and the work that Babak does here, but they don't have the stomach for his methods.

"Farhad," Babak says, entering the room. The cleric sits upon a dark green sofa, his robes spread out on the cushions beside him. He doesn't stand as Babak enters. He nods, touching the front of his turban in greeting.

"Babak," he says. He's flanked by two men who stand behind the sofa, dressed in similar robes that conceal their weaponry. These men are Farhad's bodyguards. Babak knows he would never come so close to the border without them.

Babak seats himself on a chair opposite Farhad. The walls here are white-tiled and cool. The ground is covered with rugs to soften it. The only time this room is used is on the rare occasions when Farhad Gorji comes to visit. He toured The Abattoir once, and made it clear that he would never do so again. This room was converted. It sits at the front of the building like an unused waiting room.

Babak works for MOIS – the Ministry of Intelligence

and Security. He answers to Farhad Gorji. Farhad Gorji, in turn, answers to the Minister of Intelligence.

"I've been sent for a situation report," Farhad says. He sits very still and looks down his nose at Babak. Babak knows what Farhad thinks of him. He thinks he's a butcher. Babak doesn't care. He gets results, and Farhad knows this. The Minister of Intelligence knows it, too.

Babak sits back in the chair, crossing one leg over the other. He pulls out his pack of cigarettes and takes his time shaking one out and lighting it. He offers the pack to Farhad, though he knows he won't accept one. "Smoke?"

Farhad shakes his head. Babak notices how, under his white beard, the muscles in his jaw and cheeks clench.

Babak inhales deeply and blows smoke into the air. "What I know, you know. Our trade is in secrets, but there are no secrets between us."

"I understand you have a prisoner," Farhad says.

Babak eyes the cleric, unable to resist a smirk. He wonders, briefly, which of his own men is spying on *him*, and feeding information back to Farhad. Such is this life, he supposes. But, like he said, he had nothing to hide. "I *had* a prisoner," he says.

Farhad's lip curls. There is strain in his neck as he tries not to swallow. Farhad knows only too well what the prisoner's last few hours of life would have been like. The agonizing torture he would have been subjected to as the flesh was flayed from his body. "Who was he?"

"One of the American's lapdogs from over the border," Babak says. "I've had my own men trailing him for a few weeks now. They snatched him when he was returning home from visiting his mother. She lives close to our border. It wasn't a difficult task to get him back here."

"He worked for Bill Irving?"

"He did."

"And?"

"He had no answers. Nothing useful, anyway. Nothing we didn't already know."

"But nothing on the man himself?"

Babak takes his time drawing on the cigarette. "No," he says as he exhales smoke. "He'd never met him. Didn't know his face. Didn't know where he is."

"And you're certain he was telling the truth?" Farhad asks, but Babak can see that he already knows this is a ridiculous question.

Babak smirks again. "Quite certain."

Farhad looks at Babak's hands while he smokes, as if searching them for the blood he knows coats them. He inhales deeply. "So it would seem we are no further forward."

"I'll find him," Babak says. "He can't hide from me forever."

"But how long will that take?" Farhad says, animated now, leaning forward a little on the sofa, his eyes wider. "How many of his own operatives could he be sneaking over the border into our country while you torture his subordinates with no success?"

Babak is unfazed. "I have success," he says. "I always do. They always talk. The problem is, they don't have the answers we want."

Farhad bristles. He settles back into the sofa. "There can be no other reason for an American spymaster to be so close to our border. He is there to get his people into Iran and to get information on our actions and our movements, and then to feed that information back to his masters in Washington.

Every day that goes by, he could be closer to achieving that goal. He could have *already* achieved that goal. His people could be within our borders, infiltrating our cities as we speak. We need this threat eradicated. *You* have been tasked with doing so, Babak, and yet it seems to me you have become comfortable here, indulging in your basest desires, thinking we'll permit you to continue undisturbed while you allow your bloodlust to run wild."

Babak remains calm. He takes another long draw from his cigarette and then absently plucks lint from his trouser leg. "I can assure you, Farhad, that I am all business. That everything I do here is in pursuit of the task that has been assigned to me. Don't mistake my enjoyment of my work for something that it isn't. I *will* find Bill Irving. I will root him out, and I will have him upon my table in my interrogation room. And when I do, he *will* talk, just like everyone else. If there are enemy agents already within our borders, I will find out, and I will find their locations. I will root them out like a cancer, and they in turn shall grace my table. I will extinguish the Americans' little operation over our border. I will descend upon them with such fury and carnage that the thought of returning here will give them nightmares. They will awaken in their beds shaking and crying, pissing themselves with fear, praying to their God and to their mothers that they should never have to come *near* here again."

Farhad watches him. "And how do you intend to do that?" he asks. "You killed your last prisoner. Another in a long line, I might add."

Babak smiles. He puts out his cigarette. "I'm glad you asked," he says. He drops his crossed leg and leans forward, clasping his hands. "I already have a plan. It's been in formulation for a few weeks now. Your visit today is most fortuitous."

"And why is that?"

"Because this plan involves outside help," Babak says. "And in order for them to agree to participate, deals must be struck. They're going to need certain...allowances."

CHAPTER SIX

A week is a long time. Tom has been so busy for so long, he isn't sure what to do with himself.

When he was in the Army, he didn't have a fixed address. He still doesn't. With most of his time spent overseas, there doesn't seem any point in having a permanent abode. It's not like he's ever coming back to anyone. There's no one he needs to shelter. So when he wasn't on tour, he'd either stay in a motel, or with his father and step-mother on their commune in New Mexico. Or, on some occasions, he'd stay with his brother Anthony, sleeping in his spare room. Anthony lives in a small town in Texas called Harrow.

Tom drives to Texas. He doesn't let Anthony know he's coming. Tom isn't coming to see his brother.

It takes him a day to drive from Virginia. He spends the night in a motel a few miles down the road, then sets off early in the morning. Anthony's car is at the house when Tom arrives. He parks down the block and he watches, wondering if Anthony currently has a job, or if he's enduring one of his long stretches of unemployment.

Tom loves his brother, of course he does, but that doesn't mean he can't admit that his brother is a fuck-up. His whole life, since leaving school, Anthony has struggled to hold down a job for longer than six months. Tom keeps hoping he'll grow up, but so far that day hasn't come. Instead, a string of petty offenses has occurred and been added to his criminal record, in turn making it harder for him to find work. Often, when Tom would stay with him, Anthony would disappear for hours at a time, not saying where he was going, and offering no answers upon his return. Tom never asked. It felt better that way. He had his suspicions, of course. Some light breaking and entering, perhaps. Drug dealing.

Tom hasn't stayed with his brother for a long time. Not since his second tour ended. Things changed between them then, not that Anthony knows that. But Anthony had a new girlfriend, and it was difficult for Tom to be around them both, because Tom was in love with her.

While he watches, he handles the Santa Muerte pendant he usually wears around his neck. He runs his thumb absently over her face, staring at the car and the house. It's quiet on Anthony's street. He sees a few people leaving for work, but most of the houses remain as they were when Tom first arrived.

Suddenly, he sees movement. Curtains are pulled open. Tom stops rubbing the pendant, his thumb lying flat upon it. A moment later, the front door opens. Anthony steps out. He's wearing jeans and a black short-sleeved polo shirt tucked into them. He twists slightly side to side and breathes deeply. He runs his hands back through his hair, scratching at his scalp, and then he goes to his car. He gets inside and drives off, in the opposite direction to where Tom sits.

Tom watches him go. He watches the house. He doesn't see any further movement coming from inside it.

A few minutes pass by. Anthony does not return. He was dressed smartly. Tom wonders if he has a job, or if he's going to return any moment. Tom deliberates, staring at the house. Is she even in there? Are they still together?

Tom puts the Santa Muerte pendant back around his neck. She sits on top of his T-shirt. He looks at her in the mirror and then he tucks her inside the shirt so she's out of view and pressed against his chest. He starts the car and pulls out from around the corner, crawling until he's in front of Anthony's home. He looks up at it. Still, he can't see anyone inside. He gets out of the car and goes to the door. Before he can hesitate, before he can change his mind and get back in the car, he knocks on the door and waits.

It doesn't take long before he hears movement. The door opens, just a crack, the occupant clearly not expecting anyone. For a second, Tom hopes that he won't recognize the face looking back at him. That it'll be a blonde woman he's never met before, and who has no idea who he is, save for his resemblance to his younger brother.

But then, that face fills the crack in the door, those big brown eyes settle upon him and within a moment they widen with recognition, and Tom feels both his heart skip a beat, and his stomach sink into a deep pit.

Alejandra Flores stands before him. She throws the door wide, says, "Tom!" and steps out of the house and into his arms, her own wrapping themselves tightly around his neck.

Tom closes his eyes, hugging her back, his face in her shoulder, her black hair tickling his cheeks and nose. He doesn't care how it tickles him. He can smell her shampoo in it. A familiar smell that brings back memories of when they first met. Of when he fell in love with her.

She lets go of him and takes a step back, looking him over, smiling wide. Her hands don't leave him. They rest on his arms while she takes him in, like she can't believe he's standing before her, and that if she were to let him go he'd disappear.

"We didn't know you were back," she says.

"Just a couple of days ago," he says. He looks into her beautiful face and he tries to keep from blinking. He doesn't want to miss a moment. Her long hair is loose, cascading over her shoulders. She wears a pale yellow sundress patterned with small pink flowers. Her shoulders and arms, her legs and feet are bare.

"Come in, come in," Alejandra says, letting go of him now but waving for him to follow. She looks back over her shoulder, keeping her eyes on him as he steps into the house and closes the door behind him. They go into the living room and Alejandra motions for him to sit on the sofa. She sits down beside him, folding her legs beneath herself, turning her body toward his. "You just missed Anthony," she says.

"That's a shame," Tom says.

"I wonder if I should call him," she says. "He can't have gone far. He'll be disappointed that he missed you."

"Where's he gone?"

"Work. They've built a warehouse a couple of miles outside of town. Storage and packaging. He's a supervisor. They like him there."

"How long's he been there?" Tom asks.

"Six months."

He could be looking to break an employment record,

Tom thinks. He hopes he does. He'd hoped that being with Alejandra would straighten his brother out. Make him get his head on straight and sort his life out. It's what she deserves. "That's good," Tom says, and he forces himself to smile. "But don't disturb him. I wouldn't want him to get into trouble on account of me."

"Are you planning to hang around? How long are you on leave for?"

"I wish I could," Tom says. "But I was just passing by. I've only got a couple of hours and then I need to head back to base." He doesn't tell her about his new job. About the CIA. She thinks he's still in the Army, and he'll leave it that way.

"That's such a shame," Alejandra says, and he sees genuine disappointment in her face. It stabs at him, but to wait around and see her and his brother together would stab him deeper. "Where are they sending you? Back to the Middle East?"

Tom shrugs. "Maybe. I guess I'll have to find out. How about you? Are you still bartending?"

Alejandra nods. "I am. We're saving up. We want to buy a house."

"This place seems nice."

"Yeah, but it's a rental. Anthony says that if he does another year, two at the most, they'll make him a manager and that'll come with a big pay raise. We've started saving now. I keep all my tips from the bar." She looks so happy.

"That's…that's great, Alejandra," Tom says. "That sounds great."

She chuckles.

"What's so funny?" Tom asks.

"Nothing. Well, just my name. When you said it. It

brought back a memory. Do you remember what you told me, when we first met?"

Tom remembers. She told him to call her *Ally*, that everyone did, but he said he wouldn't. He said that Alejandra Flores was the most beautiful name he'd ever heard. He nods.

She smiles. "How about you, Tom? Do you finally have a home?"

"No, not yet."

"Too busy," Alejandra says. "Always too busy. What about a girlfriend?"

He shakes his head. He'd dated a girl a few times while he was training in Virginia, but he wouldn't call her his girlfriend.

"No one can tie you down, huh?" She laughs.

Tom looks at her. "I suppose not."

"Would you – would you like something to drink? To eat?"

"I'm okay."

Tom looks at her. He can't take his eyes from her. He doesn't want to. From the first moment he met her, from that first night when he walked her home after her shift at the bar ended, he knew he was in love with her. And then, during his whole time on leave, while they talked and walked and hung out, with nothing physical transpiring between them, he wanted to freeze time so he could stay with her, despite knowing that his time was winding down, that soon he would have to return to the Army. Return to war. He'd never feared it. He'd never dreaded it. But then, because of her, he *did*. He didn't want to go back, out of fear that he might never return. That he might never see her again.

But he went. Because that's who he is. He did his job.

He saved lives. He took lives. And all the while, he thought of Alejandra. He thought about getting back to her. Of returning to Texas, taking her in his arms, and kissing her. Of telling her exactly how he felt.

Except when he returned from his second tour, Alejandra was no longer available. She was with his brother.

He'd asked himself why he hadn't already told her how he felt, why he'd allowed her to slip away. He didn't have a real answer. Those days when he first met her, they were the happiest of his life. He couldn't remember a time he'd smiled or laughed so much. A time when he'd felt his heart swelling and actual butterflies in his stomach. And if he had to guess, he hadn't told her because he hadn't wanted to ruin it.

She looks back at him. She's starting to frown, sensing that there's a tension within him, that there's something hanging between them, and she doesn't know what it is.

"Alejandra," he says. "I wasn't passing by. I came here to see you."

She lowers her eyes. She bites her lip. Tom thinks that maybe she'd already guessed this. That a part of her already knew. She reaches out a hand, a finger, the tip touching the Santa Muerte pendant where she can see the lump of it through his T-shirt. "She's kept you safe. She's brought you back."

Tom says nothing.

Alejandra raises her eyes back to his. "What do you want me to say, Tom?"

"Nothing," he says. "I just didn't want to lie to you. I just...I wanted to see you."

"You can see me any time you're back. You choose not to."

"You know why."

He can see from her face that she does. "I never wanted to hurt you, Tom."

Tom says nothing.

Alejandra breathes deeply. "Have you ever even talked to Anthony about how we met?"

"No."

"You don't care? Or do you care too much?"

"I don't see what difference it would make."

Alejandra chews her bottom lip. "I was going to wait for you," she says.

"I never asked you to."

"I know you didn't. But I was going to. And then one night, I thought you walked into the bar. And I was so happy to see you. I thought you'd come back early. I thought you'd come back for me. But I could tell that something looked different. I could tell it wasn't you, but I was struck by how much you looked alike. I was going to ask him if he knew you. I was going to tell him how much he looked like you, but before I could, I heard one of his friends call to him. He called him Rollins. When that happened, I started talking to him. I didn't even think about it. I had to know if he knew you.

"He got so excited when he found out I knew his big brother. Anthony thinks the world of you, Tom. He wouldn't admit it, but he looks up to you. He always has. You're the kind of man he wishes he was. He told me that, once, when he was drunk. He'd hate it if he knew I remembered and was telling you now."

"I told you; I don't see what difference telling me this makes."

"I've started," Alejandra says. "I'm going to finish. I want you to understand."

Tom says nothing.

"I didn't mean to fall in love with your brother. It just happened. The two of us started as friends, like we did, but we spent a lot of time together. And Anthony is very sweet. He's very like you, Tom, but he's also...*not*. He's always present. When I spoke with you, it always felt like you were somewhere else. You were always so...*tense*. You still are. You're always looking over your shoulder. It was hard to engage with you, to really get to know you, because it never felt like you trusted anyone. It never felt like you trusted me, even."

Tom remains silent.

Alejandra looks into his eyes. "I fell in love with your brother. I'm sorry that I couldn't fall in love with you."

"I appreciate your honesty," Tom says.

"I'm not trying to hurt you."

"It's what I needed to hear."

They sit together in silence for a moment. Alejandra does not turn away from him. She hesitates and then she reaches out and takes his hand. "I'm sorry," she says. "I do *care* about you, Tom. You have to know that. Whenever you're away, I worry about you. Anthony tells me I shouldn't, that you can take care of yourself, that you always pull through, but I still pray for you. Every night. I pray to God. I pray to Santa Muerte."

Tom looks down at her hand holding his. It hurts, certainly, to hear her words, but it's what he needed. He needed to hear them. He needs to know that there's no reason for him to come back here. To know that she isn't waiting for him. That she isn't holding a candle for him, the way he is for her.

"Thank you for your prayers, Alejandra," Tom says. "I

appreciate them." He takes his hand back. He prepares himself to leave.

"You don't need to go, Tom."

He gets to his feet. "I think I do. I think I should."

"But you came all this way."

"I got what I needed."

"But not what you want."

"It's not about what I want. It's about what you want. I needed to hear that." He holds his hand out to her. She takes it and he pulls her to her feet. She stands very close to him. She's not much shorter than him, but she looks up into his face. "I'm happy for you, Alejandra. For you and Anthony." They look at each other. Neither of them moves for a long time. They're very close to each other. Tom can feel the warmth coming from her body. She gasps a little, as if realizing she's been holding her breath.

Tom turns away. He heads toward the front door. There's no reason for him to stay here any longer. They've said all they need to say to each other. Alejandra follows. When Tom opens the door, she holds onto his arm and turns him around. She wraps her arms round him and she squeezes him tight. Tom hugs her back.

When she parts from him, she says, "I don't think I'll tell Anthony that you came here today."

"Tell him what you please," Tom says. It feels unnecessarily harsh, so he adds, "I hope the job works out for him. I hope he gets that promotion next year. Good luck buying your house."

Alejandra smiles sadly. "Stay safe," she says. She presses her finger to the mound of the Santa Muerte pendant through his T-shirt. "Keep her with you. Keep her close."

"I always do," Tom says. "Goodbye, Alejandra."

"Goodbye, Tom."

Tom leaves the house. He returns to his car. He can feel Alejandra's eyes watching him go. He doesn't look back. He starts the engine. He still doesn't look back.

He drives away. He doesn't know it, but he'll never see her again.

CHAPTER SEVEN

Babak gets into Afghanistan. It's not difficult for him. He crosses the border often. For work, of course. To pluck some of Bill Irving's assets from the streets and to take them back to his Abattoir. He knows they fear him. That's what he wants. It's what he wants from Bill, too. He wants them to know that they're not safe here, not so close to the border, not so close to his home.

The downside of that fear he induces is that Bill Irving keeps himself hidden. He did that already, though. It's not like Babak has caused him to conceal himself, quivering with terror. Bill already did that. He was already a coward. That's why Babak had to go undercover in the first place, pretending to be an Afghan, trying to get himself closer to the area's lead operations officer.

No luck.

Babak tried the subtle approach. Now he needs to be a hammer. It needs to be an overt, heavy-handed approach. Babak has to lure him out. Lure them all out. He has promised Farhad Gorji that he will find Bill Irving and eliminate his activities in the area, and he is determined to follow through on that promise.

Now, as the sun gradually rises, he makes his way toward the co-ordinates that have been provided by the Dutch. They've told him they'll collect him. Babak only has six miles to go. He can do it on foot.

The meeting point is in the middle of nowhere. Babak takes a seat upon a stone beneath a tree and he waits. He enjoys the peace, closing his eyes and turning his face toward the sun. He feels himself smiling. It's quiet here, but he can remember the screams whenever he wants. They're clear in his mind, in his ears. He can remember the good and happy times in his Abattoir. He'll be back there soon. He'll be back there with his prize catch. He can feel it. It's coming, finally. It won't be long now.

He hears the approach of vehicles. Opening his eyes, he sees two white box trucks coming toward him, kicking up dust in their wake. They slow as they get close, and he sees the men in the lead truck scanning the area, searching him out. Babak doesn't stand, but he raises an arm and waves. The trucks stop and the men get out. There are six of them. They're each dressed the same – khaki cargo pants, combat boots, and green sweaters with turtleneck collars. They're all armed, too. Five of the men carry H&K MP5s, and on their hips are P320s. The five men equipped with the submachine guns hold them loose but ready. They spread out around the trucks, staying close to them but watching the area.

The lead man, the man whom Babak has been talking to, comes toward him. He doesn't carry an MP5. He's left it in the truck. He does, though, have the P320 on his hip, same as the others. He stops a few paces away from Babak, places his hands on his hips and looks him over. Babak looks him over in turn. He's a tall man, over six feet, and broad. His blond hair is swept back from his movie-star good looks.

"The area is clear," Babak says, in English, remaining seated for now. "I've been here for twenty minutes."

The men ignore him. They remain on alert. The man before him raises an eyebrow like the only word he'd trust is the word of his men.

"Bram de Groot," Babak says, getting to his feet. "It's a pleasure to finally meet you in person."

"Babak," Bram says, though it's a statement, not a question. He offers a handshake. Babak takes it. He feels the strength in Bram's hand. Babak is impressed by what he sees so far. These men suit his needs well, he's sure. "The feeling is mutual, though I must make it clear that my men and I do not usually spend so much time in this area. In the country, in fact. In and out is our preferred method of travel here."

Bram is former KCT – Korps Commandotroepen – Dutch special forces. But that life is long behind him now. He retired from the KCT, but the retirement package wasn't satisfactory enough for him. And, perhaps more than that, he couldn't leave the excitement behind. Now, he makes his living smuggling drugs. He's been all around the world, but he makes his most lucrative deals from the opium grown in Afghanistan.

"I can promise that you and your men will be well compensated for your time and your assistance."

Bram grunts. "And you've explained to Khan that we'll be delayed?"

Khan is an opium kingpin on the Afghan side. He grows and sells it, and distributes it locally. Babak has been in contact with him for years. It was Khan who told Babak about Bram and his men, and how they'd likely agree to help him.

Babak nods. "I've spoken to him directly. He says your collection will be ready and waiting for you and there's no need to worry about being late. He knows what you're doing here, with me. He said you do not have to worry about being behind schedule. I assume you've told your buyers back home the same thing?"

Bram grunts again. "They'll wait." He looks Babak over. "I need you to remove your clothes."

Babak raises an eyebrow. "What?"

"I do not like to repeat myself, Babak." Bram eyes him coolly.

"But why?"

"To make sure you are not wearing a wire. Or a tracker."

"I contacted *you*."

"All the more reason to check you. One can never be too careful."

The two men look at each other, neither backing down yet. Bram's eyes are cold. His chiseled face is blank, like stone. It doesn't flicker. He doesn't blink.

"I have heard of Babak Rashidi," Bram says finally. "I have heard of the things he does. But I've never seen him. You fit his description, but so what? Any undercover agent could provide the name Babak Rashidi and reach out for our assistance with the promise of a large payday and easier traveling routes."

"Khan vouched for me."

"He did. But we're not leaving here with you until you comply."

Babak stares at the Dutchman. Bram isn't going to back down. "Fine," Babak says through his teeth. He removes his clothes. He takes his time removing his gun, making sure that Bram sees it before he pulls it out and places it on the ground. A couple of the other men at Bram's back are looking over, watching, and their fingers are close to their triggers. Babak isn't taking any risks.

Finally, he stands barefoot and naked. He raises his arms and turns in a slow circle. Bram looks him up and down, remaining impassive. He whistles and one of his men hurries over, slinging his MP5 over his shoulder, then drops to his knees and goes through Babak's clothes.

Babak stands and waits, refusing to cover himself, refusing to show any form of embarrassment, until the men are through with this farce. The man looking through his clothes looks up at Bram, nods, and then returns to the others.

"Put your clothes back on," Bram says. "I'm sure you can understand, Babak, why we would need to take such precautions. If we were to be caught doing what we do out here, we would be facing much worse than a cell and armed guards."

Babak bristles, but he does understand. "We need discuss it no further," he says, pulling up his trousers. "I'd prefer it if we got straight to work."

"I'll introduce you to my men," Bram says. "And then we'll do exactly that."

When Babak finishes dressing, he follows Bram to the trucks and the other five men. Bram starts pointing at them in turn, starting with the man who went through Babak's clothes. "This is Dirk," he says, then proceeds to point at each man in turn, his arm extended ahead of himself, never dropping, his finger gliding and never jabbing. "Hennie. Egon. Jacco. Johan."

Babak takes in their faces and their names, committing

them to memory. "I understand that some of the members of your team are also ex-KCT, like yourself?"

"Dirk and Hennie," Bram says. "Egon, Jacco, and Johan are all former Koninklijke Landmacht."

"And that is?"

"The Royal Netherlands Army," Bram says. "They were soldiers. You are in good hands, Babak Rashidi."

"I'm glad to hear it."

The man called Jacco turns his head to the side and spits something out. Gum, Babak thinks. "Why do you want to be seen?" he asks. "Your plan doesn't make sense to me. I'm not afraid to get my hands dirty, none of us are, but it feels as if you are attempting to pull us into an unnecessary firefight."

Babak looks them over. All of them are almost carbon copies of Bram, save for some differing hair and eye colors, weight and height, some scars here and there. But they all have similar granite jaws and steely eyes. They could pass for brothers, or cousins perhaps. Babak can imagine them all working out together, training together, staying sharp when they're not smuggling.

"I need to catch a fish," Babak says. "But it's not a big fish. It's a small fish. A bottom feeder. A parasite that latches on to larger fish. This fish, it remains hidden. It never comes out from under its rock, but there's a chance that if it sees the largest fish imaginable, a fish it has hunted for many years, a fish it is so *desperate* to latch onto, then it will finally emerge from under its rock. It just needs the right kind of lure. *I* am that lure. I am the bait. I am the biggest fish that Billy Irving could ever want. I'm not pulling all of *you* into an unnecessary firefight. I'm drawing *him* toward the hook. I am the bait and you are the hook."

"It still sounds risky," Egon says.

"Khan told me I should have faith in your abilities," Babak says. "Does he have more faith in you than you have in yourself?"

Bram grunts. "We'll capture your fish," he says. "But the Americans cannot know it was us. That would cause unwanted problems."

"Once I have Bill Irving, the Americans still in the area won't be for much longer."

"You think he would come out himself?" Johan asks. "He'll send men after you. An operations officer isn't going to put himself in the field like that, not unless he's particularly gung-ho. From what you've said, he's not."

"No, he's not," Babak says. "But he'll send his best men after me. Men who have met him. Who know where he is and how to find him. *That* is my key to finding Bill Irving."

"That could still take time," Hennie says. "Bram told you – we don't want the Americans to know of our involvement."

"And they won't," Babak says, struggling to remain patient, reminding himself that he's outnumbered among these men. "So long as you do your job properly. But we will have to adapt to the circumstances. If only it were as straightforward as swooping in and plucking someone from the streets, but no. I have to make myself known first, and I cannot be obvious about it. If I'm not careful they'll know exactly what I'm doing. This is why Khan told me about you and your men, Bram de Groot. He told me you'd be able to improvise. That you'd be able to handle any situation, no matter what might arise."

Bram remains cool. He doesn't rise to Babak's baiting. He just nods, once. "Of course," he says. And then he shocks Babak by smiling for the first time. "Personally, I am looking forward to the challenge."

"Okay," Babak says, glancing at the other men. Bram's smile is brief. His face soon returns to what Babak is accustomed to. The other men don't smile at all, but he notices how some of them glance sidelong at Bram, and Babak thinks – he hopes – this is because they know they should be looking forward to it, too. They should see it as a challenge, just like Bram does. "Good." Babak's tongue flickers over his lips. He looks around at the six silent Dutchmen. "Then shall we begin?"

CHAPTER EIGHT

Tom finds a motel to stay in close to Langley and he waits out the days of his leave. He passes the time by working out, as Captain Dale suggested. He does calisthenics in his room, and goes for runs in nearby woodland. He doesn't think about Alejandra. He doesn't think about Anthony. It's all behind him now. It's in the past. He needs to move on. To push forward. He has to get on with his life.

And soon, a new chapter is beginning. Life with the CIA. Running black ops missions. Cutting down the enemies of his nation, keeping safe its innocent citizens. It's something he can take pride in, at least.

He's called back from his leave a day early. It's Nathan Sapolsky who calls him. "The captain says you need to come in. We've received a call. Top priority."

"Where do you need me?"

"Langley AFB." The Air Force Base. "We're going overseas."

"I can be there in an hour," Tom says.

There's a brief pause at this, Nathan considering this timeframe. "An hour? You haven't gone far."

"I don't have anywhere to go."

"All right. We'll see you in an hour."

When he gets to Langley, Captain Dale, Simon Collins, and Nathan Sapolsky are already present. They have to wait for Zeke Greene.

"He's coming from Louisiana," Simon says when Tom asks where he is. "But he's flying up. He'll be here soon."

While they wait, Tom gets ready. He's alone in the locker room. The others are in the hangar. They're already geared up. Tom pulls on all-black clothing, then puts his Army-issue Beretta and KA-BAR into the locker with his everyday clothes and his backpack. He deliberates the Santa Muerte pendant, pressing a hand to it resting against his chest. He leaves her where she is, tucked under his T-shirt. He exits the locker room and joins the others in the hangar. Weaponry and tactical equipment is set out on a table nearby. Captain Dale, Simon, and Nathan are huddled together near a blank whiteboard. Tom wonders where they're going. So far, he hasn't been told anything.

He looks over the equipment. Maps and flashlights. Rations and canteens. Radios. There's also M4 assault rifles and spare magazines. Glock pistols. Strider Coyote knives. Tom is familiar with all of this weaponry. He's used it all before. Tom takes one of the knives. It's folded in on itself. He pops it open and checks the blade. It's sharp. He closes it again, sheathes it, and clips it onto his trousers.

There are tactical vests on the table, too. Five of them – one for each member of the team. They don't have their names on.

Before Tom has a chance to check one of the maps,

Captain Dale calls over to him. "You've been to Afghanistan before, Rollins, ain't that right? It's where Reynolds recruited you from, if memory serves."

Tom turns away from the tables. "That's right, sir."

"Then this first outing maybe ain't gonna be so exciting for you," he says. "You been to the Nimruz Province?"

"Maybe," Tom says. "Helmand, for sure, and they're right next to each other, I believe."

Robert nods. "The boy knows his geography. We're gonna be close to the border. You ever been to Iran?"

"No, sir."

"And you're not going on this trip, either. But you might catch a glimpse of it, depending on how close we have to get to the border."

"Yes, sir."

"And save the *sirs*, Rollins," Robert says. "I don't need to hear them all the time. It's just us here. If there's brass around, fine, but you don't always have to be so formal."

Tom nods.

It doesn't take much longer for Zeke Greene to arrive. He gets changed and then they all gear up and head out onto the runway, to the C-130 Hercules awaiting them. The pilots are already aboard. They've been running through their checks while the team waited for Zeke. It's a big plane for a small team, but if anyone sees its approach they'll assume it's carrying more troops than it really is. They won't suspect a small elite team to be on board.

It's a long flight to Afghanistan. Tom is accustomed to it. Robert tells them all that they'll be briefed when they arrive, that they don't know exactly what they're being called on for other than that it's a top priority. Tom settles in and gets some sleep. It feels good to be on the move. Good to be back in the air. Good to put all of his problems behind him.

They land at an Air Force base in Helmand and are transported the rest of the way by helicopter. It touches down at an airstrip in Nimruz. There's nothing else near the airstrip. It's far from any settlements. A man is waiting for them when they get out of the helicopter. Mustafa Rabbani introduces himself and leads them away from the airstrip as the helicopter takes off back into the air. Mustafa is Arab-American. He's CIA. He's an operations officer in the area. He tells them he answers to Bill Irving. Mustafa Rabbani is not his real name; it's the name their local assets know him by, and it's the name the team are going to know him by while they're here, too.

"I know Bill is glad you could all make it out here on such short notice," Mustafa says. "A target has reappeared in the area. One that we're all very eager to get our hands on. It's a serious situation. For a lot of us, Bill and myself included, this is personal. Bill said he'll brief you himself."

CHAPTER NINE

Bill Irving is a nondescript man, but out here, in Afghanistan, he'd stand out like a sore thumb.

He's of average height, thin, and pale. Very pale, like the sun hasn't touched his flesh in years. He dresses like he's still in America, with blue jeans, sneakers, and a plain white T-shirt tucked into his jeans. His pale face is clean-shaven, but his hair looks like it's a little longer than he'd like to wear it. Tom notices how he keeps brushing it back behind his ears and pushing it back from his forehead.

Bill's hideout is similarly nondescript. It's part of an abandoned clutter of houses made of stone and wood on the edge of the desert, some of them run down and collapsing, missing roofs, windows, doors. The outside walls are plastered with dried mud, their color blending into the surroundings, adding further disguise. The house Bill is in is in the center of the houses. It still has its roof. The windows are blacked out from the inside, masking the lights Bill has on. The vehicles Mustafa brought them here in are parked five miles away, concealed behind an outcrop of rocks. They continued the rest of the way at a brisk run.

Tom is at the back of the group. He keeps his mouth shut and his eyes and ears open, taking it all in. He looks around the living room. Bill has converted it into his office. It looks like he spends most of his time in here. There is a cot bed in the corner, and a hot plate on the floor beside it. Tins of food and bottles of water are under the cot. Floor lights are set up around the room, illuminating it. Outside, it's night. The walls are covered with pictures and maps. There are snapshots of people of importance – assets and enemies both, separated and distinguished by the walls they're pinned to. There are radios on tables around the room, and a couple of laptops. Piles of paper and notebooks.

"I stay on the move," Bill says. He glances at Mustafa. "This is probably my, I dunno, sixth hideout this year?"

"Fifth or sixth," Mustafa confirms. His accent is local from so much time spent amongst the Afghans, but Tom notices a hint of Alabama coming through in it. He assumes he's usually able to hide it, but in the presence of fellow countrymen it's slipping through. "Not that anyone's come close to finding you."

"And I intend to keep it that way," Bill says. He looks over the team, Robert at their fore with his hands locked on the collar of his tactical vest. "I appreciate you all coming out here. We could use some help with this one."

"Tell us what you've got going on," Robert says.

Bill lifts one leg and rests it on the back of a chair at one of his desks. He clasps his hands together before he begins. "A little background, first," he says. "I've been in this area for the last four years. I oversee the operation, but the day-to-day is run by Mustafa here. He fits into the surroundings better than I do."

The two men smirk at each other like this is some kind of inside joke between them.

"Together we've built up a network of assets," Bill continues. "Our work here is predominantly to monitor Taliban activities, but we also keep a close eye on the Iranian border. We monitor *their* activities, too.

"Two years ago, we recruited an asset by the name of Abdul Rahman. He seemed promising. Eager. Willing to get his hands dirty." Bill purses his lips like he's suddenly tasted something sour. "He was with us for a year. Around that time, another of our assets, Aalem Hussain, came to Mustafa with some troubling news."

"He told me Abdul had attempted to recruit him into spying against the CIA," Mustafa says. "Aalem is one of our best. Speaks fluent English. Former electrical engineer, so he knows his way around a gadget. He's bugged plenty of properties for us. Brought us a lot of crucial information – what he brought us about 'Abdul Rahman' was probably the most important."

"Abdul Rahman didn't fucking exist," Bill says bitterly. "Mustafa and Aalem began tailing him, along with two of his associates."

"Abdul was a sneaky bastard. Gave us the slip on more than one occasion. This was already setting off alarm bells. His two associates, they weren't as careful as he was. Aalem bugged their homes."

"Did you ever meet with Abdul?" Robert asks Bill.

"No," he says.

"Have you met with Aalem?"

Bill shakes his head. "I don't meet with the assets. They

might know my name, but that's the extent of it. Anything I have to say to them, Mustafa relays it. They don't see my face. They don't know who I am. That's how I keep it."

Robert nods, like this was what he expected and he's glad to hear it. "All right. So what happened with the bugs?"

"They confirmed some of our fears," Mustafa says. "They'd been recruited by Abdul, same as he'd try to do with Aalem. At this point, Abdul must have been on to us. He'd disappeared. So we brought in his two converts and questioned them. They cracked easily. Abdul Rahman was actually Babak Rashidi. He wasn't even Afghan – he's Iranian. They're aware of our presence here, and Babak was sent to infiltrate our operation and track down Bill here."

Bill's mouth twists, remembering the betrayal. "Babak must have fled back across the border," he says. "We believe he has spies of his own active in the area – both Iranian and Afghan."

Robert grunts. "Another reason for you to keep such a low profile."

"Exactly," Bill says. He straightens now, getting off the chair. He folds his arms. "Babak is a spy, but he's also a torturer. He has a reputation, on both sides of the border."

"He flays," Mustafa says, his mouth set grimly.

"Jesus," Zeke mutters. He's standing close to Tom. Tom's the only one who hears him.

Robert grunts. "We've gone up against worse." He's probably thinking of Oscar Murray, of what the cartel did to him. Tom hasn't forgotten.

"Babak captured one of our assets, soon after we'd discovered who he really was," Mustafa says. "He peeled the skin from his entire body and dumped him at the border for everyone to see. For *us* to see."

"It was a *fuck you*, no doubt," Bill says.

"Another of our assets recently went missing," Mustafa says. "We suspect Babak might have captured him."

"Or maybe he turned him," Robert says.

"If he turned him, he'd still be here. More likely he's dead in Iran somewhere."

"You don't know where Babak goes when he's over the border?"

"We're working on it," Bill says. "But we're yet to have found his location. And he knows it. He turns up sometimes, teasing us."

"I assume this is who you've called us in to deal with," Robert says. "How do you expect us to find him if you don't know where he is?"

"Like I said, he likes to tease us," Bill says. "But lately, it seems like he might have gotten careless. He's been spotted on this side of the border."

"What's he doing?"

"We're not sure just yet. He's been seen traveling with a couple of trucks, and sometimes on foot, but always accompanied."

"His associates?"

"We don't know yet. They're always masked. From what little we *can* see of them, we think they're white."

"Interesting," Robert says.

"Mm," Bill says. "We've had people posted up at the easiest crossing points back into Iran, and as of yet we haven't caught any sight of him, or the vehicles he's been seen with. That gives us reason to believe he's still on this side of the border, still in this area. The sightings of him have been regular enough that we're confident enough you should be able to swoop down and bring him in."

"Preferably alive?" Robert asks.

Bill nods. "We need to question the son of a bitch. We need to unearth the extent of his own spy network, and find out if any of our own assets belong to him."

"What's he been doing over here? Where's he going? Is there an obvious route to his travels?"

"There's a known drug supplier in these parts. A kingpin by the name of Khan. We try to keep close tabs on *him*, too, but he's a slippery devil. Moves around almost as much as I do. But on occasion, Babak and his associates have been seen meeting up with some recognizable faces from Khan's organization."

Robert frowns. "Is there any reason why he'd be looking to get into drugs? Has he ever had anything to do with them before? Or with Khan for that matter?"

"Not so far as we're aware, but maybe Babak has something in the works. Maybe the Iranians do. This is the kind of thing we're here to monitor. When you bring him to us, we can ask him."

"So, we sit tight until he's spotted?"

"Yes," Bill says, "but not here. Mustafa will take you back to HQ. It's closer to the areas he's been spotted in thus far. I'm afraid we don't know how long you're gonna have to wait it out. We have to do everything old school here – it's all eyes and ears, boots on the ground. If we send up drones, the Iranians on the border shoot them down."

"We've already upped the patrols," Mustafa says. "And made sure all of our most trusted assets are aware of his presence, and how imperative it is to get back to us as soon as they see him."

"Well, you've got us until we've got him," Robert says.

"Or until you think he's gone again. Either way, waiting around ain't nothing new."

"Appreciate it," Bill says.

Mustafa leaves the house first, checking that outside is clear. When he's confident it is, he motions for the team to follow him out. As they head back toward the vehicles, Tom glances back and sees how Mustafa sweeps away their footsteps, erasing all trace that they were ever here, or that there's anyone in the buildings.

CHAPTER TEN

Maryam Hussain is building a computer. Right now, she's repairing a circuit board. She was able to find most of the parts at the bazaar, but one of the boards was damaged. It's not going to take much for her to repair it. Some solder and some patience, and then she'll be able to put it into the mainframe.

She works hunched over at her desk in her room, the smell of solder and burning plastics wafting acrid up her nose. The desk is covered in electronics and manuals. Some of the manuals are not in Dari, but that's fine. She can read the English.

Outside of her bedroom, she can hear her father moving around. She thinks she heard him take a phone call earlier. One of his secretive ones that he doesn't want her to overhear because he knows how she worries. Regardless of what he wants, she's going to worry. She has to. They're the only family they have.

She focuses on her work, knowing that if it's important, her father will come and speak to her. Already, though, she can feel herself growing unnerved, knowing that something might be happening, that her father might be heading out soon. It's hard to concentrate on her work when she has these feelings.

So instead, she sits back and she waits. Waits either for her father to settle, or for him to come in and talk to her.

She looks out of her window. It's early evening. The sun is low, casting long shadows. Whenever her father gets a call this late at night, it's never good news.

Like when her mother died. It was six years ago now, almost to the day. They still lived in Zaranj back then. Maryam was sixteen at the time. Her mother had gone to the store. She never came back. There was a robbery. Her mother was caught in the middle of it. Maryam's father had returned late from work when he got the call. Maryam didn't understand as he fell to his knees, his face fracturing. Then, when he looked at her, tears in his eyes, *that* was when she understood. That was when she joined him on the ground, each of them holding tight to the other. Her father retired from his engineering job soon after that. He moved them down here, to where he grew up. He fell in with the Americans.

Maryam has often wondered at this turn of events. She's wondered at what drove him to become a spy. He loves his home. He loves his country. And yet he's not a young man, and he runs around as if he is, helping the Americans to root out Taliban insurgences, and Allah knows what else.

She thinks it's because of her mother. His wife. Something is missing in his life and he's trying to fill it with excitement and adventure – except more often than not it feels like pure terror to Maryam. She's the one who has to lie awake at night, or remain indoors during the day, and worry about him. She's the one who has to shoulder the burden of his new life.

Her father is not an oppressive man. He's no tyrant. He's taught her many things, far more than the fathers of her friends. And yet Maryam still feels herself fulfilling the obligations of her mother; she washes, she cooks, she cleans. The household chores fall to her. It's not that her father forces this upon her; it's just that he won't do it himself. If the household work is not done, he won't do it. He doesn't see the point. After her mother died, Aalem lost a large spark in his life.

It never used to be like this. Another symptom of his grieving depression. He would always help his wife around their apartment back in Zaranj. He'd help with the cooking and the cleaning. He didn't sit back and leave her to do it all. And then, when she was so senselessly killed, he lost all motivation. He doesn't care about cleanliness anymore. He'd live in a hovel, like a pig.

There's a gentle knock at her door and Maryam snaps back to the present with a start. The smell of solder is strong in her nose. She turns off the gun and swivels in her chair to face the door. "Yes?"

Her father pokes his head into her room. He's dressed to go out. Maryam feels a sinking in her stomach. "I've had a phone call," he says. "I'm needed."

"By the Americans?"

Aalem frowns as if she shouldn't throw that word around so carelessly.

Maryam rolls her eyes at him. "It's just the two of us," she says. "It's not like I would be calling it out in the bazaar."

"We should still be careful," he says. "I've bugged many

homes. I know how easy it is to do. What's to say that no one has attempted to bug us?"

"Well, I'm here most days, Papa – I think I would notice if someone tried to do such a thing. And I see you checking for them."

"Still, we cannot be too careful."

Maryam looks at him. She's not going to get pulled into a discussion about their security and how careful they need to be. They've had it too many times already. "Where are you going, Papa?"

"Mohammed has information for the Americans," Aalem says. "He's coming here to collect me and then we'll travel to them together."

Maryam suppresses a shudder. Mohammed is a friend of her father. He's lived his entire life in this area. He and her father were friends growing up. But Maryam doesn't care about any of that. What she cares about is how Mohammed makes her feel – uncomfortable. She tries to hide it from her father, and he doesn't seem to notice the lecherous way Mohammed behaves even when he's around. His eyes crawl over her. She feels them, even when her back is turned. His smile is smug when she looks at him. She's even seen him lick his lips on more than one occasion. He keeps his behavior hidden from her father. She hasn't mentioned it to him. He wouldn't ever try anything, she knows. He would never do anything to upset her father. He has to content himself with just looking, and Maryam can continue to ignore him.

"Information about what?" Maryam asks, moving on, pushing thoughts of Mohammed out of her head before they make her visibly shudder.

Aalem looks unsure about whether he's going to tell her

or not. He runs a hand down his mouth, through his beard. "You remember Babak Rashidi?"

Maryam narrows her eyes, sitting up. "Of course I remember him," she says. She remembers the stories her father told about him, at least. Babak the torturer. The flayer. "Papa, that man is dangerous. What are you going to do?"

He holds up his hands to calm her. "I won't be going anywhere near him," Aalem says. "Mohammed has seen him. We're going to lead the Americans to where he is, but we won't be getting close."

"And why do they need you? Mohammed can go alone."

"I speak English."

"And so does Mohammed."

"It's a specialist team. They need more than one escort. This is an important task, Maryam. Yes, Babak Rashidi is a dangerous man, but this is an opportunity to eliminate that danger."

Maryam knows she won't be able to talk her father out of doing this, but she still doesn't like it. She worries for him. She's going to worry for him most of all knowing that a man who already has a vendetta against her father is out there, and Aalem and Mohammed are going to be going directly to him. She doesn't care how many Americans, specialist or otherwise, are accompanying them.

"We won't be getting close," Aalem says. "That is the job of the Americans. I will not be near the danger."

Maryam sighs. "I don't want you to get hurt."

"And I won't. I've told you." He sighs in turn. "I need to go, Maryam. Mohammed will be here any moment."

Maryam gets to her feet and crosses the room to her father. She hugs him before he can go. "Just be careful," she says, feeling his beard hair tickling her cheek and ear.

"Always," he says. They part. "I will most likely be back late. Don't wait up for me."

"Always the same," Maryam says. "I'll see you in the morning."

"Yes," Aalem says, leaning forward to kiss her forehead. "You will."

He leaves her room, closing the door behind him. Maryam doesn't return to her desk. She remains standing where she is, watching the door, as if she can see her father through it. She stands there until she hears a knock at the front door, and her father answer it. She hears him and Mohammed speaking briefly and then they leave the house. Maryam remains by the door. Her stomach is in a pit. She doesn't feel good. But then again, whenever her father goes out and she knows he's doing work with and for the Americans, she feels like this.

She turns away from the door and goes back to her desk. All she can do when she feels like this is try to distract herself. To work. To put her mind somewhere else. She turns the solder gun back on and waits for it to heat up. She stares out the window while she waits. Her mind roams. She can't stop it.

CHAPTER ELEVEN

HQ is an Army base on the outskirts of an unnamed village, twenty miles south of the city of Zaranj. Mustafa escorted the team to a room with a sofa and a few cot beds where they could wait in relative comfort, and then he left to return to his assets and coordinate the search for Babak Rashidi.

It's been a day since they arrived, and so far they haven't heard back from Mustafa, or anyone else. The base is small and the soldiers stay out of their way. Meals have been brought to them and their leftovers have been collected an hour later. There isn't any need for them to leave the room. They need to keep a low profile, as if they were never here. The soldiers understand that. They know better than to ask any questions. This isn't likely to be the first time a black op or a special forces team has had to briefly wait or hide out on their base. This is a dangerous area. There's always something happening.

It turns out Tom was right in his initial observations of the team he's now a part of. There's a division, though it doesn't seem to be built on any sort of animosity so far as he can tell. Captain Robert Dale, Simon Collins, and Nathan Sapolsky form a group, and Zeke Greene is apart from them. Zeke doesn't seem to mind. He's happy enough keeping to himself. He reclines on one of the cots in the corner of the room, reading a battered Chester Himes paperback.

Tom, in turn, has been keeping to himself. He's cleaned his weapons, taking them apart and putting them back together, keeping his hands busy and his mind preoccupied. Waiting can be hard if you don't know how to keep yourself focused. Robert, Simon, and Nathan group together on the sofa, Simon and Nathan laughing sycophantically at Robert's stories. A couple of times, when their voices have lowered, Tom has noticed them looking his way out the corner of his eye. They're assessing him, gauging whether or not to invite him into their clique, trying to figure out which way he's going to fall on the divide. Tom ignores them. Groups have never been his thing.

His weapons cleaned and reassembled, he looks up at the clock on the wall. It's evening. He looks toward Zeke and his book. Tom can't see the cover or the title. He can see, though, that the front and back are bent, and the pages are fraying. Either Zeke picked it up second-hand and very cheap, or it's done a lot of miles in his travel bag.

Tom clears his throat. "It looks like you've read that more than once."

Zeke glances at him over the top of the book. He lowers it a little to speak. "A few times, yeah," he says.

"Which one is it?" Tom asks.

"*The Real Cool Killers*," Zeke says. He grins, and adds, "This is my travel copy. I've got a nicer one at home. It's not so damaged." He laughs. "I've got travel copies of all my favorite books. There's a hell of a lot of waiting around in this line of work." He closes the book with his finger inside to keep his place. "You read it? You read any Chester Himes?"

Tom nods. "I've read most of the Harlem Detective books," he says. "How many are there? Eight?"

"Nine, if you include *Plan B*. He died before he finished that one."

"Then I think I've read six of them."

"Yeah?" Zeke looks impressed. He sits up, putting the book to one side. "You got a favorite?"

Tom thinks for a moment, remembering each book. "I think I'd probably have to say the first one. *A Rage In Harlem*, right?"

"That's right."

"Yeah. It's maybe not the best, but I've got a fondness for it. You?"

"*Cotton Comes To Harlem*," Zeke says. "Pretty sure that's everyone's favorite – other than yours, apparently – but for good reason. You read much?"

"Whenever I can."

"But you didn't bring one with you for the downtime here."

"Not when I've got work to do," Tom says. "I wouldn't be able to focus on it. My mind would be elsewhere. And plus, this is my first mission. I need to make a good impression, you know?" He grins.

"Well, the important thing is that now there's a fellow reader I can talk with. The others, they don't read anything more than a manual, and even then I have my doubts. Skim them, probably. You might see them with a magazine sometime, but you can guarantee they're just looking at the pictures. Especially when you see the kind of magazines they're looking at."

"Are they the kind with naked women?"

"A *lot* of naked women," Zeke says. He casts his eyes over the room, indicating it before he says, "How are you enjoying your first mission so far?"

"It's a lot of what I expected," Tom says. "So far."

Zeke nods at this.

"I'm just wondering if, from what Mustafa said, we got here in time. If this Babak is gonna show up again and stick around long enough for us to nail him."

"Sometimes they do, sometimes they don't. Sometimes we get to go in and do our job, and other times we just have to go home. Speaking of, where's home to you, Rollins?"

"I'm from New Mexico."

"Just a couple of states away from me."

"They said you live in Louisiana."

Zeke nods. "That's right."

"I should clarify that I don't live in New Mexico," Tom says. "It's where I'm from. I don't *live* anywhere."

Zeke tilts his head. "No? What do you do when you aren't working?"

"Motels and hotels," Tom says.

"That's gotta be costly."

"I suppose it is. But I suppose losing my freedom would come with its own cost. I'm thinking, though, that when we get back from this, I might start looking at apartments to rent in Virginia. It makes sense to set down *some* roots, I guess. And if I don't like it, I can run out the lease and get back on the road."

"I take it you're not in any kind of a relationship."

Tom shakes his head. "You?"

"Hell yeah I am," Zeke says, and taps his ring finger and the wedding band there. Tom had already spotted it, but he's making conversation. Sometimes, it's possible to be *too* observant, and then you have nothing to talk to a person about. You can tell everything about them from a glance. It pays to play it dumb, like you haven't noticed telltale pieces of jewelry.

"What's her name?" Tom asks.

"Naomi."

"Been married long?"

"Few years now."

"How'd you meet?"

"At a bar. And we had mutual friends. No one's ever admitted it, but I think there was a set-up involved. Anyway, if it was, it worked out. Never looked back."

"You thinking about starting a family?"

"Already started," Zeke says. "Our boy's one year old now, nearly two. And he's gonna be a big brother pretty soon."

"Congratulations," Tom says. For clarification, Tom adds, "Naomi's pregnant right now? Or you're trying?"

"Oh, she's pregnant all right," Zeke says and laughs.

"Do you know what this one will be?"

"Little girl. You have any kids?"

"No," Tom says.

"They don't sound like they'd suit your nomadic lifestyle."

Tom grins. "Are you looking forward to having a daughter?"

"I am. I really am. Having a boy's great, too. I love being a dad."

"I assume your wife's excited, too."

"Like you wouldn't believe. She's always wanted to have kids – plural, that is. And she's a great mom. I know she's always wanted to have a little girl, and a big family, too. Personally, I think I'm happy to stop at two, but I know that if we didn't have a girl coming we'd be going until we *did*." Zeke laughs.

"What's your boy called?"

"Tre."

"Do you have a name for the girl?"

"We're still juggling a few options," Zeke says. "Nothing's solid just yet."

"My mother named me after her father," Tom says. "I never met him. He died before I was born, but she said he was the best man she ever knew. I guess when you know someone like that it makes names easy."

"Your mom know what you do now?"

"She's dead," Tom says. "She died when I was nine."

"Damn," Zeke says. "I'm sorry to hear that."

"It's been a long time."

"Still..." Zeke pauses a moment, then asks, "What about your father? Have you told him about this new life?"

"I haven't told him yet. I haven't seen him since I was recruited. It's been a couple of years since I saw him last."

"You're not close?"

"We're close enough," Tom says. "I just stay busy. And he and my step-mom live on one of those doomsday prepping communes. The people there are fine, but it's not my kind of scene. I've spent enough time around that kind of lifestyle already."

Zeke tilts his head a little, raising an eyebrow. "It ain't one of those racist militia-type places, is it?"

Tom shakes his head. "No. There's Black folk on the commune. Asians, too. It's an inclusive place."

Zeke nods. "That's good. For a moment there I was worried I was gonna have to reconsider this budding friendship."

Tom grins. "I'm glad it won't come to that."

Zeke smiles, but his eyes flicker toward Captain Dale and his group. Tom notices how his smile sours a little. Tom looks over. Robert and the others aren't looking back at them. They're talking among themselves. They don't care that Tom and Zeke are talking.

"You can't be too careful," Zeke says, turning his attention back to Tom. It seems like he wants to change the subject. "I think the scariest thing about having kids is worrying you're gonna fuck them up too bad. I mean, especially when my work takes me all around the world and I can't even talk to them about it, especially for their safety. It comes down to who you have them with. Naomi is a great mom, so at least I don't worry in that regard. But even so, you wonder, you know? When and where to draw the line. If you should be harsh, or if you should ease up."

"I have no experience," Tom says.

"But you know how your own daddy was with you."

Distant, Tom thinks. After his wife died, and before he met Sylvia, his new wife. She thawed him. Before that, Jeffrey was very focused on Tom and his brother learning survivalism. Running drills. Ensuring they could fend for themselves out in the wild. Tom thinks he wanted to make sure they would be able to look after themselves and each other if anything were to happen to him. Suddenly becoming the sole parent and carer weighed down on him.

Tom took to all of his training and preparation. Anthony

not so much. Anthony was a morose boy. He grieved for their mother for a long time. Tom isn't sure if he ever got over it, really. He was so young when it happened, even younger than Tom. Watching her wither away as the cervical cancer ate through her had a profound effect on him. A profound effect on all of them, but Anthony seemed to suffer the most and the longest. Tom and their father were able to stoically move on and build themselves back up. Anthony never did.

"He did his best," Tom says finally.

"Yeah, I guess that's all any of us can ever do," Zeke says. "I have this one cousin, though, his folks used to spoil him. Everything he ever wanted, they gave it to him. He's a few years younger than me, but growing up I was always jealous of him. I wanted all those things he got. But now, looking back, I'm glad it didn't happen like that. He's a grown man and all he does is spend his time online."

"Doing what?"

Zeke shrugs. "Damned if I know. Video games, maybe. Chat rooms. He says he knows hackers, like that's supposed to be impressive. I mean, I dunno, maybe it is. Or maybe he's just on there talking about Japanese cartoons with other grown men who always got what they wanted. Anyway, twenty-four seven, he's on his damned computer. He's never really grown up."

Before they can say anything further, there's a knock at the door. Robert responds to it, summoning the knocker in. A soldier steps inside, peering tentatively around the room. Robert stands to speak with him.

"Captain Dale?" the soldier asks.

Robert nods.

"Mustafa Rabbani has asked me to tell you that he's en route, sir, and that he has two assets accompanying him. He said one of them has the whereabouts of your target. He asked you to be prepared for his arrival, sir."

"ETA?"

"Ten minutes, sir."

Robert circles a finger in the air, looking around the room at his team. "You all heard the man," he says. "Let's go."

CHAPTER TWELVE

They meet with Mustafa off-base, traveling to him in a Jeep. The sun is low on the horizon. It's almost dark. Simon is driving. He pulls the Jeep to the side and turns off the lights. From down the road, a vehicle flashes them three times.

"Proceed," Robert says.

They roll down the road, keeping the lights off, playing it careful. This is where Mustafa told them to meet, but they're not taking chances.

Tom is in the back of the Jeep, sandwiched between Nathan and Zeke. They each hold onto their M4s, and Zeke and Nathan are both looking out of their windows, scanning the area. Tom looks straight ahead, through the windshield, toward the vehicles they're approaching. There are two of them. He recognizes one of them as one of the cars Mustafa drove them here in. Behind it is a battered, dusty Toyota Corolla. It's dark, but Tom can see at least two figures inside, both of them in the front.

"There's our man," Robert says.

Mustafa gets out of his car as the Jeep gets close. He

waves for the men in the Toyota to do the same. Tom gets a good look at them both. Two locals. Both men are bearded. One of them, the driver, wears a turban. Robert gets out of the Jeep and tells only Simon to remain inside, behind the wheel.

As the team gathers close, Mustafa points out the two men with him. "This is Aalem Hussain, and this is Mohammed. No surname on Mohammed." Mohammed is the man with the turban. Aalem looks slightly younger than him. There's less white in his beard.

"We've heard about you," Robert says to Aalem.

Aalem nods his head.

"They both speak English," Mustafa says. "They're going to be your guides and your translators, if needed. Mohammed here is one of our assets who keeps a close eye on Khan and his people. He's one of our men who first became aware of Babak being in-country, and he's seen him again."

"Recently?" Robert asks, looking at Mohammed.

Mohammed glances at Mustafa, and then nods at Robert. "Yuh-yes," he says. "Very recent, sir. I saw him and I called Mustafa straight away." His accent is thick, Tom notices. He speaks English, but he's not confident about it. He wonders if it's the same for Aalem.

"Where'd you see him?"

"Khan has many hideouts in the area," Mohammed says. "We've mapped them all. His routes, too. Babak and his companions are in one of the hideouts."

"What are they doing there?"

"I – I don't know, sir. Hiding, I think. Waiting, maybe? I saw them arrive and I called Mustafa straight away."

"How many men are with him?"

"Uh," Mohammed says. "I think... I think..." He counts on his fingers, remembering his numbers in English. He holds up all of the fingers on his left hand and the thumb on his right. "Six," he says, looking pleased with himself.

"Did you see their faces?"

"I – I'm afraid I did not pay attention to the men. I was focused entirely upon Babak Rashidi."

"Did you see if they were white, at least? Middle Eastern? What?"

"It was dark," Mohammed says. "It was hard for me to be sure. I could only be certain of Babak. I've seen his face and his picture so many times."

"Were they armed? Did you notice that at least?"

Mohammed nods, eager to please. "Yes, sir. They were armed."

"What kind of guns?"

"I do not know guns very well. I didn't recognize them. Automatic, though. I could tell that much."

Robert turns his attention to Aalem. "What about you?" he says. "What did you see?"

"Nothing, sir," Aalem says. "I have not seen the men. I was called to help by Mustafa. Mohammed was not far from me and so he picked me up on the way here." Aalem's English is clearer, more confident.

"I suppose you have a personal investment in seeing this bastard captured," Robert says. "Would you say so?"

"I suppose that I would, sir."

"Are there eyes on Babak's current whereabouts?" Robert asks, turning back to Mohammed.

He nods. "I left a fellow asset there. I told him to call me if Babak should move again, and to follow him if he did. He has not been in touch.

"All right, well, we're wasting time here," Robert says. "Let's get going before he *does* up and move." He turns to his team, splitting them. "I'll ride with Simon. Nathan, get in with Mustafa. Rollins and Greene, right with our two new friends here. Take point."

They all get into their respective vehicles. Tom and Zeke get into the back of the Toyota. Mohammed waits until everyone has gotten into the other vehicles, until their engines are running, and then he turns the car around and leads the way through the desert.

CHAPTER THIRTEEN

The hideout is much like Bill Irving's. The building looks similar, but is smaller, and was probably once used as a shepherd's hut. There are two box trucks parked near to it.

The team have left the vehicles behind and continued on foot. Mustafa told Mohammed to call the asset who was keeping watch and tell him to get clear of the area.

The approach to the hideout is easy. There are no hills leading to it, which would outline them against the sky. There are plenty of rocky outcrops for them to conceal themselves behind. The team is currently spread out, observing. Robert communicates to them via their earpieces.

"Anyone see anything?" he asks.

Tom is with Zeke. Mohammed and Aalem are further back with Mustafa. Tom looks toward the hideout. He can see some light inside, presumably from a floor lamp. There's a little movement. Some shadows against the inner walls. There's no one outside, on guard, which he finds strange. He radios back to Robert and mentions this.

"Babak is getting sloppy," Robert says. "He thinks we

don't know he's here. He's evaded capture for so long he's grown careless."

"But what about the men with him?" Tom says.

"What about them?" Robert says. "Probably non-military. Wouldn't cross their mind to put a guard outside."

Tom isn't confident about this, but he doesn't protest. It's his first mission. Captain Dale has more experience. He knows what he's talking about. Tom glances at Zeke to his left. Zeke raises his eyebrows. "You might be right," Zeke says. "But then again, the captain might be right, too. The area looks clear. I don't see anywhere around the hideout for them to lay an ambush."

Tom has to agree with that. The hut is in the middle of nowhere. There's nothing behind it and nothing around it. The grounds are clear. The only real form of approach is the way that the team have come in.

"I can see movement inside," Nathan says on the radio. "They're not doing anything. Just stretching their legs."

"Do you have a count?" Robert asks.

"I've seen three guys. It's dark in there but I think they're white."

"Does anyone have eyes on Babak?"

They all respond in the negative.

"We stay here until we see him," Robert says.

Mustafa has been listening in. He comes on the radio. "The asset Mohammed left behind said that Babak never left."

"We stay here until we see him," Robert says again. Mustafa does not respond.

The team wait, and they watch. The minutes tick by. The night is cool. Tom doesn't feel it. He focuses on his breathing, and on the windows of the hut. He's at a bad angle. It's hard to see inside. It's hard to see anything other than the outside of the building.

Nathan comes through again. "He's there," he says. "I've got eyes on him."

"What's he doing?" Robert asks.

"Same as the others – stretching his legs, stretching his back. He's talking. All right, he's sitting back down now."

"All right, look alive," Robert says. "We have a visual. Mustafa, I want you up front with us for a positive ID when we get inside. New guy, Rollins, it's babysitting duty for you. You hold back with Mohammed and Aalem. Sound off."

"Yes, sir," Tom says.

"Got it," Mustafa says.

"Everyone into position," Robert says.

Tom ducks low and heads toward the outcrop where Mustafa, Mohammed, and Aalem have concealed themselves. He sees Mustafa moving away from it, bent double, making his way toward Robert. Tom takes his place with Mohammed and Aalem. Aalem leans against the rock, peering around the side of it, watching Mustafa go, watching the hideout. He glances back at Tom long enough to nod. Mohammed stands back. He chews his bottom lip. Tom notices how he bounces on the balls of his feet, his arms folded. Tom puts it down to nervous energy. He's probably never been this close to a potential firefight before.

"Tuck in," Tom says, motioning for him to get closer to the rocks. "If the bullets start flying, you want to be close to cover."

Mohammed swallows. He nods and then does as Tom says.

CHAPTER FOURTEEN

Babak sits back down. He resisted the urge to look out of the window, despite knowing who is out there.

Bram stands close to the wall nearby, out of view of the window, fists clenched tight down by his sides. He stares at the window and the door. He bristles with restless energy. All of his men do. The ones sitting have their MP5s ready in their laps, their hands close to the triggers. Babak notices that it's the ex-KCT men who are particularly restless. Bram, Dirk, and Hennie are almost vibrating. The others are ready, prepared for what might come, but they don't look like they're about to go running out into the night, guns blazing.

Still, Babak knows how this kind of energy is infectious. He feels it a little himself, beginning to tingle and soon to course, despite his best efforts to breathe deep and remain calm. He knows he needs to say something.

"Calm down," he says, looking at Bram, and then looking at all of the other men in turn, starting with Dirk and Hennie. "You're making me nervous."

"It makes me nervous to know that they're out there," Bram says.

"Yes, but this is exactly what I wanted," Babak says. "The men out there have met Bill Irving. That's been confirmed to me. They know exactly where he is."

"Then we should go and get them."

"We have backup coming. We just need to be patient."

"We don't need reinforcements."

"You'll do as I say," Babak snaps, glaring up at Bram, losing patience. Bram stares back at him. As usual, his face is unreadable. "This is *my* operation," Babak says. "You have been hired to answer to *me*. We sit tight, and we wait for the others to arrive. I can see that you're all eager to get out there and test your mettle against the CIA –"

"Isn't that why we were hired?" Bram says.

"Only if necessary," Babak says. "You were hired to do as I say. To escort me. To assist in the capture. And in return you're going to receive a lucrative route – but *only* if you do as I say. You'll get your chance to engage, but not before our backup arrives."

He sees how Bram's nostrils flare as he inhales. Bram doesn't say anything for three breaths, calming himself, but then he nods. "Very well," he says. "We do it your way. But when they arrive, we shall be stepping outside to join them."

"That's all I ask," Babak says. "All I request is some patience. They'll be here soon."

Babak feels like the vibrations have stopped at least. He feels like their restless bouncing has abated.

"And remember," Babak adds. "This CIA team has been called in especially for me. This is a gift that has fallen into my lap. I want – I *need* – these men to be taken alive."

CHAPTER FIFTEEN

Zeke waits for Robert's command to start moving. They'll drop in fast and hard on the hut, catch them by surprise. It's open season on the men with Babak, especially if they're armed and they turn hostile, but Babak *must* be taken alive.

Mustafa is with Zeke. It's their job to secure Babak. Robert, Simon, and Nathan will deal with the men with him. Of course, knowing how Robert and the others operate, as Zeke does, he imagines that means a bullet for each man in Babak's company, regardless of whether they attempt to fight back or not. Zeke has seen it happen many times before.

He doesn't think about that right now. It's not worth the bandwidth. He has a job to do. An important job. When the hideout is secured, he and Mustafa need to get in, get Babak, and get out. Robert, Simon, and Nathan will at least wait until they're clear before they open fire on Babak's friends – that's provided they up and surrender first during the smash and grab. And then Robert et al can catch up with Zeke and Mustafa and tell Mustafa that their hostages made a move, turned violent, nothing else they could do.

Robert comes on the radio. "Let's move," he says. "Team B, on our flank."

Zeke and Mustafa are Team B.

Mustafa is armed with a Beretta. He doesn't have an automatic rifle. "Stay behind me," Zeke tells him. "Stay low."

Mustafa nods. He knows what he's doing.

Zeke sees the three dark figures of Robert, Simon, and Nathan moving forward in formation. Zeke leaves the rocky outcrop behind, slipping out from behind it, Mustafa following. They fall into position behind the point team. They make their way to the hut.

CHAPTER SIXTEEN

Tom hears the radio. He sees the team make their move.

Tom turns away. It isn't his job to watch them. He trusts their capabilities. It's his job to protect Mohammed and Aalem, and to watch their six, make sure no one tries to slip into the area and get the drop.

As he turns, he sees that Mohammed isn't watching what's happening, either. He's leaning against the rock still, his back flat against it, and he's looking back the way they've come. He's bouncing again, same as before, up and down on the balls of his feet. He sees Tom looking at him and he freezes. He flashes a bright smile. A fake smile.

Tom frowns. He looks into the darkness.

He spots movement. It's coming in low, crawling across the ground. Men, armed. He sees AK47s in their hands, out ahead of them as they crawl, sneaking closer. They're far to Tom's left, coming in wide. He can't make out who they are, but that doesn't matter. They're obviously a threat.

Tom preps his radio, to warn the others of the incoming

ambush. Before he can say a word, Mohammed reaches behind himself. He pulls out a Glock. He points it at Tom.

"Don't say a word," Mohammed says.

Disturbed by the movement and the talking, Aalem turns back from peering around the rock. He looks at Mohammed, at his gun, and then at Tom. He does a double-take, not sure that he can trust his eyes. "Mohammed?" he says, sounding shocked.

Mohammed turns his head, just a little, baring his teeth. It's distraction enough for Tom. With his left hand, he grabs Mohammed's wrist and drives it away, toward the rock, getting the gun away from himself. He slams Mohammed's arm against the rock and forces him to drop the gun, and he reaches for his throat with his right hand to silence him.

But Mohammed realizes what he's doing, why he's reaching for his throat.

Mohammed screams.

CHAPTER SEVENTEEN

Zeke and the others are almost at the hut when they hear the scream.

It comes from behind them. Zeke freezes and drops to a knee, readying his rifle. The scream is quickly choked off, but almost instantly following it gunfire erupts, the sound destroying the night's silence. This also comes from behind them. Zeke wheels toward the sounds, rifle raised, putting Mustafa behind himself.

"Spread out!" Robert says. "Get to cover! Return fire!"

Bullets hit the ground close by. Zeke lays down suppressing fire, wondering where Tom is and why he didn't warn them. Wondering, too, who screamed.

These are questions for later. Right now is about surviving this ambush.

"Simon!" Robert shouts. "Run! Get the fucking car!"

Zeke backs up, firing toward the men who are emerging from the darkness, laying down covering fire for Simon as he sprints to their right, away from the fight to circle around back to their vehicles. It's hard to count how many ambushers there are. At least a dozen, Zeke would guess, judging by the flashes from their rifles, which he thinks from the sound are AK47s. Mustafa sticks close to him, firing his Beretta into the darkness over his shoulder, one hand on Zeke's back to guide him backward. They make for the hut. It's not ideal, but it's the only cover available to them here.

Robert and Nathan are moving wider, the same direction Simon went, attempting to avoid being pinned down. In their grouping, they return a sustained fire. Robert, reloading, motions for Zeke and Mustafa to follow them, to keep up.

Before they can set off, the door to the hut flies open. Six men emerge, each of them wearing ski masks, and each of them armed with an MP5. They fire toward Robert and the others. They have to scatter and flee. Zeke sees that they're being corralled toward their mystery ambushers. He also sees how the masked men do not shoot to kill; they're aiming at the ground, toward their feet, herding them but not trying to kill them. Zeke realizes that the ambushers appear to be doing the same. They're not aiming at their bodies, despite the fact that Zeke and the others have dropped a couple of them. They're firing *toward* them, not *at* them.

The biggest of the masked men turns his attention toward Zeke and Mustafa. He fires the MP5 in their direction. While Zeke doesn't think he's shooting to kill, he still reacts to bullets coming his way. He stumbles back as they hit the ground close to him, and as he looks up he sees the man charging, knocking both him and Mustafa back and down. The man swings his rifle, driving it into Mustafa's face, bloodying him where it connects close to his temple. He stomps down on Zeke, pinning his own rifle against his body.

Zeke struggles under his boot, trying to wriggle free. He

can hear gunfire still, all around him, and cries. His earpiece has come loose when he was tackled. It hangs from his ear. If anyone is saying anything, he can't hear them.

The man, satisfied that Mustafa has been incapacitated, turns his attention fully to Zeke. Zeke looks up at him. Through the mask he's wearing, he thinks the man is smiling. He can see it in his cold eyes.

The man reaches down, both hands grabbing for Zeke's neck, his boot still pressing down on Zeke's rifle, its body digging into his tactical vest and crushing his chest. Zeke grabs at the man's leg and twists it. He manages to roll to the side, throwing the man back. The man hops, but he keeps his balance. Zeke turns, pushing himself up. He sees Mustafa close to him, blood running down the side of his face and dripping to the ground. Mustafa's Beretta is gone. Mustafa looks around as if trying to find it.

"Get up!" Zeke says, shouting almost in his face. "Run!"

Mustafa tries to push himself up. He looks behind Zeke. Zeke hears a gunshot and he flinches, expecting to feel it penetrate his body, or to burst through his skull and face and then feel nothing at all, but that's not what happens. The bullet hits Mustafa in the head. His skull snaps back. He hits the ground and lies very flat and very still.

Zeke spins. The big man is close behind him. A Sig Sauer P320 is at the end of his extended arm. His face lowers. Still grinning, Zeke is sure. He turns the gun on Zeke, pointing it at his face.

"Drop your weapons," the man says.

Zeke hears him clearly, despite the firefight raging around them. He has an interesting accent. It takes Zeke a moment to place it. Dutch. Zeke frowns. It's not an accent he expected to hear all the way out here, and especially not in this situation.

Zeke doesn't react to the demand fast enough for the big Dutchman. "Have it your way," he says, and then he swings the Sig Sauer, slamming the handle of it into the side of Zeke's head.

CHAPTER EIGHTEEN

Tom punches Mohammed, knocking him down and silencing him, but it's too late. The sound of gunfire is fierce. Tom raises his M4, pointing it at Aalem. Aalem promptly raises his hands and shakes his head. "I have no weapon," he says. "I – I – I don't know what he's doing, I swear!"

"Turn around," Tom says, keeping the gun on him, simultaneously trying to see beyond him, what's happening. He needs to help the others, but he can't turn his back on Aalem. He could be just as treacherous as Mohammed.

Aalem does as he's told. Tom throws him against the rock and pats him down. Aalem is unarmed. Tom backs off, allows Aalem to push himself off the rock, though he keeps his hands raised. Tom reaches down for Mohammed's Glock. He throws it aside, into the darkness. "Stay here," Tom says, rifle in Aalem's face. "Sit down and lace your hands on top of your head. Don't fucking move."

Tom has to leave them. He has no choice. The others are in danger. He peers around the rock, toward the battle. He can see Zeke close to the hut, fighting with one of the masked men. The biggest of the six. The others, all masked, are firing toward Robert and Nathan, who are behind another outcrop, shielding, returning fire when they're able.

Tom charges from cover, firing toward the hut, heading for Robert and Nathan. He turns and fires toward the AK47-wielding ambushers, too, driving everyone back.

Drawing close to Robert and Nathan, he doesn't duck behind cover. The masked men back up, concealing themselves behind the hut. The others in the dark scatter. Tom looks toward Zeke again. He sees Mustafa on the ground nearby, lying very still. It doesn't look good. Zeke is down, too, but there's still some motion about him. He sees the big man reaching down and grabbing Zeke by the front of his tactical vest.

A pair of hands grab him, drag him behind cover. "Are you fucking nuts?" Nathan says. "Get into cover, goddamnit! We're outnumbered!"

"They've got Zeke!" Tom says. "He looked unconscious."

He hears the roar of an engine, speeding through the night, coming their way.

"Return fire," Robert says. "Keep them at bay. That's our ride."

Tom swaps out his magazine and does as Robert says. He's lost sight of Zeke. He and the big man are gone. They must be inside or behind the hut with the others. Mustafa remains on the ground. It's clear he isn't going anywhere.

The car engine gets closer, its engine getting louder. Tom fires. He turns to Robert as it screeches to a stop close by. "We need to loop round and get Zeke," he says. "They can't have got far, especially not carrying him. We can run them down, take them out. We can potentially still grab Babak, too."

Robert narrows his eyes.

"Fucking *nuts*," Nathan says again.

"Get in the car, Rollins," Robert says, voice raised. "This mission is FUBAR. We need to go."

"But Zeke –"

"Zeke's on his own," Robert says. "Nathan, get this asshole in the fucking car." Robert turns and starts running toward it.

Before Tom knows what's happening, he feels the stock of Nathan's rifle driven into his face, knocking him back against the rock, dazing him. "This is for your own good, asshole," Nathan says, then grabs him by the vest and forces him forward, pushing him ahead, shoving him into the back of the car.

Tom's head swims. He hits the far door as Nathan forces him over, getting in beside him. Before the door can be closed, Simon speeds off, away from the battle. There's gunfire behind them, chasing them away. Some of the bullets hit the vehicle, but not enough to do damage and bring it to a halt.

Tom jostles. He tastes blood. His head bounces off the window as they bounce over the uneven terrain. He's dimly aware of someone cursing, of someone else slamming a hand down on the dash.

He thinks about Zeke, but he's not sure why. It's hard to focus.

CHAPTER NINETEEN

Babak doesn't leave the hut until the fighting ends. When he does, he takes in the scene before him, looking around, straining against the darkness. A few of the Taliban men have been killed in the battle. He sees the others dragging their bodies along the ground, gathering them up. When he takes a step forward he feels spent shells beneath his boots.

"We got one of them," Bram says. The Black member of the black ops team is slumped on the ground, unconscious, blood running down his face. Bram holds him in a seated position with a hand clasping his tactical vest.

"Just one?" Babak says, feeling disappointment. He'd remained inside the hut until the shooting was over, lying flat and covering his head. He heard all the sounds of the battle; of gunfire, screams, calls, dying men. He'd ventured out only when he was certain it was over. Babak hadn't come here to fight. He came here to capture, and he'd anticipated capturing more than *one*. "What happened to the others?"

"They had a car," Bram says. "They sped away." He

points. "You can see the tracks. Of course, if you'd been out here you would've seen it all for yourself."

Babak ignores the jibe. Something catches his eye beyond Bram and the unconscious captive. He steps past them, toward a recognizable face with a hole through its forehead. Mustafa Rabbani. He wheels on Bram. "What happened to him?" he demands, jabbing a finger down at the corpse.

"It was kill or be killed," Bram says, shrugging. "The situation called for it."

He sees how Bram's men are standing close to him, watching Babak, watching his reactions. He sees how they still have their guns out, fingers close to the triggers.

"I needed as many of them alive as possible," Babak says. He points a finger at his own temple. "Do you know how much information Mustafa was privy to? Do you know how much importance there was in those brains you have splashed upon the ground?"

"We could have killed all of them," Bram says. "But we didn't. Because you told us not to. We fired at them, the same as the Taliban men did. And look how many of them suffered for it. It's fortunate that we are good at what we do or we may have endured the same fate. You should be grateful for this one." He shakes the unconscious man to illustrate his point.

Babak puts his hands on his hips and looks out into the darkness, eyes following the route the tire tracks have gone.

There's a commotion and Babak turns back around. The Dutchmen turn, too, raising their rifles. The Taliban have found two more men whom they usher forward, AK47s at their backs. Babak can hear one of the men, the one wearing a turban, complaining.

"I'm with you!" he says, his hands in the air. "We're on the same side!"

Babak smiles, but not at Mohammed. He smiles when he sees the man beside him, arms also in the air. Babak goes to them, waving his hands for the Taliban to lower their weapons. "This one is with us," he says, pointing at Mohammed. "Keep guns on this one." He looks at Aalem, feeling satisfaction at his capture. "It's very good to see you again, Aalem."

Aalem says nothing. He sets his jaw and looks defiantly back at Babak, refusing to cower. His arms remain in the air.

Mohammed rubs at his jaw, twisting it side to side. "What happened to you?" Babak asks.

"I was hit," Mohammed says. "One of them punched me. He saw the Taliban coming. I managed to sound the alarm, but he hit as hard as a train. When I came back round, I had guns in my face."

Babak claps him on the back. "It's over now, my friend. Your days of serving those dogs are done. And you brought me a gift!" He laughs at Aalem. "The man who betrayed me."

"I brought you many gifts," Mohammed says, nodding toward the captured man. He frowns. "Is that all? Only the one?"

Babak grumbles. "Let's not talk about it. Our Dutch friends may grow touchy on the subject. Mustafa is dead, but I can make do with what I have."

Mohammed points at the captured man. "His name is Zeke Greene," he says. "He met Bill Irving. I know he did. They all did."

Babak nods. "I received your message."

"If the others got away, Bill may move again."

"This one will lead me to him," Babak says. "And even if he does not, he'll tell me everything he knows. With a member of the CIA captive, there are opportunities to mine for so much more information than just the whereabouts of Bill Irving. I'm confident about that." He talks to the Taliban behind Aalem, pointing toward the other captive – Zeke Greene – and says, "Take him over there, with the other one." He turns to Bram and his men, calls to them. "Bind these two, get them in the truck."

Bram and his men do not respond, but Bram hauls Zeke upright and slings his limp form over his shoulder.

"Here is where we part," Babak says to Mohammed. "Go with the Taliban and await further instructions. Always be ready. I could be in touch very soon."

"I was wondering," Mohammed says as Babak turns, surprising him and causing him to turn back with a raised eyebrow. There's a malevolent look upon his face. "I was wondering if I may make a detour before I go with our allies."

Babak frowns. "What sort of a detour?"

"I would like to bring a guest," Mohammed says. "A woman."

Babak feels his frown deepen. "A woman? You understand where you're going, don't you? You understand the company you will be with?"

The malevolence does not leave Mohammed's face. He smiles. "She's very special to me," he says.

Babak shakes his head. Mohammed, so far as he's aware, is not married. He has no attachments. It's one of the things that made him such an appealing option for a double agent. "I can't allow that," he says. "There are more pressing concerns. We have important work to do."

Again, Babak turns to leave, and again, Mohammed stops him. He's undeterred. "I think if you know who she is, you may change your mind."

"I'm intrigued."

"Her name is Maryam Hussain," Mohammed says. "She's the daughter of Aalem."

This does change things. Babak looks toward the Dutchmen and their captives. They're both bound now. Zeke Greene has been disarmed. His tactical vest has been cast aside. Aalem is being directed into the back of one of the trucks.

Babak turns back to Mohammed with a smile. "Very well," he says. "You may make your detour. But she'll have to behave herself."

"Thank you, Babak," Mohammed says. "And I will ensure it. But I should go alone to collect her. If I turn up with any of these men, she will grow suspicious. I can rejoin with them later."

"They won't give out their location like that."

"Then I'll call them when we're ready for collection."

"How do you intend to persuade her to join you? I assume the two of you are not already an item."

"I'll lie," Mohammed says. "I'll persuade her. And, if that does not work, I'll use force. But I don't think it will come to that, not if I tell her her father is awaiting her."

Babak places a hand on Mohammed's shoulder, squeezing it. "Go," he says. "Have your fun." He raises a finger. "But remain ready, always. Await my call."

Mohammed nods eagerly and then hurries off to discuss the change of plans with the Taliban.

Babak grins to himself. He turns and makes his way toward the trucks. He holds onto this information for now. It may come in useful later, when he has Aalem back at the Abattoir.

CHAPTER TWENTY

Tom's vision clears. His brain settles, no longer feeling like it's swimming. Memories of the battle come back to him, clear. He remembers Zeke's capture.

"Stop the car!" he says. He wipes blood from his mouth.

Robert looks back at him from the passenger seat. "We're not stopping the car, Rollins. We've only just got clear."

"Stop the fucking car!" Tom says. "They have Zeke!"

"Do I need to calm you down again, Rollins?" Nathan says beside him.

"You can try it, motherfucker, but this time I'm ready."

They glare at each other. The car does not stop. Tom takes matters into his own hands. He reaches through the front, grabbing at Simon's arms on the steering wheel.

"Jesus Christ!" Simon says, losing control of the car.

Chaos erupts inside the vehicle. Nathan grabs for Tom, but Tom back-elbows him in the face, bloodying his nose; a receipt for the blood Nathan has drawn from him.

"All right, stop the car!" Robert says as it moves wildly from side to side, in danger of tipping and rolling.

Simon stomps on the brakes. Robert spins around, staring at Tom with hard eyes. "What do you think you're gonna do, Rollins?" he says.

Nathan nurses his nose, cursing under his breath. Tom ignores him. "We have to go back for him," he says. "We can't leave him there. He has a wife, a kid, another kid on the way. We can't leave him there with that sick bastard planning on flaying him."

"That's why we get out of here and we come back in force," Robert says.

"They're probably already clear of the area," Tom says. "If we leave and come back, any trail is gonna be stone-cold. And what if they're over the border? We need to cut them off."

"We're not going back," Robert says, shaking his head, preparing to turn back around in his seat. "We were ambushed, and they have the numbers. I'm not going to lead us back into a potential death trap."

"Then I'll go," Tom says. "Just me."

Robert stops turning. He looks back at Tom. "*Why?*" he says. "What is Zeke to you? You've known him all of, what, a day?"

"I've known him as long as I've known any of you," Tom says. "And I'd do the same if it were you back there."

Robert looks at Simon and then Nathan. Simon shrugs. Nathan holds his nose still. He cuts his eyes murderously toward Tom.

Tom doesn't wait for them to come to a decision. He reaches for the door handle.

"Rollins, you've been a part of my team for a whole goddamn five minutes," Robert says. "And you're already a colossal pain in my ass."

"I'm gonna be the pain in the ass that brings Zeke back home."

"You're so determined, then you go get him if you're that desperate to get yourself killed. We'll regroup, stick to the original plan."

Tom nods. He pushes the door open.

"You've got your radio?"

"I've got it."

"And remember – we were never here."

"I won't be seen."

"You *can't* be. Anything happens to you, the government denies all knowledge. You're a mercenary running wild."

Tom gets out of the car. He shoulders the M4 and runs into the night, back the way they came.

CHAPTER TWENTY-ONE

Robert stares back through the rear window, watching Rollins disappear.

"Son of a bitch could've broken my nose," Nathan says.

"Well, did he?" Simon asks, twisting.

"No, but it's gonna swell." Nathan lets his hands drop.

Slowly, Robert turns back around. He grits his teeth, feeling a sourness in his stomach and the back of his throat. He doesn't like how Rollins spoke to him. Disobedient prick.

"I'm surprised you let him leave," Simon says.

Robert waves a dismissive hand. "Let him go. We're not gonna see him again."

"You rate his chances so low?" Nathan asks.

"Babak has Zeke, and that's the end of that," Robert says. "We'll send his wife and kids our regards, but there's nothing else we can do for him. He's dead soon, if he ain't already. As for Rollins, he's got no vehicle, no ammo, and no backup. He's not gonna be able to get into Iran, and he's outnumbered by Babak's team, whoever they are. Furthermore, this whole area is crawling with Taliban – hell, that might've even been them back there, ambushing us, in cahoots with Babak. Either way, they're gonna be on high alert for Americans. And if they find one, shit, they're gonna have the time of their lives. I don't see him lasting through the night."

Nathan laughs. He's pissed about Tom's back-elbow, despite it being a receipt. He doesn't care what happens to him. "Through the night, huh? Wanna make it interesting?"

"I could go in for some of that action," Simon says.

"Four hours," Nathan says, "tops."

"I'll be generous," Simon says. "He makes it to morning. Daybreak."

Robert grins. The annoyance he felt is subsiding now. It helps knowing that the person who's pissed him off has run toward his inevitable doom. Ordinarily, Robert likes to deal with people who piss him off personally, but in this instance he'll make an exception. The new boy can go and get himself killed and keep Robert's hands clean. He won't have to explain anything.

"Start driving," he says. "We can work out bets on the way back."

CHAPTER TWENTY-TWO

Maryam can't sleep.

She lies awake, staring at the ceiling, and she worries about her father. It's getting late. It *is* late.

She hates this. Knowing that her father is out there, and knowing that he's helping the Americans to hunt down a dangerous man. Hates knowing that she's not going to be able to sleep until she knows that he's returned home and she's certain he's safe.

It's not worth fighting. Sleep will not come for her. This isn't the first time she's suffered a night like this. She gives up, rolling out of bed and grabbing her nightgown, wrapping herself in it and going through to the kitchen. She pauses a moment, listening to the house, listening to the outside. Everything is very quiet and very still.

In the kitchen, she makes chai and pours herself a cup. Carrying it through to the living room, she makes herself comfortable on the sofa and sips at her drink while she watches the door, as if her father will immediately walk through, they can drink chai together and then retreat to their separate rooms and *finally* Maryam will be able to sleep.

It doesn't happen. She knew it wouldn't. She continues to watch the door, feeling alert, knowing that tiredness will not come until the morning, when her father is most likely to return.

The minutes pass by. They turn into an hour. The chai is long finished, but Maryam remains restless upon the sofa. She breathes deeply, trying to remain calm and to stop her mind from racing, from fearing the worst. For so many years, she's feared the worst about everything. Ever since her mother died, and before that even. Because the worst keeps coming. It keeps happening, over and over. There's no escape from it.

She hears something outside. She checks the time. It's almost ten. She sits up, hoping that it might finally be her father, and a good night's sleep is not completely off the table after all.

A car pulls up to the front of the house. She thinks she recognizes the sound of the engine – Mohammed's car, bringing her father home. The engine is cut silent. Maryam waits, listening. She frowns when, just a moment later, there's a frantic knocking at the door. It's too fast. Too soon. As if someone ran from the car to the door.

She feels her stomach sinking, and that familiar feeling of dreading the worst comes to the fore. She flashes back to the death of her mother. The constant sensation of sinking that followed her in the days and weeks in the aftermath.

Weightless, she gets to her feet and floats to the door, already numb, knowing that her father would not knock. He has his key. There's no reason for him to knock. She opens the door.

Mohammed stands before her, alone. He's disheveled, wiping sweat from his brow. His jaw is swollen on the left side, and he prods at it with the tips of his fingers. He straightens when he sees her. "Maryam," he says, and he sounds breathless.

"Where is my father?" Maryam asks, hearing the words leaving her mouth but unaware of saying them.

Mohammed holds up his hands in a pre-emptive calming gesture. "Your father is hurt," he says. "But don't worry! He's okay. He's with the Americans. He asked me to come and get you, to take you to him."

Maryam feels a sliver of hope cutting through the despair. Her father is not dead. He's hurt, but he's not dead. "How badly is he hurt? What happened?" She notices how Mohammed's eyes flicker down her body, aware that she wears only her nightgown and the shorts and T-shirt she sleeps in. His eyes linger briefly on her bare feet and lower legs. Even now, in an emergency, he can't help himself.

"It's not life-threatening," Mohammed says. "A broken leg, if that. It may just be a fracture."

"What happened?"

Mohammed shakes his head, waves his hands, snapping himself out of his stare. "We must go," he says. "Come, come." He tries to usher her out of the house, reaching for her arm.

Maryam keeps out of his reach. "I'll change," she says. "I won't be long." She closes the door on Mohammed and races through to her bedroom and grabs the closest dress to hand, stripping out of her nightgown and clothes, slipping into underwear before pulling the dress over her head. She hesitates before leaving her room, and grabs a pair of shalwar – trousers – too, pulling them up her legs before she slips into shoes. The shalwar are blue. The dress is white. She wraps her head with a thin scarf and then hurries from the house. She can hear Mohammed's engine idling. He's inside, waiting for her. He waves her to him. Maryam dreads the prospect of being in such a confined space with this man, but she thinks of her father. She thinks of how he's hurt. She swallows her disgust and gets into the car.

CHAPTER TWENTY-THREE

Tom slows only as he nears the scene of the firefight, readying his M4 and scanning the area to make sure it's clear. He doesn't see anyone lying in wait; no signs of a trap. He presses on toward the shepherd's hut.

The area is clear, as expected. He sees multiple tire tracks on the ground, more than just the two trucks that were here and the vehicle Simon rode to the rescue in. The tracks all head off in different directions. Tom checks the hut. It's empty.

The spent shells have been left where they fell. There was no point in clearing them up. He steps upon them as he scans the area. Mustafa's body has been left behind. Tom goes to him and pats him down, but there's nothing on him. Tom pulls out his radio and his map of the local area. He spreads the map on the ground, holding it down with one knee. He shines a flashlight on it and then radios Robert.

"Giving up already?" Robert says. Tom thinks he can hear Nathan chuckling in the background.

"Give me Bill Irving's frequency," Tom says.

There's a pause. "Why?"

"I need information," Tom says. "Information he should have. Information I would've asked Mustafa for, but he's dead."

"Irving's not gonna like it."

"That's between me and Irving."

Robert relays the information. Tom promptly switches channels. He radios Bill Irving.

"This is Rollins. Come in. This is an emergency."

He waits. He's about to repeat his call when Bill Irving responds. "Rollins, what the hell are you doing?" He sounds angry.

"There was an ambush, sir, we –"

"I know what happened," Bill cuts him off. "Captain Dale has been in touch. He's brought me up to date. Now I repeat, what the hell are you doing?"

"They have Zeke, sir," Tom says. "We can't leave him behind. I need–"

"I don't care what you need. What *I* need is for you to get your ass back here. Return to base immediately. There's nothing out there for you."

"I need the addresses for Mohammed and for Aalem Hussain," Tom says.

There's silence on the radio. "Did you hear a word I said?"

"I heard what you said, sir," Tom says. "I chose not to acknowledge."

"Rollins, if you don't get your ass back to base, I'll have your goddamn career, I swear."

"I'm willing to accept those consequences, sir. But Babak

has Zeke, and we both know what the consequences of *that* are. I cannot allow that to happen. He has a family. I can't leave him behind. I *will* bring him back, and then you can do whatever you want with me. Sir, I need the addresses for Mohammed and Aalem Hussain."

"Rollins, you're going to cause an international incident."

"I'll do my best to avoid it coming to that, sir."

"And if I don't give you the information you need, what then?"

"Then I'll continue my search the hard way."

"The hard way? There is no easy way in this situation, Rollins."

"I just need the addresses, sir." Tom thinks Bill is going to give them to him. The fire has gone out of his tone. He knows he can't talk Tom out of this.

There's silence, and then a sigh as Bill comes back on the radio. He gives the addresses. Tom marks them both on the map.

"It's unlikely that Mohammed is going to be at his home," Bill says. "He's exposed himself. He's going to flee."

"But there could be something there to lead me to Babak," Tom says, studying the map and the routes while he talks. "I'll see you when I have Zeke, sir. Out." Tom puts the radio away.

Aalem's home is closer, but Tom won't go there first. He doesn't believe Aalem had anything to do with the betrayal. His home is a backup. There could be people there who could help, who might have any kind of information on Mohammed, his comings and goings. He needs to go to Mohammed's; this is his priority. He lives in an apartment block. Tom needs to get there while it's still dark, while most of the occupants of the building will be sleeping.

Shouldering his M4 once again, Tom runs on, away from the scene of the firefight, deeper into the night, toward distant lights, toward civilization, heading for Mohammed's building.

CHAPTER TWENTY-FOUR

Mohammed says he needs to stop quickly at his apartment. Maryam doesn't understand.

"I need to pack a bag," Mohammed says. "Come up with me. I won't be long."

Maryam is confused. She doesn't want to go up to his apartment. "I'll wait here," she says. Despite the late hour, there is a group of men loitering at the entrance to the building. Some are sitting, some are standing. They're talking and laughing.

Mohammed sighs. "Please," he says. "It is not safe for you to stay out here alone."

Her eyes flicker toward the men at the entrance again, and Mohammed notices.

"Not them," he says. "Something much worse. Please, we will be safer upstairs. If you come with me, I will explain everything there."

Maryam looks at him. She doesn't like this. "Where is my father?" she says.

"He's not far," he says. He pleads with her, speaking

earnestly. "Please, come with me. The faster we finish here, the faster we can go to him."

Maryam finally relents. She gets out of the car and arranges her head scarf, wrapping it around the lower half of her face to conceal her features as they pass the group of men. She feels their eyes upon them as they pass, but she keeps her own lowered. One of them says something to Mohammed as they pass. It's about her.

"A friend's daughter," Mohammed says in response, and then they're inside and they're going up the stairs toward his apartment, the group left behind. Maryam uncovers her face.

Inside the apartment, Mohammed makes for his bedroom, telling her to make herself comfortable in the living room and that he won't be long.

"You promised me answers," Maryam says, steadfast.

Mohammed pauses in the hallway, looking back at her, her feet planted close to the door. He inhales deeply. "We were betrayed, Maryam," he says finally. "One of the Americans, he was a mole. He…he hurt your father. It was he who broke Aalem's leg. This is why I could not leave you out in the car. The American and Babak, they could still be out there, still looking for me. In here we're safe. The men at the entrance would never let an American through without making some noise first."

Maryam absorbs this, feeling the shock hit her like cold water.

"The other Americans were able to get us out. All your father was concerned about was you. He wanted to ensure your safety." He puffs up his chest and adds, "The Americans did not want me to come. I forced them to permit me. I made a promise to your father."

Maryam runs a hand down her face, trying to take this all in, trying to make sense of it.

"Please," Mohammed says, coming toward her, placing a hand on her back and guiding her toward the living room. Maryam steps out of his touch, enters the living room of her own accord. She does not sit. "I must pack," Mohammed says. "And then we will leave. I will take you to your father. He is receiving medical attention. You do not need to worry, Maryam. He will be all right." He smiles at her reassuringly, but she does not like his smile. It makes her skin crawl. She does not feel reassured.

Mohammed hovers in the doorway, watching her, like he's waiting for her to say something. Maryam does not.

"I'll – I'll be fast," he says. He hesitates again and then he leaves the living room and hurries to the bedroom. Maryam hears him close the door after himself.

She stands in the center of the living room, her arms wrapped around herself. She looks around, breathing deep, feeling her heart hammering inside her chest. There isn't much to see. A standard home with cheap furniture and portraits of his parents on the cabinets. Maryam barely takes it in. Her thoughts race. A deep-seated worry churns her insides. She needs to see her father, and she hates how Mohammed is dragging things out, bringing her back here first so he can pack a bag.

And there's something else, too. Something she can't put her finger on. There's something suspicious about Mohammed, about how he's behaving, what he says. But she doesn't know why. She puts it down to her personal feelings toward him. She has to put these aside. She can't allow them to cloud her judgement, not now when her father is injured and Mohammed is going to take her to him.

She still doesn't settle. She doesn't sit. She doesn't want to. Doesn't want to make herself comfortable. She wants to *leave*, as soon as possible. She starts to pace instead, arms still wrapped around herself.

From Mohammed's room, just a short way down the hall outside the living room, she can hear him talking. His voice is lowered. He doesn't want to be heard. She frowns, sticking her head out of the living room doorframe and cocking it to listen. The words are too hushed to be understood at this distance. Stepping lightly, she gets closer to the door. She listens in, but she's too late. Mohammed is wrapping up the call.

She remains outside his room, deliberating. She hears Mohammed moving around, packing. There's no point in thinking on it – she has nothing to hide. Calling through the door, she asks, "Were you on the phone?"

The movement inside the room stops. She can't hear anything. She thinks he's frozen. A long moment passes, and then she hears him coming to the door. He pulls it open. "The Americans have called," he says. "They're concerned about the betrayal. They said that they will come here and collect us."

Maryam looks at him. That sense of suspicion remains. He's too earnest. Too desperate to be believed. Maryam forces herself to clear her throat and keep her suspicions to herself. "How long will they be?"

"They didn't say," Mohammed says. "But I don't think they'll be long."

"Did they say anything about my father?"

"Just that he's asking about you. He hopes to see you soon."

"I would have liked to have spoken with him."

"It wasn't him on the phone, Maryam. It was the Americans."

They look at each other. Maryam can feel a charge in the air. It's not a good charge. There's an underlying current of threat. Maryam doesn't ask any further questions. She nods.

"Wait in the living room," Mohammed says.

Maryam does. Her skin crawls. She hates being here. She sits on the sofa and watches the door, waiting for Mohammed to finish in his room and come and join her. Something doesn't feel right.

CHAPTER TWENTY-FIVE

Tom dips into the shadows of buildings close to Mohammed's apartment block and catches his breath. The town has been quiet, he hasn't seen anyone outside so far, but there is a small gathering at the front of Mohammed's building. Five young men, lingering there.

Tom scans the area, taking in his surroundings. He doesn't see anyone else around. The apartment building is on the outskirts of town. There are only a few streetlamps through the town, some of them on the sides of the buildings, all of them solar-powered. They come to an end here. Beyond the building there is only darkness. In the dark, Tom can faintly make out the outline of a ruin; a bombed-out relic of a past war, a past invasion. The damage is maybe American, but this is a historically war-torn area. It could be from anyone throughout the years.

The building is eight floors tall. Bill said that Mohammed is on the sixth, on the right side. Most of the apartments are dark. Only a few of them have lights on. Mohammed's is one of them. Tom is intrigued by this. He can't see movement inside. Mohammed may have just forgotten to turn them off. Optimistically, though, it could mean he's inside. Either he was stupid enough to come back here and think it would be safe, or he's hurried back to pack a bag before he disappears – or else there's important information here that his new allies need from him.

Whatever the reason, Tom needs to find out soon. He slips out from the alleyway and sticks to the shadows, making his way down and round toward the rear of the building. The small gathering at the entrance don't notice him. They're busy joking around. It looks like they're mocking the smallest member of their group. He doesn't look happy about it.

Tom gets to the rear of the building and looks it over. There are balconies on this side. There's also a rear door, but there's no handle on it. A fire door that only opens from the inside. Stepping back, he looks up. The only light comes from Mohammed's apartment. Tom looks the building over and makes sure the windows and ground are all clear. He straps the M4 tight to his back and then goes to the bottom balcony. He climbs upon the railing, steadying himself against the wall, and then stretches upright, bracing his hands on the floor of the balcony above. He pulls himself up, moving as quickly, quietly, and carefully as he can, not wanting to wake or alarm any of the people presumably sleeping in the apartments within.

His arms are aching by the time he reaches the sixth floor. He pulls himself up and peers over the floor level. He saw from the ground that the curtains were drawn. He makes sure that they still are, that neither Mohammed nor anyone else who might be inside has heard his approach. It's clear. Tom gets over the railing and presses himself to the wall. He steps closer to the glass door. He tries to see through the curtains, but they're too thick. Tom pulls his Glock. He pauses before he tries the handle, thinking. If Mohammed is in there, Tom currently has the drop on him. Problem is, Tom can't see inside. He has no idea where in the apartment Mohammed could be. Tom is going to try the handle, and if it's locked he's going to have to pick it. Luckily, he can see it's a simple lock that he should be able to brute-force open with his knife. The problem with that is Mohammed will become alert to his presence. He'll have time to prepare himself for an invasion, leaving Tom a sitting duck, especially since he can't see him.

He listens at the door. He can't hear anything inside. He assumes this door leads to the living room. There's no movement on the other side so far as he can tell. There's no sound.

Fuck it. He's just gonna have to go for it. There's no time to waste.

Bracing himself, raising the Glock in case gunfire comes his way, he remains pressed to the wall and reaches out for the door handle.

It's unlocked.

Up this high, Mohammed probably isn't expecting anyone to try and walk in on him. He's not expecting someone to scale all of the balconies to get here.

Tom opens the door and steps through the center of the curtains, Glock raised. It leads him into the living room. He scans it. It's clear. He looks toward the adjoining kitchen. It's in darkness, but he doesn't see anyone there. Stepping lightly, he makes his way through the room, Glock held two-handed and close to his chest. He can hear some movement, but it's from another room.

Tom reaches the hall. He sees a closed door to his right,

the light on inside. This is where the sounds come from. Someone moving around, their feet scraping across the floor. Drawers opening and closing. Tom puts the Glock away and pulls out the Strider knife, popping the blade open. He needs to keep things quiet for now. He needs to get Mohammed out of here, out of this building, somewhere Tom can make noise when questioning him and not worry about anyone hearing.

Tom reaches the door and carefully pushes it open. He peers inside. Mohammed is at the bed, stuffing clothes into a bag. It looks like it's almost full. Mohammed pauses a moment, rubbing at his jaw, stretching it. Tom sees, with some satisfaction, that it's where he hit him.

He creeps up on Mohammed, the knife raised. Mohammed doesn't hear his approach. Tom scans the room. There's no one else here. Tom clamps his left hand over Mohammed's mouth, silencing him. He flashes the knife in front of Mohammed's wide eyes so that he knows it's there, and then he presses the blade to Mohammed's throat.

"Nice and easy," Tom whispers into his ear. "Any sudden movements and you're gonna cut yourself."

Tom forces him to turn, pointing him toward the bedroom door. He pushes him forward, keeping hold of him, keeping his hand on his mouth. Mohammed is rigid, but he moves with Tom. They move down the hall, toward the door.

CHAPTER TWENTY-SIX

Maryam heard sounds out on the balcony. They were very slight, but she feels attuned to everything right now. She frowned toward the door, waiting and watching. Nothing happened, but she got to her feet, alarmed. Was it just an animal? She couldn't be sure.

She found herself stepping aside, eyes fixed on the door, and in particular on the handle. The living room light was on and the curtains were closed. She couldn't see anything through them. She cocked her head toward the door, straining to hear anything further.

Then, barely a moment later, she saw movement at the handle. Tentative, testing. It began to lower. Someone was out there. Someone was coming in.

Maryam, stepping as lightly as she could, hurried into the kitchen and ducked behind the counter, pressing herself against it, concealing herself. She listened as the door opened and she heard the outside night clearer. A bird called. The sound of a distant car. A slight breeze. And then silence as the door closed again, and she knew that whoever it was was now inside the apartment.

She couldn't hear anything further. She stayed low, eyes open and looking ahead as if boots and legs might come into view. They didn't, and nor could she hear footsteps.

She stayed in that position for an uncomfortable time, her shins and calves beginning to tingle with restricted blood flow. Until she finally heard something.

It comes from the bedroom. A brief – very brief – scuffle. Maryam chances movement, staying low and crawling forward, peering around the counter toward the living room door. She watches the hall.

Mohammed comes into view, but he's moving funny. He's leaning back, his feet a couple of paces ahead of the rest of his body. She soon sees why. A man dressed all in black military gear is behind him, a hand over his mouth, a knife at his throat.

Maryam swallows, feeling her eyes bulge. It's the American. The American who betrayed them, who hurt her father. Mohammed was telling the truth. He's here, now. He's tracked Mohammed down and he's come to finish the job.

It takes her a moment to absorb all of this. Mohammed may have been acting suspiciously, but she supposes that's just the way he is. He's a spy, after all, or whatever it is the Americans call them. Being suspicious comes with the territory when you know what he does.

They're heading for the door, going to leave the apartment. The American has Mohammed, and he's taking him away. Who knows what he's going to do to him? Maybe he's going to use him to find out where the other Americans and her father are.

Maryam can't allow this. He's already done so much damage.

He's hurt her father. He can't go unpunished for this.

She finds herself rising to her feet when they get past the living room door. She hurries, tip-toeing to the living room door. She sees the back of the men almost at the front door. She bites her lip. She doesn't have a weapon. There's no time to find one. If she waits, they're going to leave. She'll lose her chance.

She has to act.

Without thinking, she jumps onto the American's back.

CHAPTER TWENTY-SEVEN

Tom feels someone jump onto his back. It's not a heavy weight, but it catches him by surprise and almost causes him to lose his grip on Mohammed. It's a woman, he thinks. He wonders where in the apartment she was hiding, but he doesn't think about this for long. He can't, not when she's clawing at his eyes.

Tom closes his eyes and tries to shake her loose. At the same time, he tries to keep a tight grip on Mohammed. It doesn't hold. He feels Mohammed trying to slip loose. Tom manages to blindly grasp him by the collar. He wrenches on it hard, twisting it. He hears Mohammed make a choked cry.

The woman rains punches down on the top and side of his head. Tom throws himself back, slamming her into the wall. He hears her gasp, the air blown out of her lungs. Tom manages to get his eyes open, her fingers no longer clawing at him after the impact. He feels her weight slip from his back, too, though she reaches for him still, not wanting to let go completely.

He sees Mohammed throw a punch at him. Tom

manages to block it with his forearm. The woman is grabbing for his neck and his hair. Tom presses back harder against the wall, crushing her, trying to smother her with his back but unsure if he's covering her face.

Mohammed reaches for the knife with both hands. He's still making choked sounds from Tom twisting the collar of his baggy shirt. He clutches at Tom's right arm, at his hand holding the knife. He digs his fingernails into Tom's wrist. His clawing breaks the skin. Tom drops the knife. He raises a leg and kicks Mohammed away before he can reach down for it, forcing him back to the opposite wall, letting go of his collar at the same time.

Mohammed hits the wall. Tom tries to go to him, to hit him again, but the woman leaps up onto his back once more, dragging him out of reach of Mohammed. Tom sees Mohammed realize that he has space. He tries to flee, heading for the door. Tom can't reach him. He drops to the ground and kicks out, sweeping Mohammed's legs out from under him. He topples forward and lands on his face, busting his nose.

Tom realizes that the woman is saying things while she attacks him. He realizes that she's speaking in English.

"What did you do to my father?" she says. She sounds like she's spitting the words through gritted teeth, a fingernail dragging down Tom's cheek. "I'll kill you for hurting him, you pig!"

At first, Tom doesn't understand. He thinks she's talking about Mohammed, that it must be his daughter attacking him. Tom looks toward Mohammed, sees him pushing himself up, blood dripping from his nose down onto the hallway's tiles. He's still within kicking distance. Tom lashes out, kicking him in the side of the head.

The woman's grip on him has released. Tom rolls to his side to get up. He sees why she suddenly let go of him. She'd spotted his fallen knife. She lunges for him now, wielding it. Tom moves fast. He catches her wrists, the tip of the blade an inch away from his face. Glancing up, he sees how she snarls, still pushing, still trying to drive the knife into him. Their eyes lock. She knows he's stronger than she is, but she's defiant. "I will kill you for my father."

Tom feels every muscle in her arms straining. He manages to rise to his feet, holding her in place. She tries to kick at him. She's unbalanced herself. Tom uses this against her. He forces her back and sweeps her leg, dropping her flat to the ground. He twists the knife out of her hands when she makes impact. Out the corner of his eye he sees Mohammed trying to crawl toward the door, smearing his nose blood along the tiles as he drags himself along.

"Your father's a piece of shit," Tom says to the woman. He puts the knife away and he grabs her by the wrists, pinning them together, keeping her under control. "And he's put my teammate's life in danger with some Iranian psychopath."

The woman looks like Tom has slapped her. She frowns. Tom doesn't care if this is how she finds out what her father has done. He drags her across the ground toward Mohammed. He needs to keep them both subdued. Needs to get them both gagged and bound. He has zip ties in his vest. He has enough for both of them. He can leave the woman here in the apartment, but he needs to get Mohammed out. Needs to get him somewhere he can scream.

"Wait," the woman says.

Tom ignores her, despite the way she tries to make herself heavier and how she pulls at the hand holding onto both of her wrists. He reaches Mohammed and presses a boot into the center of his back, pinning him to the ground, stopping his crawl.

"Wait, listen to me – *wait!*" the woman says, getting louder.

Tom might have to find a way to silence her before he can find a gag.

"My father wouldn't do that!" she says. "He would never help Babak!"

Tom looks at her. "I don't care what you think," Tom says. "I saw what he did."

He sees the woman's eyes flicker from side to side. She's thinking. Absorbing. But then she looks at Mohammed under his boot, then she looks back up at Tom, eyes narrowed. "Mohammed is not my father," she says. "Is that what you think?"

Tom says nothing. He looks down at her, waiting for her to continue.

"My father is Aalem Hussain," she says. "I am Maryam Hussain, *his* daughter. My father would never work with Babak Rashidi. My father gave him up to the Americans when Babak tried to turn him to his side. My father would never help a man like Babak Rashidi."

Tom listens. "Then what are you doing here?"

"Mohammed told me one of the Americans was a mole," Maryam says. "He said that the American broke my father's leg, and that the other Americans were providing medical care. He was going to take me to him."

"Your father is with my teammate," Tom says. "Zeke Greene. They were taken by Babak."

Maryam looks like she's been slapped again, or else had ice water dumped upon her. She looks toward Mohammed, daggers in her eyes. Mohammed's face is turned toward her. When she looks at him, he turns away.

"Please release me," Maryam says, her voice quiet.

Tom doesn't.

She looks up at him. "Please," she says. There's no emotion in her face, or her voice. She isn't pleading. "I am no danger to you. My actions were poisoned by Mohammed. I thought you were the treacherous American. I thought you had harmed my father." She breathes deeply. "I know what Babak Rashidi does to his captives. I know what is going to happen to my father."

Tom lets go of her wrists. She rubs them. She doesn't attempt to get off the ground. Tom is about to turn to Mohammed, to haul him from the ground and throw him into the living room where he can look for something to gag him with, but he hesitates. He looks down at Maryam. She stares blindly into the distance. She wraps her arms around her raised knees.

"It hasn't been long," Tom says. "I can still find them."

Slowly, she turns her face to look at him.

"I can stop Babak from hurting them." He points down at Mohammed. "He's going to take me to them."

Maryam's eyes narrow, considering what he says. Tom turns to Mohammed now. Mohammed grunts. Tom ignores him. He grabs a handful of hair at the back of his head, his turban lost in the scuffle, and hauls him to his feet, slamming him into the doorframe as he pushes him into the living room. He throws him across the room. Mohammed hits a chair and stumbles over it. Tom goes to him, pulling a zip tie from his vest.

Mohammed struggles to his knees. He holds up his

hands, begging off. Tom notices that Maryam has gotten to her feet and has followed them into the living room.

"A moment," Mohammed says, breathing hard. "Just one moment."

Tom ignores him. He approaches, getting closer.

"I just need to know the time," Mohammed says.

Tom pauses. An alarm bell rings in his head. He watches Mohammed.

Mohammed smiles. Slowly, his head turns to the side, toward the clock mounted on the wall above his sofa. He starts to laugh, a chuckle building in the back of his throat as he turns back to Tom, his wild eyes fixing on his. "That should be enough," he says. "You don't have long."

"What are you talking about?" Tom says.

Mohammed says nothing. He smiles, showing his teeth. He shudders with suppressed laughter. He's mocking Tom.

"I heard him on the phone," Maryam says. "He told me it was the Americans. He said they called him, that they were coming here to collect us."

Tom shakes his head. "That isn't who's coming," he says. "Who's coming, Mohammed?"

Mohammed shrugs. He holds out his hands, palms up. "You'll see soon enough."

CHAPTER TWENTY-EIGHT

Tom has gagged Mohammed with a dishcloth taped into his mouth. With the zip ties, he's bound him to a chair.

"I need to check the front," Tom says to Maryam. He wasn't intending on taking her with him when he left with Mohammed, but if someone is coming, someone dangerous, and they know where Mohammed lives, then he can't leave her behind. "To see if anyone is coming."

Maryam nods.

"He's not going anywhere," Tom says, pointing at Mohammed. "And he can't talk to you. Just ignore him. I'll be right back."

"Is my father okay?" Maryam asks. "What happened tonight?"

Tom doesn't have time to waste, but she looks so worried that he gives her a quick rundown. "Mohammed betrayed us. It was an ambush. Most of my team got out, but one of them was killed, and Zeke and your father were captured." Tom doesn't know for sure that Aalem was captured, but he doesn't know that he wasn't, either. He didn't see what happened to him, but he *did* see how they left Mustafa's dead body behind. If they'd killed Aalem, it stands to reason they would have done the same with his corpse. The condition and whereabouts of Aalem is something else he'll have to ask Mohammed about. He makes a mental note.

"Was he hurt?" Maryam asks. "Mohammed said his leg was broken."

"I didn't see him get hurt," Tom says. "And Mohammed was probably lying to you. That's what he does."

She nods at this. Tom leaves her as he exits the apartment, checking that the hallway is clear before he steps fully outside. It is. It's quiet still. No one was disturbed by the scuffle in Mohammed's hallway.

Tom goes to the front of the building. It's open. There are no windows. He can hear the men at the entrance still there, talking loudly, laughing still. If they were in America he'd think they were drunk. As it is, he doesn't know what they're doing, other than noisily hanging out in the early hours. He supposes alcohol could still be the case. People have always battled against prohibition in secretive ways, but if it *is* what they're doing, they're not being careful about it.

Tom is about to turn away, seeing that the coast is clear for him to sneak Mohammed and Maryam out, but then he hears an engine. Two engines. Their noise cuts through the night's silence, and they're coming closer. Tom can see the vehicles' headlights coming through the town, both pairs of them. Tom steps behind the cover of the wall, watching.

When they're close enough, he can see that the vehicles are open-topped Jeeps. The gathering of men at the entrance has fallen silent. They've seen the approach, too. They might be as concerned as Tom is.

He counts up the men inside the Jeeps. Three in the

front vehicle, four in the rear. Seven total. They have weaponry. AK47s. Like at the ambush.

The Jeeps come to a stop in front of the building. The men start getting out, shouldering their rifles. One of them calls something to the men at the entrance. Tom sees how he waves his hand side to side. He's dispersing them. The gathering does not argue or complain. They do as they're told. One of them leaves the building and heads toward the town. The others all come inside. In a moment, Tom is sure the armed men will come inside, too.

Tom retreats back to Mohammed's apartment. He has to be quick. He goes straight to Mohammed on the chair, pulling out his knife. He yanks the tape from his mouth. Mohammed grunts as some of his beard hairs are torn from his skin. "Who's coming?" Tom says. "Who are they? The men from the ambush, right? What are they, Taliban?"

Mohammed doesn't answer. He laughs again, and says, "Babak has many friends. More friends than you do, American. You should give up now, throw yourself upon their mercy. They may take pity on you, if you beg hard enough." He grins smugly. He raises his eyebrows. "They're here, aren't they?"

Tom slaps the tape back into place, forcing the dishcloth back between Mohammed's teeth to keep him quiet. With his knife, he cuts the zip ties that bind him to the chair. Pulling another out of his tactical vest, Tom drags Mohammed to his feet, pulls his arms behind his back, and pulls the zip tie tight on his wrists.

Maryam is watching them. She's concerned. She heard what both men have said. "Is it really the Taliban?" she asks.

"I think so," Tom says. "We need to get out of this building immediately. They're going to come right here, looking for you both. Just stay close to me and do exactly as I say, you got that?"

She swallows and manages to nod. He can see she's scared.

"Hey," he says, and she looks at him. "What happened to that girl who tried to claw my eyes out? She was right here not so long ago." He points at where he can feel a scratch still tingling on his cheek. "What happened to the girl who did this?"

She purses her lips like she's maybe trying to suppress a smile. She nods. "She's right here," she says. "I will stay close."

"Good," Tom says. "Then let's move."

CHAPTER TWENTY-NINE

They make their way cautiously through the building toward the stairs, Tom listening for anyone who might be close and coming up to cut them off. Maryam stays close on his tail. Tom has both hands on Mohammed, holding him tight, dragging him along. Mohammed tries to drag his feet, but Tom keeps him moving.

The sounds from outside, from the entrance, have fallen silent. The group descend the stairs, getting to the floor below and pausing, Tom listening, then – when he's satisfied there's no one directly below them – they descend to the next floor. They repeat. They get down three floors. Only three more to go.

Tom doesn't think they'll be able to go all the way. He just needs to get them as close to the bottom of the building as possible. If they take the main stairwell they're going to run into the Taliban. But they can't take the fire escape – the Taliban will more than likely have that covered, too. At least they should, even if they think they're just coming here to pick Mohammed and Maryam up. Tom dreads to think what

Mohammed had planned for the young woman after he took her away with him. Maryam is probably sick to the stomach at this thought, too.

Tom pauses on the third floor. He can hear voices. The Taliban, coming up the stairs. They're not shouting or calling out. They're not charging into battle. They're talking among themselves. They don't have anything they think they should worry about. Tom turns his head and strains his ears, listening. He thinks they're still a couple of floors below, like they've maybe just entered the building, tired of waiting. He wonders if Mohammed was supposed to meet them outside.

Tom goes to the nearest apartment door pointing toward the rear of the building, and tests the door handle. It's locked. He eases it back into place so as not to make noise. On the ground between the doors is an animal cage. Tom checks it. It's empty. It's not big. For a cat, maybe, or a bird.

Maryam watches him try the next door handle, confused. This door is also locked. Tom turns to her. He whispers. "I think this is as low as we can safely get without running into them."

She watches him, listening.

"We need to get out the back. We'll have to go through an apartment." There are only three doors to choose from. If they're all locked, Tom is going to have to try and break the lock as quietly as he can. "We'll climb down the balconies, the same way I got up to Mohammed's apartment."

She looks nervous about this.

"I've gotten us closer to the ground," Tom says. "Even if we fall, it's not so far to go. We'll be fine. We hit the ground, and we start running."

She still looks unsure, but she nods.

Mohammed kicks the animal cage.

Tom freezes. Mohammed's face snaps toward him, eyes gleaming.

The sound of the Taliban voices has fallen silent. They've stopped moving.

Mohammed starts to scream through his gag. The sound is muffled, but it's clear enough what it is. Tom punches him in the stomach to shut him up.

The Taliban men have heard enough. They start coming up the stairs again. They quicken their pace.

They're coming to investigate.

CHAPTER THIRTY

Tom drags Mohammed to the third door and tries the handle, not needing to worry about noise now. The door is locked. Tom isn't surprised. He throws Mohammed against the wall and then rears back and kicks the door, throwing all of his weight into it, aiming close to the handle.

The lock splinters close to the frame, but it doesn't break all the way. Tom can hear the men coming closer, running up the stairs leading to this floor. They're almost here. Tom kicks at the door again. The lock breaks. The door swings wide, hitting against the wall behind. He can hear alarmed cries coming from inside the apartment, the owners awakened by the noise of someone breaking into their home.

Tom grabs Maryam and pushes her into the apartment. "Go!" he says.

She starts running. Tom pulls Mohammed from the wall and forces him ahead as the Taliban reach the top of the stairs. Tom dives inside as they open fire. The bullets from their AK47s tear up the spot where he previously stood. Tom pulls the M4 from his back and blindly returns fire around the frame, keeping them at bay. The AK47 fire briefly stops as the men duck for cover.

Tom keeps the M4 in hand. He turns to see Mohammed flat on the floor, pressing his head into the ground, unable to cover it with his bound hands. Up ahead, Tom sees a bedroom door open a crack, someone inside peer out from the darkness. "Get back!" Tom shouts, not sure if they'll understand him. He waves a hand, ushering them back into their room to punctuate his point. "Get low! Take cover!"

They understand enough. The door promptly slams shut. Tom hears shouting inside the bedroom. He also hears shouts from the hall, the direction of the stairs. Gunfire follows, hitting the doorway again, the men outside checking it's clear. Tom grabs the back of Mohammed's loose shirt, bunches it up, and drags him from the floor. Mohammed is babbling from behind his gag. Tom can't understand a word he says. He thinks he's praying.

Tom forces him through the living room and toward the door leading out to the balcony. Maryam is by the door. "It's locked!" she calls.

Tom raises the M4 and shoots out the glass. "Go!" he says, motioning her ahead.

Maryam hurries forward, crunching through the glass. Tom glances back, sees that their pursuers have not entered the apartment yet. They're being careful. They know he's armed, and they would have just heard the gunfire, too.

Tom gets to the railing with Mohammed. Tom can't carry him down. Mohammed looks at him. Tom can see that he's wondering what he's going to do.

"We'll see you down there," Tom says. He reaches down, grabs Mohammed's legs, and flips him over the balcony railing, dropping him to the ground three floors below.

Maryam leans over the edge, watching him go with wide eyes. They both see him land. There's a thud, and then a long, low groan.

"It's not high enough to kill him," Tom says. "So keep that in mind if we need to jump, too. Go limp. If you're tight, that's the best way to hurt yourself. Go limp, and try to roll through."

Maryam nods, but it's clear she doesn't want to have to jump.

"Start climbing," Tom says. He turns and watches the entrance to the living room while she grips the railing and steadies herself against the wall to climb over.

A man appears in the doorway. Tom opens fire, strafing his torso. He hears Maryam squeal. She almost loses her grip and her balance, but she manages to right herself. The man stumbles back, knocking down the man behind him. Tom continues to fire, emptying the magazine. He presses against the wall and quickly reloads. This is his last magazine. He grits his teeth and fires a few more rounds toward the doorway. He sees how the man who was knocked down by the falling dead man has scrambled behind cover.

Tom backs up to the railing, keeping an eye on the doorway. He needs to keep the M4 out and ready, in case the men attempt to fire upon them. Climbing down one-handed is going to be difficult, and his aim will be almost nonexistent. Still, fire from an automatic rifle should be enough to spook them back into cover.

He hauls himself over the railing, checking the living room doorway is still clear. He glances back to see Maryam a floor below him. Tom begins his descent. It doesn't take him long to catch her up. She moves slower than he does. She's not accustomed to this. She's probably never done anything like this before in her life.

Before Tom can say anything to her, attempt to help her, he hears movement at the balcony above. He looks up, the M4 readied in his right hand. He braces himself against the railing in front of him with his left. A face appears. Tom fires at it. As expected, most of his shots go wild. They pepper the ceiling above and the wall beside the man, but he quickly ducks back. Tom waits to see if anyone else appears. He sees the tip of an AK47 appear and he fires, spooking them back again.

Tom waits, watching. They don't reappear. He's not sure they're going to, knowing that they won't be able to get a good bead on him pointing their rifles down, not when he's lying in wait, ready to pick him off. They don't know he's down to his last magazine.

Maryam has continued her descent while he's kept the Taliban men at bay. He doesn't think they're coming back – not to the balcony, anyway. He thinks they've given up on that plan of attack. They're probably heading back down the stairs, back to the front of the building, most likely to get their Jeeps and then come around the back of the building. They can shoot them off the back of the building with ease. It'll be harder for Tom to defend from this position. Or, if they've reached the ground already, they can run them down in their Jeeps. Tom and Maryam need to get down faster, before they can arrive. They're sitting ducks hanging off the side of the building.

Tom looks down. Two floors from the bottom. It's not so far to go.

He pushes himself away from the railing and lands, knees bending on impact, throwing himself forward to roll through and disperse his momentum. He comes up on a knee and scans the area. He sees that a lot of lights have turned on in the apartment building. He can see some people hanging over their balconies and out of their windows, trying to see what's happening.

Maryam is nearly at the bottom now. Tom looks around. Mohammed is gone from where he landed. He spots him, on his feet, trying to escape. He's moving slowly though, after his rough landing. He's not going to get far. Tom goes to the building and catches Maryam as she reaches the bottom, wrapping his left arm around her waist and spinning with her, taking her from the building. "Run for the ruins," Tom says.

Maryam sets off. She doesn't need told twice. Like Tom, she can probably hear the Jeeps roaring back into life.

Tom runs down Mohammed. He knocks him off balance from behind, but keeps him from falling to the ground. He spins him around and throws him over his shoulder. Looking back at the building, he sees that the Jeeps have split up. They're coming from both directions, a pincer formation, looking to cut them off.

Tom runs for the ruins.

CHAPTER THIRTY-ONE

The building used to be a house. A big house. It looks like a bomb fell through it.

The rooms are empty of furniture and any other signs that anyone ever lived here. The walls are blown out in places, blackened, and the roof is almost completely gone. Pieces of wood from the roof are scattered throughout the building, their edges scorched.

The Jeeps have seen where they went. Tom can hear them halt outside the building, and the six remaining men jumping out, about to charge inside.

Tom leads Maryam through to the rear of the building. He still has Mohammed slung over his shoulder.

"Through here," Maryam says, changing direction and tugging on his arm.

Tom follows her lead. She's spotted the rear door. She's taking him toward it. Tom stops, holding onto her wrist. "They'll just run us down," Tom says. They keep their voices low, knowing the men are near. "They might already be encircling us. We won't get far."

"Then what do we do?"

Tom looks around. They're in what would have been the kitchen. There's a storage room. Tom points her toward it. "Hide in there," he says. "Stay very still and don't come back out unless I come and get you." Tom drops Mohammed in with her. Before Mohammed can react, Tom strikes him in the jaw with the stock of his rifle. Mohammed falls back, hits the wall and goes limp. While he's out, Tom checks both of his shoulders, wondering if either of them dislocated in the drop from the building with his hands bound behind his back. They're both still in their sockets. Tom exchanges a glance with Maryam, then closes the door on them.

He gets away from the back door and presses himself to the wall, M4 raised. He moves slowly, sweeping the ground with his boot as he moves so as not to step on anything that would reveal his location.

There are six men left, and Tom needs to kill them all. He has to. He can't leave any of them alive. Their silence is of the utmost importance. Their silence buys him a few more hours in the area without anyone knowing he's here, especially Babak Rashidi.

Tom moves room by room, sweeping them all. He listens. The men are here, he knows, but they're moving quietly in turn. Trying to get the drop on him. They've seen how dangerous he was back at the apartment building. They know he's armed. They've already lost one of their number to him.

Tom presses his back against a wall and listens, trying to pick out movement. He pushes the magazine release button and counts how many rounds he has left. Fifteen. It's not a lot. It should be enough, but it depends on what kind of fight he's getting into. If a sustained firefight breaks out, he's not going to last very long. He needs to try and keep things quiet, to avoid it coming to that.

He spies movement out the corner of his eye, back the way he came and toward one of the blown-out windows. Tom slips toward the nearest window in the room he's in, moving sideways as he sticks to the shadows. He shoulders the M4 and pulls out his knife. One of the men outside, at the back, is searching the rooms, peering in through the windows. Tom braces, waiting for him. When the man reaches the window, sweeping the room with his AK47, Tom grabs the barrel and forces it aside, then jabs the knife through his throat, tearing it sideways to open his neck. He falls back, hands grasping at the blood gushing out from his neck.

Tom still has control of the AK47. Before he can pull it in and take control of it, gunshots hit close to him. There was a second man outside at the back. Tom falls into cover, the rifle dropping away from him. He hears a voice calling, probably telling the others where he is.

Tom runs. He puts his head down and flees back to the last room he was in, knowing it's clear, but he's careful. He also knows that someone could be coming toward him from the other end.

Gunfire hits the room he previously occupied, impacting the walls. Tom peers back and sees two men converging upon it, firing wildly, sweeping the room. Tom ducks back behind the cover of the thick walls as stray bullets fly his way. Some of them churn up the ground through the doorway.

The noise is deafening. It makes it hard to pinpoint movements. Tom heads in the opposite direction, moving toward a door opposite. As he enters, he sees movement through the darkness. There's someone here. A rifle rises. Tom throws himself back and fires toward the shadow. Bullets hit the man and he falls back, finger squeezing on his AK47 trigger, but the end of the rifle is pointing upward now.

The brief gunfight draws attention. Their shooting stops in the other room and Tom hears them coming this way. He's on the ground from where he threw himself back, and he can see them at an angle through the doorway. He fires to keep them at bay. They fall back, then resume firing wildly and blindly into the darkness. Tom scrambles away from the doorframe, toward the thick stone wall, staying low. He pushes himself up and feels his hands land on something hard on the ground. He looks down. Pieces of bone. Pieces of fingers, he thinks. Here a long time, potentially from the bombing that hollowed this house out.

Tom looks around. There's one more room at the end of the house. He runs through to it, putting distance between himself and the men firing indiscriminately. The two of them are coming his way. He assumes that must mean there are two men outside – one at the front, one at the back. Tom doesn't have many bullets left. He still has the Glock, but he doesn't like his chances wielding it going up against four automatic rifles.

Tom looks up. Through the nonexistent roof. He doesn't look so far as the stars. He looks at where the roof would have been. The walls are thick. More than thick enough to support his weight, and wide enough for him to move on. To walk on, if he wanted.

He gathers up pieces of wood and piles them against the wall, then uses them to boost himself up the wall, catching the edge with his fingertips. Kicking his boots against the wall, finding purchase, he manages to pull himself up to the top. He stays low when he's there, flat on his stomach, and he crawls forward so that he's above an empty room.

The two men have stopped their shooting. They're making their way through the ruin, rifles raised. Tom can see them. They stay together. He stays flat so that they can't pick him out. If he were to stand, his silhouette would block out the stars. This would get their attention. Tom gets above a room where neither of them is. He keeps pulling himself forward, toward the front of the building. He doesn't go all the way to it. Again, he doesn't want to make himself easy to spot. He pulls out his Glock, moving carefully so as not to knock any rubble down. The area is very quiet now that the shooting has stopped. Tom's ears are ringing.

Looking down, he can see the man outside guarding the front of the building. He stands stationary, close to the Jeeps, guarding those too. His eyes are narrowed as his head moves, swiveling left to right, looking through the windows. Trying to spot their target.

Tom levels the Glock. Aims for center of mass. He fires twice. The guard never knows what hits him. He falls back as blood erupts from his chest. He lands between the two vehicles.

The two men have heard the gunshots. They bark something at each other and then they split up. One of them comes into the room below Tom. He looks out of the window, toward their guard at the front. It takes him a moment to spot him. Tom hears him mutter something to himself. Tom doesn't understand it. He pushes himself up just a little, enough to see where the other man is. He's in another room, tentatively stepping through toward the final room of the house. Tom sees an opportunity. He throws himself down from where he's hiding, toward the man directly below him.

Tom comes down with both boots, making his legs rigid, landing and stomping down on the back of the man's neck and his head. The man collapses into a heap and Tom bounces off and lands next to him, catching his balance. He thinks he broke the man's neck, but to be sure he stomps down on his skull.

The other man heard the movement. He charges through the doorway. Tom anticipated him. He drops to a knee and fires toward the man's legs. There's only a couple of rounds left in the M4. Bullets embed in the man's thighs before the trigger clicks uselessly. The man goes down as Tom rises, wielding the M4 like a club. The man screams. Tom brings the stock of the M4 down on the back of his head, over and over, caving in his skull.

There is only one man left, but he's no longer outside, guarding the rear of the building. He could tell from the noises, the gunfire, the screaming, that things are not going well. He possibly realizes he's the last man standing.

He charges, firing. Tom throws himself to the side, scrambling for his Glock. Bullets hit the wall around him. The man is firing wild. He doesn't know where Tom is. He's screaming as he charges. Tom realizes that the man hasn't seen him; he's scared, and he's charging in blind. Tom pushes himself up, ready, and as the man comes through the doorway, Tom tackles him from the side, pressing him back against the wall, the AK47 pinned to his chest.

The man tries to fight back. Tom keeps him pinned. They wrestle over control of the rifle. Tom pushes it up his chest, toward his throat. The man snarls and pushes back. He kicks at Tom. Tom manages to avoid contact, twisting his body. He drives a forehead into the man's nose, breaking it. The man grunts, but swings the AK47 in a last desperate attempt to fight Tom off. The rifle connects with Tom's ribs, driving him back. His back no longer pressed against the wall, the man presses his advantage, swinging the rifle again, looking to bash in his skull the same way Tom did to one of his comrades.

Tom manages to duck the swings, avoiding contact. When the man tries to turn the rifle back around, to aim and fire it, Tom charges him, keeping him from doing so. The man understands that they're too close to each other for him to shoot. The rifle is no good except as a club. He swings it again. Tom ducks and it dents the wall above him. While he's down, Tom spots a piece of the charred wood. He scoops it up and jabs it into the man's ribs, then rises and swings it, smacking him across the face with the flat of it.

The blackened tip is pointed, like a stake. As the man steadies himself, Tom charges, the stake out in front of himself. He drives it through the man's soft midsection, pushing him back into the corner of the room, pinning him against the wall. The man coughs blood. It runs down his chin and through his beard. Tom shoves it in, twisting it, until the man falls limp. Tom lets him drop.

He takes a moment to catch his breath, one arm outstretched to lean against the nearest wall. His body aches from the fight. He feels various scrapes and grazes crying out to him, and his ribs throb where the stock of the AK47 connected.

He knows he can't stop for long. He breathes deep and straightens, and goes to each of the bodies, searching them. He finds both keys for the Jeeps and takes them. He picks up one of the AK47s. Not the one that was swung at him. It could be damaged now.

Tom isn't a big fan of AK47s. Poor sighting, prone to overheating, and their accuracy isn't as reliable, especially at long distances. But beggars can't be choosers, and the AK47 ammo, unfortunately, is not compatible with his M4. Not that it matters too much, considering he broke the M4 beyond repair bludgeoning one of the Taliban men to death.

Tom straps the AK47 to his back and retrieves all of their magazines. He swaps bullets over in a couple of them, making sure the magazines he keeps are all fully loaded. One of the men is also carrying a Glock. Tom takes it, keeping it in his hand as he goes to the storage room at the back of the building. He opens the door and finds Maryam ducking low, covering her head. Slowly, she lifts her face, dreading who she might see in front of her. Tom sees relief flood her when she sees that it's him. He holds his hand out to her. She takes it and stands. Mohammed remains slumped against the wall in the corner, still unconscious.

"I brought you a gift," Tom says, holding the spare Glock out to her. "You ever used one of these before?"

Maryam shakes her head, but she takes the gun. She holds it delicately. She looks scared of it.

"Hold it tighter than that," Tom says. "Your clothing is loose – use that to your advantage and hide it somewhere you can easily pull it out but where people aren't gonna notice it. When we get clear, I can show you how to use it properly."

"The men?" Maryam asks.

"Don't worry about them," Tom says. He reaches into the storage room, grabs Mohammed, and slings him back over his shoulder. "Let's get out of here."

CHAPTER THIRTY-TWO

Zeke's face feels like it's been split in two. Like it's in danger of cracking in half and collapsing in on itself.

As he wakes, he probes tentatively at his features, making sure they're still intact. He can feel dried blood on the side of his face. It cracks in places and flakes off. His head aches. The too-bright lights above stab into his eyes. His stomach turns like he might throw up. He forces himself to turn over, rolling onto his side in an effort to keep the nausea at bay.

Turning, he realizes he doesn't have much room for movement. He's in a cage. Like a cage for a large dog, or maybe for transporting a tiger. He concentrates on his breathing for now, trying to focus, to unblur his vision. The last thing he remembers is getting hit by a big guy. A big *strong* guy. He struck like a truck. But it wasn't just his fist – he was holding a gun. And that gun – it had killed Mustafa. *Shit*. And the voice – something about his voice. It was unexpected. He had an accent.

"Dutch," Zeke mutters to himself.

"You're awake." The voice is familiar. It's close.

Zeke blinks, alarmed that he hadn't noticed there was someone so near to him. Looking to his left, he sees a cage identical to his own. Sitting cross-legged in the corner is Aalem.

Zeke doesn't respond straight away. With his vision finally returning to normal, he looks around the rest of the room. It's white. *Too* white, and too bright. Sterile, like an operating theatre. The floor and walls are all shining tile. He holds onto the sides of his head, trying to suppress the pain that resounds within it. There's one door in and out of the room, no doubt locked. In the top corner, pointing toward the cages, there is a camera. A red light flashes on top of it.

There's very little else in the room. The walls are bare. In the center, directly opposite the cages, there is a stand, like a dentist would use. Zeke can't see the top of it. Can't see what kind of tools it's holding. There's a chair next to it, pointing toward the cages.

"How long have we been here?" he asks Aalem.

"I'm not sure," Aalem says. "There is no clock. A couple of hours, perhaps. Maybe longer."

"And I've been unconscious the whole time?"

Aalem nods.

"Fuck." Explains the headache. Zeke hopes there's no lasting damage in his brain from being knocked unconscious and left unattended for so long. He hopes he's not concussed, though he doesn't think he is. His head and vision are clearing. The pain inside his skull isn't quite as sharp as it was when he first awakened.

Of course, knowing what he does of Babak Rashidi, brain damage is probably his furthest concern right now.

"How is your head feeling?" Aalem asks.

"Not great."

"What do you remember from the ambush?"

"Enough."

"Mohammed betrayed us." Aalem shakes his head, like he's struggling to believe that this is what happened. A man he worked with. A man he trusted. A man who was perhaps his friend.

Zeke nods. He isn't surprised that they were betrayed. How else would Babak have known they were coming? How else could he have laid his ambush? "Where are we?" he asks.

"I don't know," Aalem says. "They had me in the back of the truck with you. I couldn't see anything until we arrived."

"Are we still in Afghanistan?"

"I do not know. But we were driving for a long time. Long enough to have crossed the border."

Zeke clenches his jaw, despite the waves of pain it sends through his skull. If they're on the Iranian side, that's basically a death sentence. If they're in Babak's hideout, his team will never find him. They don't know where it is, hence the game of cat and mouse that has been running between Babak and Bill Irving for the last couple of years.

"I'm not gonna lie to you, Aalem," Zeke says. "This doesn't look good for us."

Aalem purses his lips. He nods once, grimly. It's clear he'd already reached this conclusion.

Zeke is aware of how dire the situation is, but that doesn't mean he's giving up. He edges forward in the cramped confines of the cage, unable to get any higher than a seated position, and he tests the door. There's a padlock on the outside. He could potentially kick the door through, but the camera is watching. He'd kick it through and within minutes armed men would no doubt flood the room. It's a big if, though. The hinges look like they've been reinforced. The bars are thin, but plenty of them.

While he's inspecting, the door into the room opens. Babak enters. He's not alone. Two men flank him. They're in civilian clothing, but they have military bearing. Their lack of uniform again makes it difficult for Zeke to know which side of the border they're on. They leave the door to the room open and stand at either side of it. They're locals, not the Dutch from the ambush. Potentially the other ambushers who attacked from the darkness.

Babak takes a seat on the chair next to the tool table and he looks at Aalem and Zeke in turn, smiling at them both. He runs his hands down the thighs of his trousers, smoothing them out. "You've tried so hard for so long to find this place," he says. It's unclear whom he's talking to specifically. "And now here you are. I hope it can live up to everything you hoped it would be."

Neither of them responds.

Babak is unfazed. "I'm sure you've heard the stories about what happens in this place. Even you, Zeke, despite your brief time in the area. I know you've heard all about me. I'm why you're here, after all."

Zeke isn't surprised that Babak knows his name. After the capture, Mohammed probably gave him a rundown of everything he knew about the team. He knows their faces. He knows their names.

And, from what Babak has said, Zeke has his answer. They're in Iran, as he suspected. As he feared.

"Do you know what we call this place?" Babak asks, shifting on the chair, leaning forward a little and pointing a finger toward the ceiling, indicating the whole building. "I did not name it myself, but I'm pleased with the moniker. It fits. This is The Abattoir. Even without your prior knowledge, I'm sure the name would give you some kind of idea as to what we do here."

He pauses. He pauses a lot, Zeke notices. He wants his words to sink in. Building anticipation. Building fear.

"But you're in luck," he continues. "I'm here to give you – both of you – an opportunity that not many people who pass through The Abattoir are ever granted. In fact, this offer is unprecedented. I am going to give you both the opportunity to tell me where Bill Irving is. To tell me where Bill Irving is, the extent of his operations in this area, and anything else of interest you may feel is pertinent to our conversation. I'm going to give you this opportunity, but if you choose not to take me up on it… Well, if you do not care for this generous offer, that is when things will have to turn ugly."

Again, a pause. A long one this time. He waits, looking at them each in turn.

"Now is the time," he says. "Now is your chance."

Zeke says nothing. He breathes deeply through his nose and keeps his mouth shut. He has no intention of saying anything. He clears his mind. Does not think about Noami, or Tre. Does not think about his unborn daughter. A daughter he may never get to meet.

This is the job. He's been trained for this. Prepared for this possibility. Whatever comes, he will not break. He will not speak. He will tell Babak nothing.

Babak seems aware of this. His attention is focused intently on Aalem. "Well?" he prompts.

Aalem has not had the same training, Zeke knows. He can't expect him to stay silent.

"I do not know where Bill Irving is," Aalem says. "I do not know anything more than Mohammed has no doubt already told you."

"Mm," Babak says. His head slowly turns toward Zeke. He points. "But you know where he is," he says. "You've met with him. Seen him in person. You know what he looks like. I know this for a certainty."

Zeke breaks his silence to say, "He won't hang around. He's probably already gone."

"I have no doubt," Babak says. "But, as I said, you know what he looks like. You've spoken with him. You may even know his next intended hideout. You have so much information that is so valuable to me, Zeke Greene. And I will pry it out of that bloodied skull of yours." Babak slides off the chair, getting to his feet. "But would you look at me," he says, suddenly upbeat. "I'm feeling generous. Today is a day for unprecedented acts. You see, ordinarily, if I were to make an offer and it was so unceremoniously thrown back into my face with such ingratitude, I would set to work. I would set to work with glee. But I'm willing to grant you both a second chance. Don't worry – this one does not require an immediate response. I want you both to get comfortable first. To acclimatize."

He moves toward the door. Zeke watches him, not liking what he says, knowing that nothing good can come of this second opportunity.

Babak flicks a hand toward his two men guarding the door. In unison, they step out of the room. They're not gone long. Babak wriggles his eyebrows at Aalem and Zeke, like a magician about to unveil a new trick.

The two men wheel a gurney into the room. There's a man upon it. He's local – either Afghan or Iranian. He struggles frantically against the binds. There is tape over his mouth, silencing him, though he's making noise in his throat, his cheeks puffing out. The gurney is wheeled next to the table and the chair. Babak does not sit back down.

"A demonstration," he says with a flourish.

Zeke understands. Babak is trying to break them psychologically first. The information he needs from them, particularly from Zeke, is too valuable. He can't jump straight to hurting them. He has to pace himself.

"Giving you an opportunity to avoid torture is one thing," Babak says, circling the tool table. "But it means very little before you can *see* exactly what it is you'll be avoiding."

Zeke glances at Aalem. Aalem is trying to be firm, to be strong, but Zeke can see how he's trembling.

"I want you to pay close attention, gentlemen," Babak says. "I want you to watch, and listen, very closely. You need to both understand that if you throw away this golden opportunity to just *talk* to me, then this is what is coming for you." He picks up a scalpel from the table. It gleams. Babak smiles at the instrument.

Zeke steels himself.

Babak turns to the two guards. "You may leave us." He speaks in English. It's all for Zeke's benefit. The two men leave. They close the door after themselves. Zeke looks toward the camera. It's pointing at the cages still.

Babak rounds the gurney. He tears at the sleeve of the man's left arm. The arm closest to the cages. "I want you both to have a good view," he says. "And I want you both to hear." He tears the tape from the man's mouth.

The man screams. It fills the room, echoing off the walls. As Babak cuts, the first incision in the flay, the scream, somehow, gets louder. Aalem covers his ears.

CHAPTER THIRTY-THREE

Tom checks both of the Jeeps, sees which one has the most gas. He uses the keys he took off the men to start it up and discards the other, tossing it aside. He starts driving, getting clear of the area, Maryam sat up front beside him and Mohammed laid out across the backseat.

It's late, very late, and the area is clear. Tom checks the mirrors while he drives, making sure no one is following them.

"Why were you with Mohammed?" Tom asks when he's confident they've gotten clear and no one is in pursuit.

"Because he said my father was hurt," Maryam says. She's already told him this, Tom remembers. Back at the apartment. The last hour has been a blur.

"Where were you before that?"

"I was at home. He came and told me that I needed to come with him."

"And you trusted him?" There isn't any accusation in the question. It's genuine.

"No," Maryam says, surprising Tom. "I've never trusted Mohammed. But he said my father was injured, that he was with the Americans, and I needed to go with him to be with my father, to be safe, so what else was I supposed to do?"

"Why did he need you? Do you know something? Has your father told you anything about his work?"

"I don't think that's why Mohammed tried to take me with him."

"No?"

Maryam breathes deeply. "I...I fear what Mohammed planned for me. He's always had an...an unhealthy infatuation with me..."

"Is your father aware?"

"No."

"Why didn't you tell him?"

Maryam looks at him while he drives. "Tell him *what*, exactly? That his friend looked at me in a way I didn't like? I had no evidence. Just a feeling. My father is a good man, he's nothing like Mohammed, but he's also a very practical man. He would require an explanation. He would need evidence, evidence that I did not have."

"Your word wouldn't have been enough?"

"Perhaps it would have." Maryam sighs. "I didn't want to risk finding out that it wasn't."

Tom nods. He doesn't say anything to this. It's not his place to. "I need a destination," he says instead, changing the subject. "I need somewhere I can question Mohammed. Find out where Zeke and your father have been taken. It needs to be a private place. Out the way. No one else around for miles. You know of anywhere like that?"

Maryam thinks. "Yes," she says, nodding. "Yes, I do.

There is an old hospital not far from here – it's abandoned. A new one was built. The old one is awaiting demolition."

"That sounds good," Tom says. "You know the way?"

"I do."

"Then lead on."

CHAPTER THIRTY-FOUR

The torture felt like it went on forever. Zeke knows he'll never forget the sound of the screams. They're echoing in his ears still. It feels like they'll never end.

Babak has left the room. Has left them with the aftermath of his work, the stench of blood thick and cloying in the air, splashes and pools of it on the floor, the walls, and even the ceiling. It drips from the gurney, plinking into the blood puddle below.

When he left them, he was coated in blood from his fingertips to his elbows. There were smears of it on his face and elsewhere on his clothing. "Please excuse me," he said as he made his way toward the door. "You must allow me to go and get cleaned up." He stripped off his bloody clothes and dumped them in a heap close to the door for one of the guards to clear up. Naked, he paused before he left them, smiling toward the man on the gurney. "Please admire this work of art that I'll be leaving with you for now. And please think on my offer. If your response is not satisfactory, the next person on the gurney could be either one of you."

The man himself is no longer screaming. He whimpers. He makes choked sounds in the back of his throat. Despite the extensive damage that has been done to his arms and his legs, he's still alive. Babak has kept him alive throughout. Has kept him from bleeding out as he peeled the flesh from his body, dumping it on the ground next to the gurney, no further use for it. The man lies on the bed, its sheets soaked through with blood, his nerves and muscles exposed to the world. He's in shock. His breathing is shallow and rapid. What Zeke can see of his face, the parts not coated in blood and gore, looks pale.

Zeke breathes deeply, ignoring the smell and the sight. He keeps himself composed. Compartmentalizes what he's seen and what he's heard, the way he was trained. It's harder for Aalem. He hasn't had any such training. Zeke can see that he's been deeply affected by what he's seen. Like the man on the gurney, he's pale, too. He rocks back and forth a little, eyes fixed upon the flayed man, at the way his exposed veins pulse and his muscles twitch.

Aalem tried to cover his eyes during the torture. Babak noticed. He didn't allow it. He flicked blood at Aalem through the cage and told him, "Eyes up here, Aalem. This is for your benefit. If you don't comply, I'll summon my men back through. They will take you from your cage and bring you up here next to me. They'll force your eyes open and *make* you watch. You'll have the closest, clearest view you could ever want."

Aalem forced himself to watch. And now, he looks like he might throw up.

"Aalem," Zeke says. He has to repeat himself to get his attention. "Babak is trying to break us," he says when Aalem finally looks his way. "This is how he wants you to feel. This is psychological warfare. What we know is too important, too valuable to him. He can't risk hurting us straight away. He needs us too much. He needs us to talk."

Aalem watches him, he listens, but it's unclear how much he takes in and if it makes any kind of difference.

Zeke looks around the room again, still searching for a means of escape. The red light continues to blink atop the camera. It never goes off. The men on the other side are always watching.

There are instruments on the table that Zeke knows he could pick the padlock to his cage with. He got a good look at them all while Babak was working. The problem is, they're too far out of reach. The man on the table could reach them if it wasn't for the binds holding him tight to the gurney bars. And if it wasn't for the agony he's in. The man on the gurney is of no help to them right now. Poor bastard probably doesn't even know where he is. Zeke hopes he doesn't.

"Aalem," Zeke says, but Aalem has zoned out again, staring at the man, staring at all of the blood. Staring at the discarded pieces of skin dumped on the ground. Zeke snaps his fingers until Aalem looks at him. "Stay with me," he says. "Don't let him get into your head."

Aalem forces himself to nod. He moves in slow motion.

"The man on the table – it sounded like he was speaking sometimes," Zeke says. "What was he saying?"

"It sounded like he was begging."

"You couldn't understand him?"

"I could understand *some* of what he was saying," Aalem says. "Not much. He was speaking Farsi, as I do, but his dialect was Iranian Persian, whereas mine is Dari. I could not understand everything he was saying, not when he was screaming like that. If he had been screaming in English it would have been the same for you. You would understand what I mean."

"So the man on the table is Iranian?" Zeke asks. "Not Afghan?"

"He sounded that way, yes."

Zeke looks at the man. At his exposed and bloody limbs. "I wonder what he did to end up here."

"We may never know," Aalem says. "Zeke, I need to ask you..."

Zeke looks at him, waiting. Whatever he wants to ask, it's clear it's a painful subject.

"My daughter," he finally says. "I am concerned for her. I worry that Mohammed may have gone after her. I don't know why. Perhaps to bring her here. To wage further psychological warfare, as you say."

Zeke says nothing. He hasn't heard a question.

"Mustafa knew about my daughter," Aalem says. "I can only assume that Bill Irving knew about her, too. Do you think they would have gone to her? That they might have got to her before Mohammed could? That they would protect her?"

Zeke thinks about Captain Dale. He knows that Aalem's daughter would not be a priority for him. "I don't know," he says. He can't lie to Aalem. There's no point.

Aalem waits, as if he's expecting Zeke to say more, and he deflates when he realizes no more is coming. "What about us?" he asks. "Will the CIA be looking for us?"

Zeke doubts it. "I don't know," he says again. "But, Aalem, they don't know where we are. They don't know where this place is."

Aalem nods like he already knew this. He was just hoping for a different answer.

"But we don't give up," Zeke says. "We're on our own out here, but we don't quit. You got that? We've gotta hold on, even when it doesn't seem like there's any hope."

"There is no hope," Aalem says.

"That's how it looks," Zeke says.

Aalem is silent for a while. He sits slumped in the rear corner of the cage, looking down at his hands. Eventually, he looks up again, frowning. "Do you have a plan?" he asks.

"Working on one."

"What are you going to do?"

Zeke flashes him a smile. "I haven't decided yet."

Aalem blinks. Then he laughs. Zeke laughs with him.

CHAPTER THIRTY-FIVE

Babak showers and changes his clothes, putting on his pajamas. They're silk, and they feel good against his skin. *He feels good.* His mission was a success. He's tired now. After a couple of days over the border, and his time spent in the torture room with his captives, he's ready for some sleep.

But first, he has to call Farhad Gorji. To update him. The hour is late, but he knows that Farhad will want to hear from him. He calls him. It rings for a while.

When Farhad answers, it's clear that he was sleeping. Babak has woken him. "I have returned to The Abattoir," Babak says.

Babak can hear Farhad shifting around. Thinks he can hear him sitting up in his bed. "Babak?"

"Who else?"

"How did it go?" Farhad sounds fully awake now, eager to hear what happened.

"There was a slight change of plan, but I'm sure it'll be to your satisfaction."

"What kind of change?"

"It was straightforward. My Afghan mole kept me up to date on what was happening after I exposed myself over the border. Bill Irving called in a specialist team to help capture me. We ambushed them, and I have one of them in captivity now, along with one of the Afghan assets."

"The team, were they CIA?"

"Yes."

"And you have one of them?"

"I do. And through him I have a better chance of finding Bill Irving."

"And you can get him to talk?"

"I'm certain of it. I always am. You know how I work."

"They're trained for torture. To withstand it."

"No one is trained against flaying," Babak says. "They can't be. He will be a challenge, I don't deny it, but I have every confidence I will break him. He will tell me all about Bill Irving. He will tell me everything I want to know."

He can hear Farhad breathing on the line. "What about your allies?" he asks. "The Dutchmen. Where are they?"

"They're gone from here," Babak says. "For now. They are making their return to Khan. Doing what they came here for."

"Okay. Well, it would seem like things are moving well so far."

"Things are exactly as they should be."

"Good. Keep me updated, Babak, regardless of the time of day or night."

Babak grins to himself. "Certainly."

The call ends and Babak stretches, feeling his joints pop as he raises his arms above his head, reaching for the ceiling. He yawns, and goes to the door to his quarters before he settles onto the bed. There's a guard outside. "Monitor the captives," he says. "Keep a close eye on them. Especially the American. I'm going to get some sleep. Wake me if there's anything urgent."

"Yes, sir," the guard says.

Babak retreats back inside. He stretches again. It has been a long day. It has been a successful day. He has earned his rest.

CHAPTER THIRTY-SIX

When they reach the abandoned hospital, Tom does not get straight out of the Jeep. He circles the building first, checking the perimeter with the aid of the headlights, making sure there is no one lingering outside. When he sees that there isn't, he parks the Jeep behind a bush, concealing it, then tells Maryam he'll go inside and check the building over, make sure there's no one inside, either.

"What about him?" Maryam says, tilting her head toward Mohammed in the back. He's awake now, groaning with a headache.

"Just keep an eye on him," Tom says. "Make sure he behaves himself. I won't be long. And remember – you have the Glock. If he starts acting up, don't be afraid to beat him around the head with it. I won't hold it against you."

Tom readies the AK47, flicks on his flashlight, and heads inside the building. It's pitch-black inside. There are many shadows and many rooms. Tom is as thorough as he can be, but he doesn't have the time to search every single room. No one jumps out at him. No one tries to attack him. This is what's important. He can't hear anything, either. Nothing that sounds larger than a small animal, anyway. The building is clear enough, and the basement is empty. The basement is where he'll work.

He goes back outside and pulls Mohammed to his feet, pushing him ahead, toward the building. Maryam follows them. When they reach the steps leading down into the basement, Tom turns to her.

"You should stay up here," he says. "Keep watch. If anyone comes, let me know."

Maryam wraps her arms around herself and looks at the darkness surrounding them. She's scared, he can tell. He doesn't blame her. It's dark, and they've already been through a lot. He wishes he could leave her a flashlight, but he only has the one, and he'll need it down in the basement. The abandoned building no longer has any electricity.

"Remember that you have the gun," Tom says. "You don't have anything to worry about."

"You haven't shown me how to use it yet."

"You're right," Tom says. He pushes Mohammed down so he's sitting cross-legged on the ground, then pulls out his own Glock and hands it to her. "Both hands," he says. He talks her through it. How to hold it. Stance. How to aim. He points to the center of his chest. "This is where you want to hit. This will stop them in their tracks. You got that?"

Maryam nods, though it's clear she has doubts about her own capabilities.

Tom points at a nearby pillar. "Shoot it," he says. "See how it feels."

She does. The sound of the gunshot echoes around the building. He sees Mohammed flinch. Tom takes the gun back. Maryam's hands are shaking. She's never fired a gun before.

"Think you could do that again?" he asks.

"Y-yes," Maryam says. "If I had to."

Tom pulls Mohammed back up from the floor, and takes him down the stairs into the basement.

It's a wide space. It smells like dust. The corners are filled with detritus – stones and pipes and discarded tools. There are some plastic chairs stacked up in the corner, leaning against the wall. Tom takes one of them and sets it down, then forces Mohammed into it. Tom tears the gag out of his mouth.

Mohammed smacks his dry lips together, running his tongue over them and then stretching out his jaw. He looks up at Tom but he says nothing.

"We need to talk," Tom says.

"I have nothing to say to you," Mohammed says.

"I figured, but we still need to talk."

Mohammed is silent. He smirks, like he has something to be satisfied about.

Tom doesn't have time for games. He can't wait him out. Mohammed needs to talk, right now.

Tom takes a step back and folds his arms, staring at Mohammed while he thinks, considering his best options.

Mohammed shrugs, still grinning. "Are you trying to intimidate me? It will not work. I don't fear you, Rollins. You can't kill me. I am too valuable to you."

Tom ignores him.

There's not enough time for Tom to utilize some of the more cumbersome enhanced interrogation techniques he's been taught. Or torture methods, to be blunt. He runs through them in his mind – he doesn't have the tools needed for waterboarding. Doesn't have the time to subject Mohammed to hypothermia. He could twist Mohammed into a stress position, but again, that requires time. Time that he doesn't have. He needs to use the more immediate techniques.

Mohammed raises his eyebrows, watching, waiting. Still grinning. Still smug.

Tom slaps him.

Slaps him so hard he almost falls from the chair.

Tom catches him, and slaps him again, left-handed this time, striking his other cheek. The sound is like a sudden gunshot in the basement's silence. Mohammed gasps at the abrupt violence. Tom grabs him by the front of his shirt, shines the flashlight directly into his eyes, shakes him.

"Speak to me, Mohammed," he says. "I've got some questions for you."

He pushes Mohammed back into the chair, taking the flashlight out of his eyes. Mohammed blinks hard, seeing spots.

Tom doesn't give him a chance to recover. He delivers abdomen strikes – hard, open-handed slaps to Mohammed's torso. Mohammed coughs. He gasps for breath. His shoulders heave. As his breathing levels, Tom strikes him again.

He stops and waits for Mohammed to catch his breath. It's clear that he's pained, and his voice trembles when he speaks, but he shakes his head and says, "Is that it? That's all you can do? You cannot kill me, Rollins."

He's trying to be defiant. Tom doesn't buy it. He's hurt and he's scared. It won't take much more to break him. "I don't intend to kill you, Mohammed," Tom says. "But I'm going to continue hurting you until you tell me what you know."

Mohammed gulps, but he says nothing.

"I don't have time for this," Tom says.

Mohammed tries to laugh, to sound unbothered. "I have all the time in the world."

Tom leaves him. He goes to the rubble and the waste piled up around the basement, pressed against the walls. He retrieves a pipe. It's steel, and dotted with rust. Tom clasps it tight and turns back to Mohammed. Through the darkness, he can see how Mohammed's eyes widen.

Tom goes to him. He doesn't say a word. Mohammed starts to babble. Tom grabs him by the back of the neck and throws him roughly to the ground, onto his front. Mohammed sneezes as disturbed dust wafts up his nose. Tom follows him down. He presses a knee into Mohammed's lower back and holds the piece of pipe in front of his face.

"Talk to me," he says.

Mohammed stares at the pipe. He doesn't speak.

Tom shifts his weight. His right knee is in Mohammed's back. Flipping open his knife, he cuts the ties loose. He presses Mohammed's left arm to the ground, bringing up his boot to pin it by the wrist. He grinds his heel down to open up Mohammed's fingers. He presses his heel into the center of Mohammed's palm, keeping him from closing his fingers again.

Tom readies the pipe. "I'm aiming for one," he says. "Let's see how many I hit."

Mohammed continues to babble. It's not all in English.

Tom raises the pipe. He brings it down. He aims for the left pinkie. He connects with it, and the ring finger. Their tips burst and blood sprays. Mohammed screams. The bones twist and break. The fingers are mangled.

Tom steps back, giving Mohammed a moment to fully

embrace the pain. Tom kicks him onto his back. "You've got eight left," he says, peering down into Mohammed's twisted face, streaked with tears and snot. "And then you've got toes. And then you've got every other fucking bone in your body. How long do you want to draw this out?"

Mohammed gasps, trying to suck down air. He grits his teeth, clutching his broken fingers protectively to his chest. "No – no more," he says, his voice barely above a whisper. "I'll talk."

CHAPTER THIRTY-SEVEN

Tom sits Mohammed back in the chair, his wrists bound again behind him. Tom keeps the piece of pipe in his hand, its tip coated in blood. Mohammed sucks in breaths, trying to control the pain. Even in the dark, he looks pale. "Please," Mohammed says. "Please... I need water. I am so thirsty. My fingers...they hurt so much..."

"I don't have any water for you," Tom says. "All I have is this." He levels the pipe. Mohammed almost recoils from it. "Is that going to be a problem?"

Mohammed shakes his head.

"Good," Tom says. He lowers the pipe. "First things first. Maryam's father. Aalem." Tom glances toward the stairs, checking that they're clear, that Maryam has not crept down to investigate the screams. "Is he still alive?"

"I believe so," Mohammed says.

"You *believe* so?"

Mohammed flinches. "He was alive when I last saw him. I do not know if that is still so." He smacks his lips and swallows what little spit there is in his mouth.

"I... I think Babak would want to keep him alive. At least for a little while. Aalem gave him up to the Americans, back when he was pretending to be Abdul Rahman."

While it isn't ideal for Aalem to be held captive by Babak, Tom is glad to hear he's probably still alive, if only for Maryam's sake. "What is Babak's objective?"

"He has to eliminate all American presence in the area. To do that, he needs to find Bill Irving. He does not know what Bill Irving looks like. *I* do not know what Bill Irving looks like, and I have worked for him for many years. Bill remains hidden, always."

"But Zeke saw him recently," Tom says. "We all did. I assume you told him that."

Mohammed nods. "Babak set a trap. That trap brought you and your team. I alerted him to this. Babak saw an opportunity – not just to finally find Bill Irving, to know what he looks like, but to find out further American plans and objectives, too. He wanted to capture all of you."

"Zeke won't talk. He's trained not to."

Mohammed bites his lip. "Babak will make him talk."

"You sound confident."

"I am confident because Babak is confident. He makes everyone talk because he does not threaten them with death. He threatens them with a prolonged life while he strips the flesh from their bodies. Everyone talks when he flays them. He has told me this himself."

Tom grits his teeth. "How long have you been working for him?"

"Since before Aalem exposed him."

"Why?"

"You and your people are an invasive force in this land,

Rollins," Mohammed spits. "The better question is *why not?*"

"When they caught the others who were working for Babak, how come they didn't catch you?"

"Because the others did not know about me, and I did not know about them."

"So there could be others still working for Babak?"

"I don't know. I could be the only one left. I don't know."

"You wouldn't lie to me, Mohammed, would you?"

"No, I swear, this is the truth. I do not know."

"All right. Where is Babak now? Where did he take Zeke and Aalem?"

Mohammed takes a deep breath before he answers. "I do not know this, either."

Tom stares at him.

"I swear. I do not know if he is still in Afghanistan, or if he went back to Iran. I would assume the latter – is that what you want to hear? Do you want me to make guesses?"

"No," Tom says. "I only want you to tell me what you know. How do you contact Babak?"

"I don't. He contacts me. It is always this way. There were times I would not hear from him for months."

"Where were you gonna go after all of this, Mohammed? It's not like you could remain in the area."

"I was to stay with the Taliban."

"Join them?"

"Yes."

"And you were planning on taking Maryam along with you for that."

Mohammed says nothing.

Tom grunts. "Where would Babak go in Iran? Do you know that much?"

Mohammed shakes his head. "Only that it is called The Abattoir. He let this slip once, while we spoke. It has always remained with me. Its name. It's such a terrifying name."

Tom thinks. Mohammed doesn't have the answers he needs, but Tom isn't prepared to give up yet. He feels there could be something he's not asked yet, something that could lead him to more information. Another lead.

It occurs to him. "Who were the men helping him, at the ambush?" he asks. "Not the Taliban. The others. They were wearing masks but what little I saw of them, they looked white."

"Drug smugglers," Mohammed says.

Something connects in Tom's mind. "Khan, right? He's the kingpin around here."

"Khan was not there."

"But the drug runners, they do business with him?"

"Yes. They have for years. Khan recommended their services to Babak when he was hatching his plan."

"Where are they from? The runners."

"They're Dutch. They're dangerous men. Half of them were part of the special forces in their country."

"Well, we're not in their country. Do you have names for them?"

"I only know one. Their commander. The man in charge."

"What is it?"

"Bram de Groot."

Tom didn't see any of their faces. "Big guy? He captured Zeke?"

"So I'm told."

"Where are they now? Are they gone?"

Mohammed hesitates. Tom raises his eyebrows. He

squeezes the pipe. Mohammed notices. "They're still in the area. They were not planning to go with Babak. But I don't know this for sure – things may have changed. Babak may have wanted them to accompany him–"

"I only want to hear the things you know," Tom says. "The things you were told. The plan as it was described to you."

"The Dutch were to meet with Khan, to continue their business."

"Why were they helping Babak? A payday?"

"Yes, but Babak has also promised them a clearer path for transporting opium. He has promised them assistance in the future, and a clear, undisturbed route through the border."

"Do you know where the Dutch are meeting with Khan?"

Mohammed nods.

Tom pulls out his map of the area. He spreads it on Mohammed's lap and shines the flashlight down on it. "Where?"

Mohammed tells him. Tom makes a mark. It looks like the middle of nowhere.

"How long will they be around?" Tom asks. "How long will it take?"

"I do not know."

"Do you know when it's happening?"

"I believe in the morning. I wasn't paying much attention to this part of things. It had nothing to do with me."

Tom nods. He believes him. "You've done good, Mohammed," he says. "Did that really have to be so difficult?"

CHAPTER THIRTY-EIGHT

Tom leaves the basement, returning to Maryam upstairs, bringing Mohammed with him. There's too much debris in the basement, too much that he could use to free himself and make himself dangerous. Tom can't leave him alone.

Maryam gives a start as they approach. "I heard screams," she says. "And then I didn't hear anything for a long time. I thought you might have killed him."

Tom pushes Mohammed down to the ground so he's seated cross-legged again. Mohammed grimaces, trying to keep his hands off the ground. "It was touch and go for a while, but Mohammed saw sense and found his voice."

"And? What did he tell you?"

"He doesn't know where your father and Zeke are," Tom says. Before Maryam can deflate, he adds, "But he knows about some people who might."

"Who?"

Tom tells her about the Dutch drug runners. About their upcoming business meeting with Khan. "I need to go there,"

Tom says, showing her the location Mohammed gave him on the map.

"You'll be outnumbered," Maryam says, studying the area.

"No other choice," Tom says. "And I'll be careful. I'm not planning on charging headfirst into battle against some Dutch ex-special forces and a bunch of Afghan drug dealers. But listen, it's going to be dangerous out there. You should stay here. It'll be safer. And I need you to guard Mohammed."

Maryam shakes her head. "No."

"No?" Tom says.

"I will not be staying behind," Maryam says.

Tom raises an eyebrow.

"I know this area," Maryam says. "I know it better than you do, than you ever could. And I speak the language. You do not. You need me."

She has a point, Tom thinks. She has a couple of good points.

"And Mohammed could be lying about where they've gone, about where they're meeting with Khan. You can't leave him behind. We have to take him with us."

Tom notices the 'we.' He doesn't argue with it. There's no time, and he can see that Maryam has already made up her mind. "All right," he says. "But out there, you answer to me. What I say goes."

"Okay."

"I'm serious, Maryam. It's going to be dangerous out there. If I tell you to hide, you have to hide. If I tell you to run, you run."

"It's already been dangerous, Tom," she says. "And I've done what you said so far, haven't I?"

He can't deny that she has. "Keep your gun close," he says. He picks Mohammed back up. He sees how Maryam spots his mangled fingers, wincing at the sight. They leave the building and return to the Jeep. It's been a long night. Dawn is still a while away. Tom is tired. He doesn't think about it.

CHAPTER THIRTY-NINE

Aalem is sleeping. He's curled up on his side in his cage, as comfortable as he's able to get. Zeke does not sleep. He forces himself to remain awake. It's not hard. The lights overhead are achingly bright and have not been dimmed. The stench of blood remains thick and Zeke has not acclimatized to it. He doesn't want to.

The flayed man is trying to sleep, but he's clearly in too much pain. He groans. When he tries to shift position, to get comfortable, he winces, cries out a little. Zeke can hear him sob from time to time.

When the flayed man moves, something catches Zeke's eye. The binds that hold him to the railing. On his right forearm it's come loose. The lack of skin and the slickness of his blood have created a gap. He could slip his arm out. He could reach the tools on the table.

The red light atop the camera remains on. It's not going to turn off. It's constantly watching them. Zeke isn't going to be able to avoid it. Whatever move he attempts to make to get out of here, it's going to be with the knowledge that he's under observation. With that in mind, when the time comes he's going to have to work fast.

Zeke takes a breath, preparing to wake Aalem, but as he does so, the door to the room opens. Zeke's eyes flicker toward it. He recognizes the man who enters. He guarded the door earlier when Babak first came to talk to them. The man looms over Zeke's cage, frowning. When he speaks, his English is broken, but he's able to make sense. "Why you not sleep?" he asks.

"The lights are too bright," Zeke says.

The guard does not reply straight away, mentally translating Zeke's response. When he does, he smirks. "You should rest," he says. His frown is gone, and his tone and demeanor are gloating now. "Tomorrow will be long day for you."

"Aren't they all," Zeke says.

He thinks the guard's visit could be a continuation of Babak's psychological torture. If Zeke *had* been sleeping, the guard probably would have woken him up.

The guard smiles, almost as if he can read Zeke's mind. He mutters something in his own language, his smile never fading, and then he leaves the room.

Zeke looks toward the camera and its red light. He decides against waking Aalem right now. After the guard's visit, they're probably watching him closely to see what he does next. The guard could still be close to the door. Zeke has to bide his time.

CHAPTER FORTY

Tom gets close to the location Mohammed has given him. As he suspected, it's in the middle of nowhere. Scrubland, as far as he can see. The land rises and dips. He can see bushes, and trees that look almost dead. There are no buildings. He slows the Jeep and pulls it to the side where there's a rocky outcrop. They're still a couple of miles away from the location.

"We're going to have to continue on foot," Tom says, gathering up the rifle and getting out of the Jeep.

"Why?" Maryam asks, sliding out of the Jeep and standing close to him.

Tom pulls Mohammed out of the back of the Jeep. Mohammed is gagged. He winces as he's moved, and Tom sees how he tries to keep his broken fingers close to his body to avoid them getting knocked. He flinches when Tom manhandles him. He's sweating. He's scared of Tom, remembering how Tom beat him and shattered his fingers. Good. Tom isn't trying to be gentle with him. He wants him to be scared.

"Because this place is desolate," Tom says. "We run the risk of running right into them if we continue in the Jeep. We need to keep the element of surprise on our side."

Maryam understands. They start walking.

The night is cool. Tom is thirsty. He has a little water left. He shares it with Maryam. They don't give any to Mohammed, despite how he stares at them like a hungry dog. If he wasn't gagged again, he'd probably be smacking his lips in desperation, pleading with them for just a drop.

They walk for more than two miles. Tom is eyeing Mohammed, beginning to suspect that, as Maryam suggested, he might have been lying. Mohammed pleads with his eyes, raising his eyebrows, nodding to push on just a little further. Tom stops. He pulls the gag loose. "Don't waste my time, Mohammed."

"I'm not, I swear," he says. "I said they'd be in this *area*. I didn't say I knew the exact *location*."

Tom puts the gag back on him and they resume walking, Tom worrying that they're wasting time. If they are, if the Dutch aren't meeting with Khan out here, then he's out of leads. If Mohammed was lying, Tom will break the rest of his bones and leave him for dead out here.

But then, in the distance, Tom sees light, concealed behind a dip in the landscape. He points it out to Maryam. The light flickers. A campfire, perhaps. "We stay silent from here," Tom says. "Mouths shut, eyes and ears open. There could be lookouts." He stares at Mohammed. "*Silence*," he says again. "You try something like that bullshit you pulled back in your building, I'll twist those fingers straight off your hand."

Mohammed swallows.

They move slower now, approaching the flickering light

carefully. Tom takes hold of Mohammed's arm and grips it tightly, burying his fingers into his bicep, pinching him. He holds the AK47 in his right hand, ready to swing it to bear if needed. He scans the area, searching for a lookout, or anyone on patrol. For movements in the shadows. He doesn't see any.

As they near the dip, he can hear voices. They're not loud, but they carry. He can hear the faint crackle of the fire. Tom indicates for the group to turn to the right, toward a smattering of bushes and trees. He pushes Mohammed down. "Watch him," he tells Maryam, whispering. "Don't let him make any noise. I'm going for a closer look."

He leaves the bushes and gets close to the dip, lowering himself to his stomach and crawling to its rim. He peers over the edge.

He sees two familiar trucks. The box trucks from the hideout where they were ambushed. He sees the two men he heard talking, sitting close to the campfire. They're not masked. The other four men are lying on the ground around the fire, sleeping. There's no sign of Khan or his men. Only the Dutch. This must be the meeting point. They've come here early, and they're waiting. Tom assumes the business transaction must be happening by daylight. Mohammed suspected it was in the morning.

Tom watches, looking over the six men. They all look alike, but one of them is bigger than the others. Taller and broader. He's on the ground, sleeping. Flat on his back, his blond hair falling back from his face upturned toward the stars. He looks like he's been carved from stone. Tom thinks this is the man Zeke was fighting with. The leader of the Dutch group. Bram de Groot.

One of the men on guard stands and picks up his MP5.

Tom freezes, knowing he hasn't made a sound but wondering if the men have felt his eyes. But no, it's not that. He's going to take a patrol. Do a sweep of the area.

Tom slowly and carefully slides back down the dip. At the bottom, he bends double and hurries back to the bushes. As he reaches Maryam and Mohammed, he presses a finger to his lips. He motions for Maryam to lie down flat, concealing herself under a bush. He drags Mohammed into another bush with him and they lie on their sides. Tom is behind Mohammed. He pulls out his knife and presses its tip to the side of Mohammed's neck to ensure his silence.

Tom peers through the branches. He sees the guard come into view. The man pauses as he comes around the dip. He looks around, scanning the horizon, his MP5 held low at his waist. He's not pointing it anywhere in particular. He starts walking again, coming toward the bushes. Tom is tense, ready to spring into action if he needs to.

The man pauses at the edge of the bushes. Tom thinks he's looking in, but it turns out he isn't. Instead, he unzips his trousers and takes a piss on a nearby tree. Tom holds his breath. He moves his head, ever so slightly, making sure he doesn't make a sound, and looks toward Maryam. She's lying very still and very flat. He can barely see her through the dark. He thinks she's holding her breath, too.

The man finishes pissing, zips himself back up, and continues on his route, making his way around the dip, past an outcrop, and eventually returning to the campfire.

Tom leaves Mohammed in the bush, but crawls out to meet with Maryam. He tells her what he saw, keeping his voice at a whisper.

"Khan is not here?" she asks, matching his volume.

Tom shakes his head.

"Then we should take this opportunity to rest," she says. "It has been a long night, for all of us."

"I don't need Khan," Tom says. "I need to talk to the Dutch."

"And you're outnumbered, and Khan could turn up at any time. You're exhausted, Tom. I can see it. You need to rest, same as I do. I know you want to do more, I know you want to save your friend, the same as I want to save my father, but you cannot pour from an empty cup."

"We don't have the time. Neither do your father and Zeke."

"It has been a long night for Babak Rashidi, too. Do you think he will not rest? He is not a machine."

Tom knows she's right, but it's hard to accept. It's hard to not push himself, knowing that lives are on the line, and because of this he'd push on if it wasn't for something else Maryam said. He *doesn't* know when Khan and his men might turn up. He's assumed it'll be in the morning, the same way Mohammed made that assumption, but there's no guarantee of this. He could potentially get the drop on the Dutch, but they're all close together around the fire. He'd quickly lose his element of surprise. If he was looking to just kill the six of them, it would be easy. But he needs to keep them alive, the same as he did with Mohammed. He needs to question them. They might have an idea of where Babak – of where The Abattoir – is. And then, if Khan were to turn up with his men, Tom would be heavily outnumbered. All he has is the AK47, a few spare magazines, and the Glock. It wouldn't take much for them to overwhelm him.

"Tom?" Maryam prompts.

He nods. "All right," he says. "You're right. Let's rest. I'll take first watch."

CHAPTER FORTY-ONE

Tom does not need to sleep to rest. He has no intention of giving up watch. He likes Maryam; she's capable, but he can't trust that she's up to the task, and he doesn't have time to train her.

He listens to the night. For approaching vehicles. For sudden alarm coming from over the hill, inside the dip, around the Dutch campsite. Nothing comes. He sits propped against a tree, the AK47 laid across his lap should he need it. He hasn't seen either of the guards do another patrol yet, but it hasn't been so long since the last one.

Mohammed is sleeping. He remains under the bush, lying on his front with his face turned to the side, his wrists bound behind him now. Tom rebound him now that they're stationary to make him easier to control. Mohammed lies with his hands away from the ground so he won't hurt them in his sleep; so he won't roll over and crush them. Maryam is close to Tom. She's trying to sleep, but he can tell she's having trouble settling. She rolls onto her side, facing him.

"I'm sorry," she says. "I cannot sleep."

"It'll be the adrenaline," Tom says.

"I felt like I was ready to pass out earlier."

"It'll come back with a vengeance."

"May I sit with you?" she asks.

Tom shrugs. "Sure."

She gets off the ground and joins him at the tree, pressing her back to it. She looks at Mohammed. "He does not have any trouble sleeping."

"I guess people like him rarely do."

She's silent. Tom keeps an eye on the edge of the dip, where the guard first stepped out from when he did his sweep.

"I am tired," she says. "I do not think it is the adrenaline keeping me awake. I… I am thinking of my father."

"It makes sense to worry about him."

"This man, Zeke, are you and he very good friends?"

"We've just met."

Maryam pushes herself off the tree a little so she can look at him, studying his face. Her eyes narrow. "I cannot tell if you are joking."

"I'm not," Tom says. "Would you believe that this is my first mission?"

She continues to stare at him like she's struggling to comprehend. "Your first?"

Tom nods. "I've spent the last couple of years training, since I got recruited. This is my first time overseas with the CIA."

"Is it your first time in Afghanistan?"

"No," Tom says. "I was in the Army before this."

"Oh. I see."

"I've never been in this province before."

Maryam sits back. "If you do not know Zeke so well, why are you risking your life for him like this?"

"Because that's what you're supposed to do," Tom says. "In the Army, we were brothers. No man left behind. How could I do that to Zeke?"

"If it were you who had been captured instead of him, would he have done the same for you?"

"I don't know, but it doesn't matter. That shouldn't be a reason to do anything. I'm here because it's right. I'm here because he has a family, and his kids want their daddy to come home to them. If I wasn't here doing something, if I'd left with the others when they tried to escape, I wouldn't be able to live with it, knowing I hadn't tried *something*."

"He has children?"

"He has a son, and a daughter on the way. He told me."

"Do you have children?"

"No."

"Are you married?"

"No."

"Is there someone waiting for you back in America?"

Tom hesitates. "No," he says.

"It is good of you to do this," she says. "For Zeke. And for my father. I am grateful to you."

"You're here, too. You don't need to thank me."

"If you had not come to Mohammed's, I would be his captive right now. Things would be very different for me."

"I came to Mohammed for answers. I can't take praise for rescuing you. I didn't know you were there."

"But that doesn't matter. You still did it, and you are still helping. And that's what matters, isn't it? That is what you said."

"Tell me about your father," Tom says. "I didn't get much of a chance to speak with him."

"I wish you could have. He's a good man. Things are... things are difficult in my country, as a woman. My father has taught me things outside of the system. Things he should not have taught me."

"Like how to speak English?"

"Yes, exactly. And electronics. He used to be an engineer. He spent a lot of time in America, too, when he was younger. In Europe, as well. He has taught me everything that he knows."

"Oh really? That's impressive. So, like, computers and stuff?"

"Yes, *and stuff*." She grins at him.

"I'm not great with computers. Never have been. My father taught me about the outdoors. I mean, I can handle them all right. Computers, that is. I can turn them on and off. Send an email. All that basic stuff. I assume you can do more than that."

She smiles at him. "Yes," she says. "Just a bit more."

They look at each other in silence for a moment, in the dark. Maryam opens her mouth to say something but Tom stops her, spotting something at the edge of the dip. One of the guards is on patrol. Maryam sees him, too. Tom glances at Mohammed. He's still asleep, no doubt exhausted from everything Tom has done to him, from being thrown from his building to having his fingers smashed with a pipe.

Tom and Maryam sit very still. Maryam leans into Tom. Tom puts an arm around her. He watches the guard as he patrols. Tom keeps a hand on the handle of the AK47.

The guard doesn't come toward the bushes. It's a different man from earlier, but Tom recognizes him. He was talking to the other next to the fire. They're taking turns on patrol and sweep. This man doesn't stop for a piss. He continues on his way, passing by the trees. Tom watches him go, disappearing back where he came from.

He looks down at Maryam. Their faces are close. Before either of them can speak, Maryam kisses him. Tom doesn't stop her. After a moment, she reaches for the button on his trousers, glancing back over her shoulder to make sure Mohammed remains unconscious.

"You've only known me a few hours," Tom says.

"What does it matter?" Maryam says, whispering. She kisses him again.

"I thought there was a stigma around premarital sex over here. Especially for women."

She pulls back enough to look at him, but keeps her face close to his. She grins a little and raises an eyebrow. "You won't be my first, Tom," she says. "So many things here are forbidden, especially for women." She shrugs. "And so what? We could both die tomorrow. This is a night for last chances."

Tom agrees with her. For a brief, flashing moment, he thinks of Alejandra. And then he doesn't, and he places a hand on the back of Maryam's neck and draws her to him again. She slips down her own trousers and climbs atop him, straddling him against the tree.

When they're done, she sits back beside him, and she yawns. She rests her head against his shoulder. After a couple of minutes, Tom notices a change in her breathing. She's asleep. He doesn't join her in sleep. He keeps watch.

CHAPTER FORTY-TWO

Zeke has spent some time lying back against the rear of the cage, his arms folded and his legs stretched out ahead of him, trying to look as relaxed as possible for the benefit of the ever-watching camera.

In reality, his body is tensed, coiled, like a spring. He thrums with energy waiting to be expelled. He's preparing himself. Mentally and physically. He's going to make his move, very soon.

He has to hope, at this late hour, that the men watching the camera are bored. That they're only checking in intermittently, and not glued to it watching every little movement like a hawk. That couple of minutes, or even couple of seconds, of them looking away from the screen could make a lot of difference to what he has planned.

He calls to Aalem in a whisper, waking him. Aalem, still on his side, comes round with a start. He opens both eyes and looks toward Zeke.

"Stay exactly as you are," Zeke says, talking quickly out

the side of his mouth. "Don't get up. Don't sit up. Stay just like that so they think you're still asleep."

Aalem does as he says.

"The man on the gurney, he's still awake," Zeke says. "I need you to talk to him."

Without moving his head, Aalem's eyes turn downward, toward the flayed man. Zeke doesn't think he'll be able to see him from his current position.

"The cuff on his right arm has come loose," Zeke says. "I don't think he's realized. Or if he has, I think he's scared about how much it might hurt pulling his arm free. But I need you to point this out to him, and persuade him to do it."

"Why?" Aalem asks, keeping his own voice lowered.

"On the table, next to him, there are tools that I can pick the padlock with. I need him to pass them to me."

"What about the camera? What about the guards?"

"We have to take this chance. And we have to do it *fast*, do you understand? You need to make that clear to him, too – *speed*. It doesn't matter how much he hurts, he has to be *fast*. No one is coming for us. If we don't try to get out of here, we're going to die here. That goes for him, too. Can you do that, Aalem?"

"What tools will you need?" Aalem asks.

"I spotted a pair of tweezers; I'll need those. And the thinnest scalpel there."

"When?"

Zeke takes a deep breath. "Now," he says.

Aalem calls to the man on the gurney. He speaks his own language. Zeke can't understand it. He watches. Aalem remains on his side, not moving. Zeke sees the man on the gurney raise his head, grimacing toward Aalem's calls. Aalem speaks to him. Zeke assumes Aalem is detailing the plan.

The grimace never leaves the flayed man's face. He says something.

Aalem translates to Zeke. "He says he's in too much pain."

"Tell him he's going to die if he doesn't do what you've told him," Zeke says.

"I already have."

"Tell him again. Tell him that the only hope he has of getting out of here is passing me those tools. Tell him if he doesn't, Babak is going to come back and he's going to peel the flesh from his torso, and from his back. Tell him he'll tear it from his face and his scalp. Tell him whatever he needs to hear that's going to get him to pass me those instruments."

Aalem does. He speaks for a long time. Zeke can see the fear in the flayed man's face. Aalem falls silent. The flayed man's eyes flicker toward Zeke. He says something.

"He's going to do it," Aalem says. "He told you to be ready."

"I'm ready," Zeke says.

The flayed man, shaking all over, pulls his trembling right arm through the loose padded cuff. He whimpers. Bares his teeth. Breathes hard. Spittle hangs from the corner of his mouth. He gets his arm free and reaches for the table. His fingers are bloody and exposed. He can't use them properly. His hands are shaking badly. The man whimpers in the back of his throat. Tears stream down his cheeks. He tries to keep himself from screaming. He struggles to get a grip on the tools Zeke needs. Gritting his teeth, he seizes the tweezers. His eyes bulge.

"Throw them to me," Zeke says.

The man understands enough of what Zeke has said. He throws them. His limbs no longer work properly. His dexterity and aim are gone. The tweezers land closer to Aalem's cage.

"I can reach them," Aalem says, spinning and crawling toward the front of the cage. He reaches through, grabbing the tweezers with his fingertips. He tosses them over so they're in front of Zeke's cage.

Zeke grabs the tweezers. He watches the door. The handle. It doesn't move. No one is coming, not yet.

The flayed man is grabbing at a scalpel. He throws this over, too. This throw is better. It lands in front of Zeke's cage. The flayed man flops back on the gurney, exhausted, breathing hard through his gritted teeth, straining sounds escaping his throat, still trying not to scream.

Zeke makes his move. He's able to reach both instruments. He slides them into the padlock, having to work blind, by touch. He bites down on his bottom lip while he works, his arms straining, trying to find the best positions to get the padlock to open.

It clicks. The padlock opens.

Zeke pushes the cage door open and scrambles out. He goes to Aalem's cage and picks the padlock. He's faster when he can see what he's doing.

As he gets it open, he hears frantic footsteps outside the room, boots pounding down the corridor, coming their way. It took time, time that Zeke silently prayed for, but they've finally been spotted on the camera. The door is opening.

CHAPTER FORTY-THREE

Zeke bolts for the door, armed with the scalpel. He slices the throat of the first man through, aiming for his carotid. It severs and blood sprays against the white wall. The man spins, flailing, and his blood sprays into the face of the man behind him, blinding him.

The guard was carrying a Masaf-2. The rifle of the Iranian army. Zeke grabs it from the falling man and opens fire on the blinded guard, the gunfire deafening in the torture room. Zeke throws the door wide and checks the corridor. It was just the two men, but anyone else in the building would have heard the shots. They'll get ready and then they'll come running, too.

Zeke wishes he knew where he was. Wishes he knew what they could be escaping into – the middle of nowhere, or the middle of a city? Whatever it is, he likes his chances better out there than waiting in here for the inevitable.

Aalem cuts the flayed man free from the gurney. He takes one of his arms around his shoulders and helps him to his feet. The flayed man screams with every step. Aalem looks at Zeke, horrified, the flayed man's blood getting onto him. There's a smear of it on his cheek. "I don't know what to do," he says. "We cannot leave him."

Aalem is right, Zeke knows. They wouldn't be out of the cages if it wasn't for the flayed man. Unfortunately, the flayed man's chances of survival are slim. With the muscles of his arms and legs exposed like that, he's wide open to infection. He's already as good as dead.

But he fought through his pain, through his agony, to help them get free.

"*Fuck*," Zeke says.

He checks the corridor again – still clear – and hurries to Aalem and the flayed man. He stoops down and lifts the flayed man onto his back so that his exposed feet aren't touching the floor.

"We're probably all going to die," Zeke says to Aalem. He holds up the Masaf-2. "But we're going out guns blazing."

Aalem closes his eyes briefly, making peace with this. He nods. They start running. Aalem gets the door. The flayed man on Zeke's back does his best not to scream. He whimpers into Zeke's ear.

Zeke hears men at the end of the corridor, shouting, barking orders. An alarm sounds. He presses on. Two men appear at the end of the corridor. Zeke guns them down, the automatic fire throwing them back against the wall behind them, leaving an imprint of their blood. He presses on. Aalem follows. He doesn't know where he's going. He has to find the way out. It's not over until it's over, and he's not giving up yet.

As they reach the end of the corridor, gunfire comes their way. Zeke ducks back into cover. With the man on his back, he's already breathing hard and there's an ache in his lumbar. The man is crying. Zeke can feel his tears soaking into his collar. Zeke has to lower him, to prop him against the wall. Zeke returns fire around the corner. He can't see how many men he's shooting at. At least three, he thinks, but there could be more. He looks back down the corridor they've come from, but there's nothing to see down there. He has to assume that if they're blocking the opposite corridor, then that must be where the way out is.

"We should go another way," Aalem says, covering his head.

"That's the way," Zeke says, jerking his thumb back toward the shooters. "We either have to go through, or find a way around them." He nods toward the flayed man. "What did he see when he was brought here? Did he see another way out?"

Aalem asks him. He looks back at Zeke after he answers. "He was brought here with a bag over his head."

Zeke fires back down the corridor and then stoops down and picks the flayed man back up. "Come on," he says. They need to explore, to try and find a way to get behind the shooters.

Another couple of shooters emerge at the end of the corridor. Zeke opens fire and they dive for cover. Zeke looks up. There are cameras everywhere. They can track their movements. Zeke shoots out the camera.

It's too late. A nearby door opens and a man charges out, barreling into Aalem. Zeke spins toward the movement. The man comes up, pressing a gun to Aalem's temple. "Drop the rifle!" he screams.

Zeke doesn't. He points it at the man holding Aalem, but as he does he hears footsteps pounding down the corridor behind him, the men who were in hiding running him down. He turns toward them but he feels the butt of a rifle driven into his midsection as they catch up. He doubles over, and the butt is slammed across his jaw. He feels the flayed man fall from his back and land hard on the ground. The flayed man screams.

Zeke falls to a knee, dazed. The Masaf-2 is pulled out of his hands. He feels himself kicked in the ribs, knocking him over, onto his side and then onto his back. He protects his head and tries to kick back at them.

A boot comes down hard, burying into his stomach. Zeke feels the air driven out of his lungs. The protective barrier of his arms around his head comes loose. As they do, the boot comes down again, into the side of his face, driving his head into the floor.

CHAPTER FORTY-FOUR

Dawn is encroaching, the top of the sun creeping over the horizon, casting long shadows across the ground.

There were a few more patrols through the night, but Tom and the others were never in danger of being found. The Dutch believe they are secure here. They must have already searched the bushes when they first arrived, and then they didn't expect anyone to find them out here. Sloppy of them, Tom thinks, but he's grateful for it.

No one else approached the area through the night. Khan did not show up while it was dark.

But now, as the sun slowly rises, Tom can hear engines. They're distant, but they're getting closer with every second. He wakes Maryam. She blinks her eyes open, seeing that it's light now.

"You didn't sleep?" she asks him.

"There are trucks coming," he says. "It could be Khan. I need to go and check it out."

Mohammed stirs. The trucks are getting closer. The sounds of their engines wake him.

"You've got the gun," Tom says to Maryam. "Keep an eye on Mohammed. Make sure he doesn't try anything."

Tom leaves them. He crawls back up the dip to the rim, looks down over the other side. The Dutch are all awake now, standing and waiting for the arrival of Khan and his men. The campfire is out. It's been smothered. The men stand armed with their MP5s, holding them loose. They're not expecting a fight, but if one comes they're ready.

There are two trucks approaching. They start to turn as they get close to the camp, reversing until they're within the camp. One of the Dutchmen waves them in, then signals for them to stop.

The new arrivals get out of their own trucks. They're armed with AK47s, same as the Taliban that Tom has confronted. Tom counts them up. There's eight of them. With the Dutch, that makes fourteen total. One of the Afghans goes up to the biggest of the Dutchmen. Tom guesses that this new arrival must be Khan. He has a thick beard and wears a turban. He's smiling broadly. He holds out a hand and he and the Dutchman shake. Tom thinks he was right in his assumption last night when he saw this man sleeping – he must be Bram de Groot. The leader of the Dutch team. The biggest of them. The man it would make sense for Khan to approach directly. Bram towers at least a foot over Khan, and is just as much wider. They talk briefly. While they do, the other Dutch drug runners open up the backs of their two box trucks, and Khan's men do the same to their own.

Bram goes to the back of one of the Afghan trucks and inspects the product within. Khan continues to talk to him. Bram doesn't show any signs that he's listening. The Dutchman nods to his men. Khan and Bram take a step to the side and oversee the work. Bram and Khan's men unload the trucks that the Afghans have arrived in, swapping the contents. Opium, Tom guesses. It's packed into boxes. They load up the Dutch trucks. It looks like it'll take a while.

Tom slides back down the dip and returns to Maryam. Mohammed is sitting up now, cross-legged, his back against a tree. Tom takes Maryam aside and talks to her with their backs to Mohammed.

"There's too many of them for me to tackle head-on," he says. "I'm gonna have to wait until Khan and his men have gone, and then I'll deal with the Dutch. I might have to take a ride with them."

Maryam frowns. "What are you going to do?"

He shakes his head. "I don't have time to explain. Just know that I'll come back for you. Stay here, stay low, and keep an eye on Mohammed. I'll be back as fast as I can. Can you do that?"

"Yes," Maryam says, no hesitation.

"Good," Tom says. He starts to turn, but then he pauses and looks back at her. He kisses her. He sees how Mohammed's eyes widen at this. Tom returns to the dip.

CHAPTER FORTY-FIVE

Babak knows what happened this morning.

Of course he does – how could he not? The gunfire woke him up, for a start. He came to with a start and quickly rolled off his bed, got underneath it and watched the door, clutching his PC-9. Nobody came for him. When things had eventually calmed down he ventured out of his room, gun raised, and found one of his men who explained what had happened.

Babak wasn't impressed. They broke free? Despite the camera? Unacceptable. Heads will roll.

But not yet. Babak doesn't have the time to punish his own men. That can come later. First, he needs to break Zeke. He needs answers. *That* is his priority.

For now, knowing that Zeke and Aalem are locked safely back in their cages, guarded in the room under constant supervision, Babak can let them wait. Keep them fretting. Allow them to stew in their own juices, fearing what he's going to do to them now after killing some of his men. After the chaos.

Babak keeps himself busy. He goes to the surveillance room and watches them on the screen, noticing how the men around him are nervous and trying to look busy. Babak purposefully ignores them. He stands cross-armed, plucking at the hair on his chin while he observes. The man on the gurney, his binds tightened, struggles to get comfortable. There is no volume, but he looks like he's crying out. He looks like he's in pain. *Good*. Babak wants them to see how he feels. Wants them to *hear* it. Wants the sound to course through them, reverberating in their guts.

Zeke is not defeated yet, he's sure. He's been trained for these situations. One failed escape attempt will not deter him. He's probably already plotting his second. Babak sees how he props himself at the back of the cage, and how his eyes never stop moving, roaming the room. Babak's instruments have been moved far out of reach of the tortured man, and Zeke will have to look longer and harder for another way out.

Aalem does not look the same. He looks closer to defeat. He's at the back of his cage, too, but his arms are folded and his head droops, his chin touching his chest. Babak can see his lips moving. He's muttering to himself. Praying, probably.

Prayer cannot save him.

There are no Gods in this place. Babak has heard so many prayers. So many pleas. No matter the worship, there has been no intervention. There is no salvation in this building.

He checks the time. He has another matter to attend to.

He leaves the surveillance and returns to his room. He has a call to make, to the border guards. Bram and his men will be meeting with Khan now. They're probably done loading up. They'll be setting off for the border soon.

"When the Dutch contact you, close the border," he says. "Shut down the traffic. Hold it up a couple of miles down the road in each direction so the border can't be seen. Let the Dutch straight through, unheeded. Two trucks. Do not trouble them. They've provided me with invaluable assistance. Is this all understood?"

It is. It's not the first time the border guards have been told this, but Babak wants to ensure that Bram de Groot and his companions have a smooth journey. They've been good allies. Who knows when he may need to call on them again.

CHAPTER FORTY-SIX

The trucks are almost fully loaded. Tom can see that there are not many boxes left in the back of the Afghan vehicles. The Dutch have already closed up the back of one of their own. They won't be here for much longer.

Tom has already plotted his route to the trucks. He needs to get there without being seen. Seeing that the end is near, he starts moving. The AK47 is strapped tight to his back. He goes to his left, to the end of the dip. When he reaches the corner, staying low, he peers around it. Bram and Khan have stepped aside, conversing. The other men are finishing up. They're busy. They're distracted.

Tom bursts from cover and races to the front of the truck they're still loading. This one is parked slightly further back than the other. When they set off, this should be the rear vehicle. He needs the rear vehicle.

He drops to his stomach and looks under the truck, down the length of it. Sees that no one spotted him. The men are continuing on as they were before. Tom crawls forward, under the truck. He remains on his stomach for now, watching the legs moving around. He can hear footsteps above him in the truck. The scraping of boots and boxes. Notices how the truck bounces up and down on its suspension as men climb in and out.

He waits. It doesn't take long. The rear door of the truck is slammed shut and locked. The men are no longer moving back and forth, loading and unloading. They're waiting for Bram and Khan to conclude their conversation and then each group can go their separate ways.

Tom rolls onto his back and reaches up, grabbing the undercarriage and pulling himself off the ground. The men are more spread out now and there's a risk of them spotting him underneath. He pulls himself up close to the underside of the truck, holding on tight. He can't see as well as before anymore, but he hears movement close to the trucks. Hears the men talking to each other in Dutch. Hears parting calls to Khan and his men.

Trucks start. The Afghan trucks. Tom hears them leave. The Dutch separate into two groups of three. They each get into a truck. Tom tightens his grip on the undercarriage. He braces himself for what comes next, knowing this is going to get bumpy.

The truck doors slam. The truck vibrates as the engine starts. Tom turns his head and sees the other truck leave first. As he thought – as he needed. The second truck, his truck, starts moving, following the first. Tom starts moving, too. He can't stay where he is, especially not when off-road, already jostling side to side and hitting bumps. It's time to strike.

CHAPTER FORTY-SEVEN

It's time. Babak has given them long enough.
He returns to the torture room, motioning for the guards to remain where they are for now. He sees how Aalem and Zeke become more alert at his arrival, watching him. The flayed man, too. He turns his head to look toward Babak, recoiling and groaning as he does so.
Babak remains in silence for a moment, not acknowledging anyone or anything. He takes in the room. The fresh bloodstains that weren't here when he last exited. He can see where the two men were killed. Their bodies have been removed. Loaded up on a truck to be returned to their loved ones, with only a minor explanation provided as to what happened to them, and where.
Now, still taking his time, Babak looks toward Zeke and Aalem. He keeps his face expressionless, his lips pursed, his nostrils flaring with each breath. They're both beaten and bloodied, Zeke more so. He resisted for long, Babak has been informed. His face is cut up and swollen. Nothing wrong with a little tenderizing, Babak

thinks. Make him more sensitive to what is coming his way.

Zeke turns his head and spits blood through the cage.

Babak smirks. He turns to the flayed man on the gurney. The man is looking back at Babak, his bottom lip quivering as if he's about to cry. Babak has seen it all before. He pulls out his PC-9 and shoots the flayed man through the head.

He hears how Aalem jerks at the sound and the sight, how his rigid body hits the side of the cage, the sound resounding through the room along with the gunshot. Zeke doesn't react. With a flick of his wrist, Babak motions to the guards to take away the body.

"And clean this mess up," he says, indicating all of the blood. "When that is done, bring a fresh gurney."

The guards wheel the dead man out of the room.

Babak crouches in front of the cages, looking both captives over. "I am not going to berate you for attempting to escape," he says. "It stands to reason that you would. But I would like to think that your failure has made it clear to you that escape is impossible. You are trapped here, in this room, alone with me and my men. Your only way out is through your words. You must speak to me. You must answer my questions. Then, and only then, will you find release. If you continue to resist," he points toward the dried pool of blood in the center of the room, where the flayed man's limbs bled as the skin was peeled from him. "This is what awaits you."

He pauses a moment. Neither man speaks.

"The hard way it is," he says. "Very well, my friends. You have made your choice. But understand this – you *will* talk. Everyone does. I will peel the skin from your bones, and I will do it *slowly*. I will keep you alive for as long as it takes. I will make sure you feel everything, until you are begging me to put a bullet through your head, as I have just done to your cellmate. But, until you answer my questions, the answer will be no. There will be no respite. You will remain alive in your agony. Take a good look at this room, gentlemen. This room is *Hell*. You will talk. Everyone does."

He straightens, looming over the cages.

"There is nowhere for you to go," he says. "There is no escape. Only the truth shall set you free. Answer my questions. It is your only salvation." He goes to the door, and pauses before he exits. He smiles at them. "No one is coming to save you."

CHAPTER FORTY-EIGHT

Tom drags himself to the rear of the vehicle, silently praying that they hit no rocky outcrop or large mound that could squash him between it and the underside of the truck.

Reaching the rear, he holds on tight and pulls himself up and out from under the truck. He holds onto its locked back door. The truck hits a dip and Tom almost falls. For a moment, his legs dangle freely, his boots trailing through the scrub. His grip upon the door is white-knuckled. He pulls himself up, getting his boots onto the back bumper. This is why he needed the rear vehicle – so that his movements would not be seen.

Gritting his teeth, Tom continues his climb, getting a foot on the handle and pushing himself up so he can catch the roof. His fingers and hands are aching, but he ignores the pain. There's no other choice. He gets up onto the roof so he can take in their surroundings.

They remain in the middle of nowhere, but, judging from the sun, Tom can see that they're heading west. Toward the border. Luckily, the border isn't in view yet. They still have a far way to go.

CHAPTER FORTY-NINE

Maryam saw the trucks leave. Saw the Dutch go in one direction, and Khan and his men in another.

Now, she waits. She remains concealed in the bushes, but she stands and paces, hoping that Tom won't take long.

Mohammed grunts at her. He shuffles back and forth from his seated position, trying to get her attention. He wants her to remove the gag. Maryam tries to ignore him. He keeps rocking and grunting behind his gag. Annoyed, Maryam tears it roughly from his mouth.

"What do you want?" she asks, hissing. She speaks their language. Tom isn't around. If he were, she would stick to English.

Mohammed sucks in breaths, stretching out his mouth. "Just to breathe," he says. "There's no one around. I don't need the gag. It's not like I'm going to scream, is it?"

Maryam stares at him, still clutching the gag.

"Please," Mohammed says, bowing his head. "Leave it off, just for now. When Rollins returns, you can put it back. It'll be our little secret."

Maryam isn't sure. She doubts Tom would allow him to sit without the gag. He doesn't deserve any kind of comfort. She makes a move to put it back on him.

"Wait, wait, wait," he says, leaning back, away from it. "Just a moment, just a moment – allow me to talk to you, first."

"I'm not interested in anything you have to say."

"But you *should* be," Mohammed says. "What if Rollins doesn't come back?"

She pauses at this. "What do you mean? What do you know?"

"I don't *know* anything. Only what he said. He was outnumbered, correct? Even with Khan and his men gone, Rollins remains outnumbered. I tried to tell him – the Dutch are highly trained, incredibly dangerous men. They make their way through his area regularly, without backup, without government assistance. Do you understand? This is a dangerous area – we both know it. And yet still they come, fearless. And then they smuggle their opium back the other way, toward Europe. I doubt they go all the way back to the Netherlands; they probably have connections far earlier than that, but that's still a mighty journey with many borders to cross. They must have nerves of steel for such an undertaking. They're not going to feel threatened by one lonesome American."

"Tom went alone against the Taliban that were coming for us," Maryam says. "He's used to being outnumbered."

"You can try to persuade yourself, but you know that what I've said is true. He's in danger. There's a very good chance he isn't coming back. For all we know, he could already be dead."

Maryam shakes her head.

Mohammed shrugs. "Either he comes back or he doesn't, but my question to you is what do you do if he does *not*?"

Maryam says nothing.

"You'll be on your own," Mohammed says. "But I could help you, Maryam. You have done nothing to hurt me. Your father and I *were* friends. That was true. I never meant for him to get captured. It was only the Americans who were supposed to be captured. But I can ensure that he doesn't get hurt. Babak will listen to me. I've done so much to help him. Babak does not like your father, but I can promise that he won't hurt him if I tell him not to."

"If you *tell* him? I doubt you hold that kind of sway over the man."

"Fine – if I *ask* him. And I *will* ask him, Maryam. For you. I will beg him, if that's what it takes. No harm will come to Aalem. You and your father will be reunited."

Maryam doesn't believe a word of what he says. He's just trying to keep the gag out of his mouth and talk his way out of his situation.

"We don't need to wait for the American," Mohammed says. "We don't need to wait to see if he lives or dies. We don't have to remain in this place. We can leave now. I can take you to your father."

"You told Tom that you didn't know where he is," Maryam says.

Mohammed grits his teeth, knowing he's been caught out. "I could contact Babak–"

"You told him you couldn't do *that*, either," Maryam says. "Tom has told me everything. Were you holding out on him? Do I need to tell him you were lying?"

Mohammed shakes his head, defeated. "I was not lying,"

he says quietly. "But I can find a way to contact Babak. The Taliban that he is in touch with, they–"

"I'm not going anywhere near them," Maryam says. She frowns. Mohammed is still rocking back and forth ever so slightly, like he has an itch somewhere, like he feels ill. "What are you doing? What's wrong?"

Mohammed stops moving. He looks up at her, like he's been caught in the middle of something he shouldn't have been doing. But then, slowly, his face begins to melt into a smile.

Maryam doesn't understand, but instinctively she feels herself take a step back.

Mohammed stands. His hands come from behind him to land at his sides, no longer bound. Maryam sees the zip tie fall away from him, a broken piece of black plastic, useless. She sees Mohammed's broken fingers on his left hand. They're twisted beyond ever being able to heal back to how they were. They're discolored. The fingernails on them both are blackened and peeling away.

Then she sees what's in his right hand. A jagged rock. A rock that he has used to cut himself free. A rock that he's now raising above his head, attacking her with.

CHAPTER FIFTY

Tom lies flat on the roof of the truck, not wanting to be spotted in the mirrors by the truck ahead. He drags himself forward, the wind in his face, the rising sun beating down on his back. He needs to get near the front. He needs to take control of the truck. And then he needs to run the lead truck down and get some answers.

Tom feels himself jostled roughly side to side, the trucks still traveling on uneven scrubland. He pulls out his knife and drives its tip through the roof, holding onto it while they pass over a particularly rough patch of land. The men inside the truck shouldn't have heard. They shouldn't hear any of his movements. It's a box truck. There's a divider between the front cab and the box. And plus, judging by the way they're getting thrown around, there's probably enough noise to distract them already.

Pulling out the knife, he lunges forward and stabs it through again, breaking the thin aluminum. He drags himself forward. He's almost at the front. The truck maintains speed. It doesn't swerve. It doesn't slow or stop. It does nothing to imply that the men inside know he's on top, and likewise for the truck leading the way.

He reaches the front rim of the box. Peering over the edge, he can see that the passenger side window is open. The man there rests his arm upon it. The driver's window appears to be closed.

Knife in hand, Tom makes his move. He drops down onto the roof of the cab. This probably gets their attention inside. He doesn't stay on the roof long enough for them to investigate or react. He moves toward the passenger side. He reaches it in time to see the man there leaning out to look up. Steadying himself with one hand against the roof, Tom drives the knife straight down into the man's face, through his eye.

The man begins to convulse. Tom pulls the knife out. He swings down over the side of the roof, into the cab of the truck. He lashes out with kicks, driving his boots into the faces of the two men remaining. Neither of them is Bram de Groot. Tom isn't surprised. He expected him to be in the lead vehicle.

The man in the middle grabs at Tom, trying to reach his throat. Tom gets his arms inside the cab and drives the knife into his chest, through his ribcage and into his heart. The man looks down at it, as if shocked to find it there, and then blood bubbles out of his mouth.

Tom can see the driver reaching for the Sig Sauer at his hip, but he's struggling to latch onto it with the bodies so close to him, and while maintaining control of the vehicle. Tom strikes at him with the knife. The man manages to catch Tom's arm. There's strength in the grip. He holds Tom at bay. Tom sees his other hand, his steering hand, reaching for the horn. He's trying to alert the others in front.

It's hard for Tom to maneuver while atop two dead bodies. He manages to lash out with his leg, kicking the driver's hand away from the horn, pinning his arm against the window under his boot. At the same time, he pulls himself back, attempting to free his arm from the man's grip, but the driver holds on tight. No one is steering. The driver does not take his foot off the accelerator. He bares his teeth at Tom as the truck begins to waver, rocked from side to side by the uneven terrain.

Tom has to release the driver's pinned arm. He has to end this quick, before the truck can topple and he's trapped within. He brings his leg back fast, driving his knee into the side of the driver's jaw. The driver is rocked, but he refuses to let go of Tom's arm. He forces Tom's arm to the side, toward the dashboard. He slams Tom's wrist against it, breaking his grip. The knife drops from Tom's fingers.

With his other, freed hand, the driver blasts the horn.

Tom sees the lead truck's brake lights flashing. The situation is getting out of hand. The driver is grinning at him. They're pushing against each other in a stalemate, but the lead truck is slowing and the driver is soon to have reinforcements.

Tom twists his arm, not to break the driver's grip but to drive his elbow into the driver's ribs. The blow catches the driver by surprise. Tom does it again, finally breaking the driver's stronghold on him. The driver coughs. He tries to grab his handgun. Tom dives at him in the cramped space. He takes a grip on his head, holding his chin in his left hand and placing his right on the back of the driver's neck. Tom twists. The driver attempts to resist, the tendons and veins in his neck bulging. He's still reaching for his gun. Tom headbutts him. His resistance goes momentarily slack. Tom twists. Hears the satisfying crunch as he snaps the driver's neck.

Tom forces the door open and kicks the driver out, dumping him in the scrubland. Tom takes his place behind the wheel. They've gone off course during the fight with no one steering. Tom rights it, pursuing the lead truck, which is no longer braking. They've seen how they went off course. They've seen the body fly from the cab. Instead of braking, they're speeding up. Tom does the same. The wind as he accelerates blows the door closed. He slams it the rest of the way. He gains on the lead truck.

CHAPTER FIFTY-ONE

Mohammed throws himself against Maryam, his weight knocking her off balance and then driving her down to the ground. He's on top of her. He attempts to pin her, the rock still in his hand.

"Don't make me use this," he says, snarling through his teeth.

Maryam struggles against him. He's heavier, taller, and stronger than she is, but she sees how he favors his left hand and its two broken fingers. How he tries to keep it close to his body, away from her. How he's not able to pin her right arm because he's scared to use his left hand. She strikes at his face, pushing him back from her, and then she throws punches toward his left hand. One of them manages to connect with his damaged fingers.

Mohammed screams. She sees tears squirt from his eyes. He rears back. Maryam gets a foot free from under him and kicks at his chest, knocking him back. He lands on his backside, away from her, cradling his left hand. Maryam thinks she can see drops of blood fall from the fingers.

She pushes herself back, scrabbling across the rough ground, trying to put distance between them. She reaches for the concealed Glock, for the gun that she doesn't think Mohammed knows she has.

Mohammed sees her moving away from him. He tries to ignore his pain and launches himself at her again. Tears stream down his face, and mucus matts in his moustache hair. Saliva drips and hangs from his snarling mouth. Maryam panics, unable to get a grip on the gun. She tries to kick at him again but he bats her leg aside. He strikes her in the side of the face with the rock.

Maryam feels herself fall back, her head spinning. She can taste blood. Can feel it running down her face, too.

Mohammed falls atop her again. He snatches breaths, his broken fingers still throbbing from when she hit them. He looks down at his shaking left hand, then grits his teeth and uses it to clasp her neck, pinning her. He screams as he presses his broken fingers to her throat, but he doesn't let go.

She gasps, sucking in what breath she's able. He can't get a grip tight enough on her neck with his mangled hand to fully choke her, but it's enough. He presses his weight down onto her through his arm. She looks up at him. He drops the rock, grinning now, satisfied. She doesn't like the way he smiles. She's terrified of the thoughts that must be running through his head right now, while atop her.

Almost tenderly, he strokes her bloodied cheek with the back of his right hand. "Oh, Maryam," he says. "Do you know how long I've waited for a moment just like this?"

He leans down close to her, his face next to hers. He breathes deeply. Maryam tries to struggle, but the blow from the rock, and his hand at her neck, have sapped her of her strength.

But then he reaches for her legs, pulls on her trousers, trying to get them down, and Maryam feels a surge of strength as she realizes what he's trying to do.

"Hold still!" he says, growing frustrated with her struggles. "Hold still, or I'll beat your skull in!"

Maryam doesn't. She fights against him. Mohammed strikes her with the back of his right hand. Maryam's face turns to the side with the blow. She spits blood. She sees the jagged rock that he used to bludgeon her, to bloody her left cheek. It's just out of reach.

Maryam stretches for the rock while Mohammed distracts himself with her trousers, still trying to get them down. The Glock is tucked into the back of them. She feels it digging into her lower back. With Mohammed's weight on top of her, she's pinned. She can't reach it. She kicks her legs to make things difficult for him. She kicks her legs and throws herself to her left. Her fingertips graze the rock. She can see her blood upon it. She has a better chance of reaching the rock than the gun beneath her.

Mohammed grunts angrily, raising his hand to strike her again. "I warned you!"

Maryam stretches again, bucking her hips to shift his weight from on top of her. Her left hand lands on the rock. Mohammed realizes what she's doing, but he notices too late. As he turns his head toward her reaching hand, she brings the rock up and slams it against his temple.

Mohammed is shaken, but he remains on top of her. His left hand lets go of her neck. He presses both hands to the temple. Blood runs down the side of his face. Maryam swings the rock again, harder this time, with all the strength she can muster. It connects with the side of his skull. It knocks him off her.

She rolls away and then follows him to the ground, raising the rock in both hands and bringing it down twice more, seeing blood splash from the wounds she inflicts. She sees pieces of his hair clinging to the blood-matted rock. She drops it and falls back, lying flat on the ground, breathing hard, pressing a hand to her chest and feeling her heart hammering there.

Minutes pass. She thinks she's killed Mohammed. After a while, she finds that she hasn't. He stirs. He pushes himself up and struggles to his feet. Dazed, he stumbles away from her without looking back, walking unsteadily away.

Maryam sits up and watches him. He sways, drifting from side to side. He almost trips a couple of times, but he manages to keep himself upright. Blood streams from the back and side of his head where the rock has split him open. The same rock he used to cut himself loose. The same rock that he has wounded Maryam with.

Maryam gets a handle on the Glock. She pulls it out and stands up. She walks after Mohammed, hurrying, the gun raised. She grits her teeth, her arm shaking, scared to use it. Scared to fire it upon a person.

But then she thinks of what he was trying to do to her. Of what he would be doing right now if she hadn't managed to reach the rock.

She fires into his back. He goes down as the first bullet penetrates him. He lands on his front. Maryam stands over him. She shoots into him three more times, until she's certain he's dead.

CHAPTER FIFTY-TWO

The lead truck tries to get away from Tom, but they're matched for speed.

He doesn't think they're fleeing, not entirely. They're probably trying to create some distance, buy themselves some time while they arm themselves, prepare for a confrontation. Mohammed said some of these men were ex-KCT. Dutch special forces. Tom can't know which ones, other than Bram. But what about the three he's already killed? Can he expect an easier time of the men remaining?

Whether he can or not, he won't. Tom doesn't take any opponent for granted. It's a good way to get himself killed. There always has to be an understanding that if you underestimate anyone, then your next opponent could be your last. Tom doesn't underestimate anyone.

The lead truck hits a particularly deep dip, slowing them, and Tom takes advantage of it. He rams the truck from behind, throwing it off balance. As it skids to the side, kicking up dust and dirt, Tom presses on, the pedal flat to the floor under his foot, and he drives himself into the side of the truck, pushing it back. He can see its brake lights flaring, but they won't do it any good now.

It rocks, almost toppling. Tom jams the truck into reverses and rears back, then throws it into drive and rams the teetering truck again. This is enough. He sends it rolling.

The truck hits its roof, but its momentum carries it through and it falls onto its side, landing flat. Tom slams the brakes. He's done enough damage, and he needs the truck he's in to return to Maryam.

He retrieves his dropped knife and then jumps out of the truck, AK47 raised, covering the scene. The wheels of the truck, the two that aren't pressed to the ground, continue to spin. Tom avoids the wheels and uses the undercarriage to climb up onto the side of the truck. Covering the door, he makes his way closer. The window is open. He steps carefully, lightly, to get the drop on the men inside.

Despite his best efforts, they hear him coming. Gunfire erupts from the open window, angling toward him. Tom throws himself off the truck, landing and rolling on the ground below. He twists, raising the AK47, pointing it toward the front of the truck. An MP5 appears there, fires blindly around in a circle. Tom presses himself to the truck for cover. He hears more gunfire, but it's not coming toward him. It sounds like it's firing away from him.

Too late, he realizes why. He hears banging follow the extra gunfire and then he hears someone coming his way. They shot their way through the roof of the cab, weakening it, and then kicked their way out. The first of the men reaches the front of the truck, MP5 raised, searching the area. Tom drops to a knee and strafes the man's knees. He bolts from the spot and charges, kicking the rifle out of the man's grip. He turns to the right, making sure it's clear.

The man on his knees, his kneecaps blown out, doesn't scream. He grits his teeth and his face reddens, and he reaches for the Sig Sauer on his hip. Tom kicks him across the face. He could just shoot him, but he has to try to keep him alive.

There's gunfire from behind him. Tom doesn't turn toward it. He's lucky the bullets didn't connect; he's not going to risk hanging around and give them a second opportunity by turning. He hears the bullets ping off the underside of the truck and some of them hit the ground near to him. He bolts right and starts running, heading round the truck, toward the back where the shooting came from, to get the drop on the shooter.

The shooter is ready for him. He lies in wait. As Tom reaches the rear of the truck, the shooter emerges from where he's ducking down and drives the butt of his rifle into Tom's midsection.

Tom manages to keep his feet, cursing himself for rushing in. The shooter turns his MP5 toward him. Tom is able to knock it aside, batting it away with the AK47 like parrying swords. The MP5's gunfire goes wild. It peppers the man on his knees. He jolts with the impact, then falls onto his face. Tom throws himself at the shooter, standing upright headfirst, driving the top of his skull into the man's face. He knocks him back. They drop their tangled rifles. The Dutchman hits the underside of the truck and rebounds off it, throwing a punch at Tom. Tom manages to block his punch and then, as the Dutchman throws a kick, Tom manages to stomp it down.

The Dutchman is relentless. He strikes at Tom with an

open-handed slap to the side of the head, causing a ringing in Tom's ears, then jabs at his ribs with a left. Tom tries to cover up, to block and parry, to protect himself, but the Dutchman is fast, and he hits hard. Tom almost feels as if the Dutchman is toying with him. Another jab bloodies Tom's mouth, and another rocks his skull. Tom throws a punch back and the Dutchman blocks it. He takes control of Tom's arm and starts to twist it. Tom sees that they're close to the still-spinning rear wheel of the truck. Tom doesn't fight the man's twisting of his arm. Instead, he uses it to his advantage. He rolls with the movement, surprising the Dutchman with how easily he's taking control, but then Tom twists through, ducking under so he takes control of the Dutchman's arm. He pushes him forward, face-first into the rotating tire.

The man's face connects with the metal rim. It continues to spin. Tom sees blood spraying as the friction tears off the man's face. The Dutchman screams. Tom pulls out his Glock and puts a bullet through the back of his head. As the man falls, Tom sees the damage that the wheel did to his face. His eyes are gone, and his nose. All that remains of the latter is a flap that hangs down over his mouth.

Tom keeps the Glock out, keeps it raised while he retrieves the AK47. Two down. Neither of them is Bram de Groot. He makes his way back around the truck, carefully, not wanting to allow the leader to get the drop on him the way one of his men did. Tom drops to a knee as he nears the cab. He sees where they burst through it to get out. When he ran past earlier, he was moving too fast to take it all in. He sees how they've peeled it back after shooting through it to weaken it. He gets to the gap, sticking the AK47 in ahead of him.

The cab is empty. Bram de Groot is not inside.

Tom wheels, checking the area, then looks down at the ground. He sees some tracks. He follows them, but he doesn't get very far. Bram has covered them, ensuring his escape.

Tom falls back to the truck, continually scanning the area, wary of a gunshot ringing out. He watches for movement. He can't see any.

He was fighting the two men for only a short time. He doesn't know how fast of a runner Bram is, but Tom supposes he could have gotten at least a klick away, maybe even a mile. And now he could be lying low, hiding out, waiting to ambush Tom, or for him to leave so he can continue his escape. Tom checks inside the cab again. There's a phone. Tom takes it. He notices there's a handgun, too. Bram's?

The area is too broad for Tom to search it all. Tom considers his options. He has no one to question. Five of the men are dead, and one of them is missing. He goes back to the nearest bodies and pats them down. He finds phones on them. He takes the phones. He takes their ammo and one of the MP5s, too. They also have water canteens. He drains one off and gathers up the others. Maryam will be thirsty. If they're feeling generous, they'll maybe give some water to Mohammed, too. Tom goes to the upright truck and searches the dead men still inside. He takes their phones and their water, and drags one of the bodies out. Tom pauses before he drags out the other. Looks at his clothes. Tom is all in black. The Dutchman isn't. He wears khaki trousers and a green sweater. The man is a similar height and build to Tom. Tom leaves him in the truck, just in case. He gets inside and starts it up, turning it around. He goes back to where he dumped the driver out and takes his phone, water, and ammo. He has all six phones. Bram must have lost his in the crash, didn't retrieve it as he made his escape. Maryam said she knows about electronics. Tom hedges his bets. He's not going to be able to find Bram here, and even if he does, there's no guarantee he'll talk. The electronics provide a better chance of getting answers. He drives back to Maryam.

CHAPTER FIFTY-THREE

Tom pushes the truck as fast as it's able to go over the rough terrain. The inside of the cab smells of blood, and of the dead man propped upright next to him.

Maryam is in the trees still, where he left her. But, as Tom enters, bringing her water, he can tell that something is different. Mohammed lies on the ground. He lies very still, but his wrists are no longer bound. There's blood on him, too. A large wound to his skull, and bullet holes in his back.

Maryam looks up at Tom as he approaches. There's a deep gash on her left cheek, and dried blood beneath it. The cut has scabbed over. She uses a tree to get to her feet and throws herself into his arms.

"Are you okay?" Tom asks. "What happened?"

"Mohammed got free," she says. "He attacked me. He tried to…"

She doesn't need to finish. Tom understands. He can see, though, that she was able to defend herself. To stop him. He squeezes her tighter.

"What about you?" she asks. She touches his face, the various cuts and bruises he's accumulated there.

"I'm alive," Tom says. He gives her one of the canteens and she drinks gratefully. "Five of them aren't. Bram got away during it. He's probably heading for the border. He'll try to find a way to contact Babak. We're going to have to try and cut him off. So far as I'm aware, he's on foot. We should be able to beat him there. The problem is, the border's a big place and I have no idea which direction he would've gone. Beyond that, I don't even know if it's in our best interests to cross the border."

"You didn't get any answers from them?"

"They weren't very talkative."

"We still don't know where Babak is?"

"No, but I got all of their phones. They're in the truck. Six of them, so I figure one must be Bram's. Do you think you could get into them, get into their messages? It could lead us to Babak."

"Probably," she says. "Maybe. I'll see what I can do."

"Then let's go," Tom says, taking her hand, preparing to lead her out of the trees. "We'll head for the border for now in lieu of having any other idea where to go. That seems like our best option. And be warned – there's a dead man in the truck."

"What about him?" Maryam asks, meaning Mohammed.

Tom shrugs. "What about him?"

Maryam leaves the body behind. "What were you going to do with Mohammed, eventually?"

"I hadn't decided yet," Tom says. "But I was probably gonna have to kill him. Only when we were certain we didn't need him anymore, though." He looks at her. "Are you all right?"

Maryam slows, her hand dragging in his. "I've never killed anyone," she says. "Before today. Shouldn't it... shouldn't it feel worse than this?"

"Not for a man like Mohammed," Tom says. "You did what you had to do. You know what he would have done otherwise. He isn't worth any kind of grief, or guilt."

"You're right," she says. She nods. She points to the cut on her cheek. "How does it look? Is it bad?"

"Barely noticed it," Tom says. He smiles reassuringly. "It's fine. It'll heal, and it'll leave you with a story."

"I'm not sure it's a story I'll be eager to share."

"Then it'll make you a woman of mystery. Let's go. We don't have time to waste."

CHAPTER FIFTY-FOUR

Babak sends his men into the torture room first. He waits outside, down the corridor, giving them time to drag Zeke out of his cage and secure him to the gurney.

Zeke is going to be hard to break, he knows. As much as he'd like to, he can't rush things with him. He needs to be patient. Needs to continue breaking him psychologically first. It's the only way. Build his fear and his anticipation until his nerves are stretched almost to snapping.

Babak runs his hands down his face. There are bullet holes in the walls and the ceiling. The bloodstains are gone. His men have been cleaning the building. They're still in the process of doing so. Babak paces the corridor, considering how to play his next move. Farhad Gorji will no doubt want quick results, but Babak has watched Zeke, has looked into his eyes, and knows there's not going to be anything quick about this.

Aalem, though. Aalem hasn't had the same training. The only training he's had is how to spy for the Americans. It won't take long to make him scream. It won't take long to have him begging for his life, and swearing to give up his own parents and daughter for just a moment's respite.

Aalem could be the key, Babak thinks. Zeke broke himself out of the cage first, but he didn't leave Aalem behind. He could have. It would have been so easy for him. He could have gotten away had he not freed him, too. He even tried to save the flayed man, despite how futile it would have been.

Babak considers this, leaning against the wall and stroking at his beard. Zeke is clearly a compassionate man. He can't know Aalem well, and yet he still risked his life, and his time, to try and save him. It shows a strength of character for Zeke, but his strength will prove to be his weakness.

Yes, Babak thinks, Aalem could be the key. The key to making Zeke talk.

He looks down the corridor and sees his men emerge. They close the door to the torture room after them. One of them sees Babak and gives a thumbs-up. Babak nods. He waves for them to go to surveillance. Babak waits. Allows a few minutes to tick by. Waits for Zeke to acclimatize himself to the gurney, knowing what is soon to come.

Except, it isn't. Still, he can't know that. Babak grins to himself. All part of the plan. All part of the torture. Sometimes, the waiting is the hardest part.

Babak *will* break him. Babak *will* find where Bill Irving is hiding. He will rid this area of the Americans, all of them, and he will ensure that it's such a glorious slaughter that they will never dream of coming back.

He makes his way to the torture room, walking slowly, whistling a jaunty tune on his way. He continues to whistle as he enters the room, sees how Zeke struggles against the binds, how he stops as Babak enters.

Babak rounds the room to him. He stops whistling. "Here we are," he says, pausing a moment to allow the words to hang in the air. "How does it feel, to be the subject of my operating theatre?"

Zeke says nothing. He lies flat and very still on the gurney, staring back at Babak. His face is blank. His eyes stare straight through Babak.

Babak leans on the side of the gurney and looks down at Zeke, smiling. He watches his chest – the rise and fall of his breaths. It barely moves. His breathing is shallow and controlled. He watches Zeke's neck, the veins in the side of it, watching for tell-tale pulsing. He doesn't see any. Zeke is calm. Cool. Collected. Prepared for whatever is coming.

Babak doesn't allow any disappointment to show in his face. This was expected. Zeke was always going to be a challenge. Babak's biggest challenge. He feels his smile broaden at the thought. This is all part of the fun.

He takes his hands back from the gurney and runs his fingers over his instruments. Again, he takes his time. He does everything slowly, drawing it all out, before finally settling on a scalpel. He raises it to the light, allows Zeke to get a good, long look at it and how it gleams.

Zeke's face does not change. His breathing does not change. Nothing about him changes.

Aalem is at his cage door, fingers through the gaps, clutching the bars, watching wide-eyed. Babak sees how he swallows. Unlike Zeke, he wears all of his emotions on his face.

"I'm going to take it slow with you, Zeke," Babak says. "I'm going to take my time, and I'm going to enjoy myself." He lowers the scalpel toward Zeke's right hand. Toward his fingers. Zeke does not move.

Before the scalpel makes contact, Babak stops. He raises his head, looking toward the cage. Toward Aalem. Again, he keeps his movements deliberate. Aalem flinches back. Babak straightens up. Puts the scalpel back on the table. Turns to Zeke, smiling.

"So defiant," he says. He taps a finger against his lips. "I wonder." Steps away from the gurney. "Will you be able to remain so stoic, so *heartless*, when you have to bear witness to someone else being hurt in your place?" Babak calls for his guards, tells them to switch the two men. "The man who was here earlier, the man I flayed, he meant nothing to you. But you've had a little time to get to know Aalem, haven't you? Watch closely, Zeke. See what I'm going to do to him, and know that you can stop me hurting him at any time. And if you don't..." Babak shrugs. "Know that you will be taking his place soon enough."

CHAPTER FIFTY-FIVE

Tom drives for the border while Maryam breaks into the phones. Tom can see how she's uncomfortable being next to a dead body, but she does her best to ignore it.

"What are you doing?" Tom asks her.

"I can't begin to guess at their passwords. When a password is gone, forgotten, whatever, usually the only way to get in is with a factory reset, but that would wipe the phone. That would erase everything we need. But these phones also have fingerprint ID. The men just weren't using it. If I use the forgotten password option, and I can figure out which phone belongs to this guy, I can use his print to get in. I've simplified it, but that's basically what I'm doing."

"What about the other phones?"

"If I can get into one, if I can get into his emails, I'll be able to work out theirs, and from there I'll hack into their accounts. I can change the passwords of their phones online and get in that way. I'll be able to control all of their backups and their fail-safes because I'm in possession of their phones." She's talking fast, excitable.

"Will it take long?"

"I don't know. I've never actually done anything like this before, but I'm going as fast as I can."

Tom leaves her to it, driving on. He stays away from the roads, sticking to the scrubland. He scans the area as they go. He doesn't expect to spot Bram, but he still has to look. They've passed a shepherd who watched them go, but other than that it's been quiet.

Out the corner of his eye, Tom sees Maryam tentatively lift one of the dead man's fingers to the phone. "He's getting stiff," she says.

"Did it work?" Tom asks. "He hasn't been dead too long. He should still be warm enough to activate it."

Maryam is silent for a moment. He sees her finger tapping at the screen, exploring. He doesn't interrupt her. She starts going through the other phones. "I need to find which one is Bram's," she says.

Tom can't help her with that. He continues to drive. A part of him wonders what Zeke and Aalem might be going through right now. If this is all worth it, or if they're going to finally reach their destination and find two dead bodies.

From what he's heard, that's not Babak's style. It's too fast. He'll torture them first. Flay them. It might buy Tom and Maryam some time, but it's gonna be hellish for Zeke and Aalem if they have to undergo that.

He pushes the thoughts aside. Compartmentalizes. It's not worth thinking about. He has to focus on the task in hand. It's all he can control. Has to push on and see it through to its conclusion, no matter what that may be.

Maryam works at the phone. Time passes. Every minute, they get closer to the border.

"I have something," Maryam says, almost giddy. Tom

looks at her. Sees how her hands are shaking holding one of the phones. "I couldn't understand the Dutch. I had to find any communications in English and read through those." She looks back at Tom. "I know where Babak is."

Tom slows the truck, bringing it to a stop. This is important. It needs all of his attention. "Where?"

"He's in Iran," Maryam says. "There's a village called Milak. He's south-west of there. He's provided Bram with co-ordinates."

"How far over the border is it?"

"It's not far at all. From Zaranj – that's the city I grew up in – to Milak is only twenty minutes. To these co-ordinates it will only be another ten or twenty minutes."

"That's good," Tom says. "That just leaves the problem of getting over the border. If we can find a quiet spot, we might be able to sneak over –"

Maryam is looking at the dead man. "I read something else," she says. "A message to Bram, from Babak. He has organized a crossing for them. He's provided a number for Bram to contact when he's on his way. He says that the guards have been told not to bother them."

Tom looks down at the dead body, at his clothes. One of the reasons Tom kept the body around. What Tom's wearing might not be known to the guards, but there's no need to take that risk. "We can take their place," Tom says. "Drive straight through. Go straight to Babak – to his Abattoir."

Maryam looks around, getting her bearings. "I don't think we're far from the border now," she says. "Another fifteen minutes, perhaps. I shall message the border guard now."

Tom pushes the door open and grabs the dead Dutchman, pulling him out of the truck. "I'll get changed."

CHAPTER FIFTY-SIX

Maryam can smell blood on the clothes that Tom has switched into. He's kept his own nearby, folded under the seats. They left the body behind. She does her best to ignore the smell and hopes none of the guards pick up on it. They've driven with the windows down to try and air it out. They wiped the blood from the seats and the windows before they set off for the border.

As they near, they notice how the traffic has been held up. They drive down the side of the road, through the dirt. One of the border guards at a barricade holding up the traffic notices them coming. He squints inside, then waves them through. It's another couple of miles to the border crossing.

The waiting vehicles are impatient. As Tom and Maryam pass by in the truck, they hear horns blaring, and people cursing, demanding to know why they're being let through, and why the rest of them are being blocked. Tom glances at her, raising an eyebrow, but he doesn't ask what they're saying. Road rage sounds much the same in every language, she's sure.

Maryam has covered her face and head in her scarf, leaving only her eyes visible. She made sure the cut on her cheek was covered. Didn't want it to raise any questions.

They're hoping they'll pass through unbothered, as Babak has promised, but Tom doesn't want to bank on it. If the guards approach, Maryam will do the talking.

They slow as they near the crossing. There's a handful of guards blocking the way, armed with automatic rifles. Most of them move aside to let the truck through. One of them looks a little more surprised. He looks into the cab of the truck. Maryam can feel his eyes on her. He frowns, then looks beyond the truck, behind it, sees nothing following. He raises a hand for them to stop. Tom does.

The guard makes his way to the driver's side of the truck. He looks up at Tom through the open window. Tom looks back at him, keeps his face empty.

"Open the door," Maryam whispers to him. The man is too low down for her to see.

Tom motions for the guard to back up, and then opens the door. Before the guard can react to this, before he can be surprised, Maryam talks to him.

"We were told we wouldn't be stopped," she calls to the guard in Dari, knowing he'll understand.

The guard looks at Maryam, at Tom, then back at Maryam. "Who are you?" he demands. "We weren't told anything about women. Are you Afghan?"

"I am one of Khan's women," Maryam says. "I was sent to talk, in case there were any questions. We thought it would help streamline things."

The guard seems to buy it. "All right," he says. "Where are the other men? Where is the other truck? We were told six men, two trucks."

"The other truck damaged a wheel on the way here. The others remained behind to repair it. They told us to continue on, to tell you that this had happened. They have the same number to contact that we did – they will let you know when they're on their way."

The guard looks down the length of the truck. He doesn't say anything for a moment. Maryam watches him. At the same time, in her peripheral vision, she watches Tom. Sees how he remains relaxed in the seat, like this isn't anything to be worried about. She notices how the hand that the guard can't see rests close to his handgun. He looks relaxed, but he's ready in case anything goes wrong.

"All right," the guard says eventually, scratching lazily at his chest. "Go on through."

Tom pulls the door shut. They continue on in silence, getting clear of the border crossing and its guards. When they are, when they've put them behind them and she knows she won't be seen, Maryam pulls the scarf from her face.

They're in Iran. They know where they're going. Now they just need to get to Babak, and then, afterward, figure out a way back into Afghanistan.

CHAPTER FIFTY-SEVEN

Aalem screams.

Zeke sits in the cage, grits his teeth, and watches at Babak's insistence. He keeps his face immobile. His expression blank. His eyes empty, staring through the bloody scene before him like it's something playing on the TV.

Babak is taking his time, not like with the unnamed Iranian. He's drawing this out. Prolonging Aalem's agony. So far, his work has mostly concentrated on Aalem's right foot, the top of it, peeling away strips of his skin an inch at a time. Babak waves them in front of Aalem's face. He waves them toward Zeke's cage and then grins before he discards them, dumping them on the floor, treading on them while he continues his work.

"I don't know where Bill Irving is!" Aalem screams. "I swear to you...please...I don't know where he is...I've never even met him..."

"Tell me where you met with Zeke and the other Americans," Babak says.

Aalem tells him. Zeke knows this is not where Bill Irving

is, or was. He says nothing. No matter what, even when it's his turn to go up onto that gurney, he won't say anything.

Babak pauses in his work, his gloves and blood-dripping hands hovering above Aalem's foot. "Do you have anything you wish to contribute, Zeke?" he asks. "Anything that would help put an end to Aalem's suffering?"

Zeke says nothing.

Babak clucks his tongue and shakes his head. "How heartless of you, Zeke," he says. "How cruel. Do you have no compassion for this man? This compatriot?"

Zeke says nothing.

"Well," Babak says. "It's early yet, I suppose. There's an entire body to work with. We'll see how long Zeke's lips remain closed."

"Please..." Aalem says. Sweat pours from his face.

"Don't worry, Aalem, my friend," Babak says. "He *will* talk. It might not be until he's up here himself, and by then it will be too late for you, but he *will* talk to me. He'll tell me everything I want to know, and more besides."

Babak is enjoying himself with Aalem, Zeke can see. He doesn't want Zeke to talk, not yet. Maybe not at all. He wants to take his time flaying the man who gave him up to the Americans.

"Is there anything you might want to tell me before I continue?" Babak asks Aalem.

"I've told you everything I know!"

Babak chuckles. "We'll see about that."

As he raises the scalpel, Zeke talks, against his better judgement. "You won't find Bill Irving," he says. "The second he found out you captured us, he would've moved. Where I met him doesn't matter anymore. I don't know where he is now."

Babak smiles at him. "I'm no fool, Zeke," he says. "I'm already aware of this. I'll find him eventually. The information you provide me today will see to that. But I want to know *everything* about what you Americans have going on on that side of the border. But I appreciate your sudden candor. Do you wish to share anything more?"

Zeke does not. He resumes his silence. It doesn't matter what he says. Nothing will help. Babak *wants* to do this.

"And there I was thinking we were getting somewhere," Babak says. He pats the bottom of Aalem's foot. "Back at it then, I suppose."

CHAPTER FIFTY-EIGHT

The border is far behind them. Tom detours before they can reach Milak, pulls off the road and parks the truck by some trees. The road here is quiet. There's no one around. Tom gets out of the dead Dutchman's clothes and slips back into his own. He gets on the radio and reaches out to Robert.

Robert doesn't answer straight away. Tom spends a couple of minutes hailing him, starting to wonder if Robert and the others are still in the area or if they've cut their losses and shipped back to America.

Still in the cab of the truck, Maryam watches him, concerned.

Tom leans against the truck and looks around, making sure the area remains clear. It is. There are no signs of life anywhere near here. According to the co-ordinates, they continue down the road to find The Abattoir. There'll probably be some off-roading, too, which they may need to leave the truck behind and continue on foot for so as not to give away their approach. The Abattoir will be concealed, Tom has no doubt. It has to be.

"Rollins?" Robert comes on the radio, making no effort to hide the surprise in his voice.

"Captain Dale," Tom says, snapping to attention.

"You're still alive," Robert says.

"I am," Tom says. "And I've found Zeke and Aalem."

"You have them?" Robert's disbelief mixes with surprise.

"Not yet, but we've tracked them down to –"

"*We?*"

"I'm with Maryam Hussain, Aalem's daughter. I found her with Mohammed. He was planning on taking her with him when he went into hiding with the Taliban."

"Where's Mohammed?"

"Dead."

He hears Robert whistle. "You've been busy."

"It's been a long night."

"Where are Greene and Aalem?"

"We've tracked them down to Babak's hideout."

There's a pause. "Say that again?"

Tom repeats it.

"Where are you, Rollins?"

"I can send you the co-ordinates."

"Which country?"

"Iran."

There's another pause. Longer now. "How did you get across the border? Have you made noise?"

"Not at the border, no."

"Tell me how you did it."

Tom tells him. Explains about the Dutch. How they crossed the border in their place. "We're maybe ten or fifteen minutes away from The Abattoir right now. I can send you the co-ordinates."

"Send them, but Rollins, I can't make any promises."

Tom expected this. "We're on our own."

"Probably. I'll have to have a conversation, but don't hold your breath."

"I can't hold this position," Tom says. "I need to get Zeke and Aalem out."

Robert says nothing to this.

"I can't wait, Captain. I have to get moving again. I'll send you the location."

"You've gotta do what you've gotta do, Rollins," Robert says. "Good luck to you."

"They're not coming?" Maryam asks as Tom puts the radio down.

He climbs back into the truck. "There were no guarantees," he says. "But that was always a possibility." He starts the engine and pulls away from under the trees. "We've been on our own up to now, and we've come this far. We'll find a way in and we'll find a way back out again." He holds a hand out to her. She takes it. He squeezes her fingers to reassure her. "You trust me?"

Maryam nods. "Of course."

"Then let's get this over with."

CHAPTER FIFTY-NINE

Robert looks at Simon and Nathan.

"Sounds like we're all losing the bet," Simon says.

Nathan sneers and his fingers instinctively dab at his nose where Tom hit him.

"Not quite," Robert says. "Not yet. Get up. We need to see Bill."

Bill Irving isn't far. They find him in his temporary quarters, lying back on his cot, fingers laced behind his head. He stares thoughtfully at the ceiling, turning his face and raising an eyebrow as they enter.

"We have news," Robert says. "From Rollins."

Bill sits up. "He's still alive?"

"He's found Babak."

Bill stands. He tilts his head. "What? Tell me everything."

Robert does, telling him what Rollins told him on the radio.

Bill folds his arms, stroking his chin while he listens, his eyes narrowed. He doesn't say anything until Robert is through. "He's in *Iran?*"

"That's what he said," Robert says.

Bill falls silent again, staring at the ground while he thinks. "And he wants us to get him out."

"That was the request. Potentially to give assistance in liberating Zeke Greene and Aalem Hussain, too."

"From the hideout. Babak's hideout. It's called The Abattoir?"

"That's what he said."

"The name makes sense, at least." Bill begins to pace. "I've been trying to find him for years," he says, quietly, more like he's talking to himself than the room. He stops, shaking his head, grinning to himself. He looks at Robert. "This is a golden opportunity we've been presented with. We need to call in more forces for assistance. We can't use the soldiers – more black operatives, like yourselves. This has to be entirely clandestine. We take soldiers, it's going to look like an invasion. We can't have that."

"You want to go in?" Robert says, a little surprised. "You want to help Rollins?"

"I want Babak," Bill says. "I've hunted the son of a bitch for years. This is our chance. Rollins is going in whether we're there or not. If Babak doesn't die today, he'll find a new hideout. Security will tighten all along the border. We may never get another chance like this again to finally deal with this butcher once and for all."

"It's not even midday yet. It's not like we can wait for the cover of darkness – it's still hours away. Rollins is going to make a move, and he's going to make it soon."

Bill nods. He understands this.

"There'll be consequences," Robert says.

"Fuck the consequences," Bill says, the most animated that Robert has seen him. "There'll be a furor, certainly, but Babak shouldn't have crossed the border into Afghanistan in the first place. He's killed our people – he's *captured* our people. They can't be shocked if there's retaliation. It has to be expected. We just have to be careful that this doesn't become an international incident. This is why we can't use soldiers. We localize any assault to The Abattoir. We don't get into an altercation with the border."

"We'll have to fly over," Robert says. "But doing that, we run the risk of being shot out of the sky. We'll need crossing points that aren't so heavily guarded."

"I have places," Bill says. "Locations where security isn't so tight. They might take us out the way a little, add a little extra time to our journey, but it'll ensure we get there in one piece. We zip over, and it'll have to be low so as not to alarm their radar. But we get in, we get our people, we get *Babak*, and we get out."

"I'll take point on this," Robert says. "They're members of my team."

Bill nods. "Gear up and get ready. Alert the pilots, give them the co-ordinates Rollins has sent you. I need to make some calls. Any operatives in the area, I'm calling them in. Let's nail this bastard."

CHAPTER SIXTY

Babak is enjoying himself. He's enjoying the sound of Aalem's screams. He's enjoying the smell of his blood, and the feel of the scalpel in his hand as it cuts through the delicate flesh of Aalem's foot.

He's not enjoying Zeke's continued stoicism so much, but he's looking forward to seeing how stoic he's able to be when he's up here in Aalem's place. That prospect in itself is enough to bring an expectant smile to Babak's face.

But then there's an interruption, and he doesn't enjoy that very much, either.

Babak looks up at the guard hovering nearby, trying to get his attention. "What is it?" Babak snaps, irritable, as if he's been interrupted while making love and he's close to climax.

"I must speak with you, sir," the guard says.

"Then speak." Babak makes no effort to hide his annoyance.

"Outside," the guard says.

It must be important. Babak notices how Zeke has picked

up on this, too. How he's watching the guard intently, listening to a language he doesn't understand but will no doubt get Aalem to translate as soon as Babak has left the room.

"Get another guard in here," Babak says. "I don't want these two talking."

When another guard enters, Babak leaves the room. The guard who summoned him waits until the door is closed and the men inside can't hear. "Bram de Groot is in contact," the guard says.

Babak shrugs. "Okay."

"He's demanding to speak to you. He will not speak to anyone else."

"What's happened? Is there a problem?"

The guard shakes his head. "He won't speak to us."

Babak pushes past the guard, heading down the corridor. "I'll take the call in my quarters." He peels bloodied gloves from his hands as he goes, dumping them in the corridor for someone else to pick up as they pass.

Babak takes a seat at his desk and picks up the call. "Bram? Is the crossing not to your satisfaction?"

"I've only just made it to the fucking border," Bram says. He sounds furious. The tone takes Babak aback. He's never heard Bram express any form of emotion. He'd begun to suspect the man was a robot. "We were ambushed."

"*What?* By whom?"

"An American. He's killed my men, all of them. I was able to get away. At the time, I thought there would be more of them. It was just the one man. If I'd known that, I would have confronted him. He destroyed one of my trucks and took the other."

Babak's spine stiffens. "Where is he now? Which direction did he go?"

"He drove away from the border, but I've spoken to the guards here and he's passed through. Like I said, when he left me he was going in the other direction; he must have doubled back for some reason. He may no longer be alone."

"How long ago did he pass?"

"About half an hour, they say."

"Was he one of the Americans from last night?"

"I vaguely recognized him. He was dressed the same as the others, and I believe I saw some of the others drag him away during the ambush. He obviously did not go far, and perhaps the others did not, either."

Babak slams a hand down on the desk. "He's in Iran?"

"He'll be coming for you."

"How could he know where I am?"

"He had one of our trucks. He had our electronics. You discussed your location with me."

"You're saying he could have hacked them?"

"I don't know the man, Babak. But why would he have crossed the border otherwise?"

"If he passed through a half-hour ago, he cannot be far from here."

"That's why I'm calling you."

Babak curses.

"Send someone to pick me up," Bram says. "I want this man. He killed my men. My friends. I must kill him in turn."

"I have men near the border already. I'll contact them. They'll bring you straight to me."

"Tell them to be fast," Bram says. "I want to get there before the killing begins."

CHAPTER SIXTY-ONE

Tom pulls the truck off the road and conceals it behind a rocky outcrop. He runs back to the road to make sure it can't be seen. Satisfied, he returns for Maryam and the guns.

He makes sure both the AK47 and the MP5 are fully loaded. He has a couple of spare magazines for each of them. He checks the Glock Maryam has. She emptied a good portion of the magazine into Mohammed. He exchanges it for a magazine from his tactical vest.

"I need to get a good look at this place before I can decide on a plan of attack," Tom says. "When the time comes, you might have to stay behind, in cover."

"You'll need me when you get inside," Maryam says. "To find your way around. To read any signs. To ask questions."

"I know," Tom says. "But I need to see the place first. If it's too fortified, I'm not going to risk leading you to your death."

Maryam doesn't object. Tom thinks she understands that he's not trying to push her aside and leave her behind.

Where they're going, it's going to be dangerous. They just don't have any idea yet how dangerous it might be.

They start moving, staying away from the road. Tom travels at a light jog. Maryam is able to keep up with him. Tom has the AK47 strapped to his back and the MP5 in his hands. He prefers the MP5 to the AK47. It's more reliable. The latter, though, has a longer range. When they actually reach The Abattoir he might have to swap them out.

Tom spots another rocky outcrop up ahead, dotted with trees and bushes, and a dip beyond it. They're gaining on the co-ordinates. This must be the place. They slow as they near the outcrop. Tom motions for Maryam to duck low and they crawl through the bushes and trees together. He looks down into the dip.

Two klicks away, at the bottom of the dip, concealed from the surrounding area, is a building. It would look like a nondescript one-floor office building, were it not for its location. Smaller than a superstore, but bigger than a bodega. Its stonework is sun-bleached. The roof is flat. It has windows, but they're all obscured. Some of them have bars over them. Outside the building, toward the rear, is a mix of parked vehicles. No road leads here, and the cars and trucks are all dirt-spattered and coated in dust.

Tom ponders on its size. There could be a lot of men inside. A couple of dozen, at the least. And Zeke and Aalem could be anywhere in there.

There are some men outside, on patrol. They cover all four points of the building. They're thorough. More thorough than the Dutch were at their campsite last night. Tom wonders if this is how it always is. If they're always so careful. He wonders, too, if they've found out by now that he's in the area, that he's on his way. If Bram has managed to get in contact.

There's a couple of guards posted on either side of the main entrance. A man on each face of the building, and two who walk a slow patrol around the perimeter. Tom spots men on the roof, too. Covering all four points. They lie flat, under blankets to conceal themselves and keep cool, protecting themselves from the merciless sun. Tom spots their slight movements, though. Sees the glint of their rifles. In all, he counts eleven men outside.

"There's so many of them…" Maryam says, her voice a whisper.

Tom doesn't answer. He's thinking. He can't just storm the place, but nor can he wait around for nightfall. Their people don't have that long. He needs to get in there, ASAP. He studies the men and their weaponry. The guards not on the roof carry Masaf-2s. They have handguns on their hips; probably PC-9s. He spots that they also have grenades strapped to their fronts. A couple on each man. The grenades catch his interest. They could come in useful. Tom can't tell what the men on the roof have; their weapons are obscured under their blankets. Watching, he starts to formulate a plan.

His thoughts are interrupted by his radio. He's being hailed. Tom slides back from the edge of the bushes to answer it. It's Captain Dale. Maryam slides back with him, lying close, listening in.

"Rollins, Bill Irving has given the go-ahead," Robert says. "We're coming in for you and the others."

"That was a quick turnaround," Tom says. "I'm glad to hear it."

"Let's not get ahead of ourselves. It's still going to take us a couple of hours to get there. We're waiting on reinforcements getting here."

"You're coming in force?" Tom asks, surprised considering Robert's earlier reticence.

"We're bulking out our numbers," Robert says. "Specialists only. No uniforms. We're already prepared to have an incident on our hands, but we don't want it to spiral into a gross misunderstanding. We need to keep this situation controlled. Where are you now?"

"We're at the location. Scoping it out."

"What do you see?"

Tom tells him.

"What are the chances of you holding your position until we get there?"

"No can do," Tom says. "We have people in there, and every second counts."

Robert pauses a moment before saying anything else. "When this is over, Rollins, you and I are going to have a long conversation about chain of command and how to follow an order."

"And I'll listen intently, sir, and we can both hope that nothing like this ever happens again."

Robert laughs. "You're lucky I ain't a stickler for rules, Rollins. But let me tell you this. If you survive today, if you ever go against my orders like this again, I'll kick your ass."

Tom grins. He'd assumed that striking a colleague – even if technically Nathan had been the one to hit him first – and insisting on returning into enemy territory to rescue another would have put an end to his brief and unofficial career with the CIA. It sounds like Robert is saying otherwise.

"We'll see you soon," Robert says. "Try to stay alive until then."

Tom puts the radio away. Maryam is looking at him. She looks back through the bushes, to The Abattoir. "What are we going to do?" she asks.

"I have an idea," Tom says. "It's loud and it's reckless, but it's the only way I can see us getting in there. First, we need to go back and get the truck."

CHAPTER SIXTY-TWO

Babak has contacted his Taliban allies. They sent seven men to collect Mohammed and Maryam last night. They never came back.

"Mohammed isn't with you?" Babak demands.

"That's what I said. None of them have come back. We're still in the process of searching the area."

Babak resists the urge to hurl the radio across the room. He grips it tightly, speaks into it through gritted teeth. "This would have been very helpful to know before now."

"Mohammed insisted on bringing the woman with him. We assumed he wanted to have some fun first. We saw no cause for concern. It was this morning, when we heard nothing from them, when we couldn't get in touch, that we became worried and decided to make our way out there."

"It matters very little now," Babak says, "but keep me updated." He puts the radio down, pushes it away from himself.

He's placed the building on high alert. Doubled the

guards outside. Ensured that everyone is heavily armed, and that the men inside are prepared for anything, too.

The Abattoir is a hard building to find. It's even harder to get inside of. No one can approach without being seen from at least a mile away. Babak knows he shouldn't be so concerned, but the fact that a seemingly lone American has come this far already, wiping out Bram's team, getting across the border, and potentially tackling the Taliban en route, too, doesn't sit right with him. The man is obviously dangerous. Whether he's on his own or has a team with him, Babak cannot underestimate him.

He spoke to the border guards who let the American through. They told him the American was not alone. There was a woman with him. She claimed to be one of Khan's mistresses. Babak does not need to contact Khan to know that the woman has nothing to do with him. He wonders who she might be. He wonders if she could be Aalem's daughter.

Babak knows about Maryam. Knows what she looks like. He knows everything about Aalem and his home life – it's a vengeance he's longed for ever since Aalem's betrayal. And if Mohammed is not with the Taliban, it stands to reason that the American intercepted them, and that Maryam is with him. And that Mohammed is dead.

Still, it shouldn't make too much difference. If the only backup the American has is Maryam Hussain, then that's nothing to be concerned about. It's not like she has any kind of military background. She wasn't even one of Bill Irving's assets. She's no threat.

In fact, as frustrating as this situation may be, Babak has an opportunity to turn this in his favor. Another American to capture, and the woman, Maryam, another tool to facilitate their talking. She'll certainly make Aalem scream everything he knows, though Babak feels like the minor torture he's administered to his foot is doing a good enough job of that already.

They'll have to leave this place, of course. And fast, once they've dealt with the potential threat. If the American has found Babak's location, he'll have sent those co-ordinates back over the border. Back into the waiting, eager, grubby hands of Bill Irving. And if the American is nearby, Babak can't take the risk of him following them to a new hideout. This problem needs to be squashed here, and as quickly as possible.

Bram is on his way, though. It won't be long before he arrives. This gives Babak some confidence. The American may have killed the rest of Bram's team, but this will just make Bram extra motivated. Babak will feel safer with Bram around.

Well, Bill Irving may have won this round, but once Babak has regrouped, he will redouble his efforts to nail the bastard. Bill Irving upon his gurney will be the sweetest flaying of them all.

Babak returns to his torture room. He barks orders at the men standing guard on the prisoners. They roughly drag Aalem from the gurney and throw him back into his cage. Aalem lands on his side and grabs at his bloody foot, holding it tight at the ankle, too scared and too pained to touch it anywhere near where it's wounded. Too terrified at seeing what is beneath his skin.

Zeke watches them all. Babak grows annoyed at his blank expression, but he ignores it for now. They leave the men in the room, locking the door on them.

"Get to the surveillance room," Babak says to one of his

men. "Watch the prisoners. No matter what, don't take your eyes off them. The rest of you, help the others. Fortify the building. If anyone attempts to approach, I want them cut off at the knees before they can get within ten feet." He pauses, then adds, "But keep them alive. Wound them if you have to, but I want them for my gurney."

CHAPTER SIXTY-THREE

Zeke stares at the locked door. Babak came in and out, hurrying. The fastest that Zeke has seen him move.

He turns to Aalem. "How you holding up?"

Aalem responds through his teeth, clutching tight to his ankle. "As well as can be expected."

"You did well up there."

"Don't lie to me, Zeke," Aalem says. "If I had the information he wanted I would have given it to him a long time ago." He breathes deeply through his nose, letting go of his ankle and pushing himself up so he's seated, pressing his back against the side of the cage. "You won't speak, will you?"

"No, Aalem." Zeke shakes his head sadly. "I'm sorry, but I won't. And when he has me up there, I won't talk then, either."

"We will both die here."

Zeke looks toward the locked door. "Maybe..."

Aalem picks up on his protracted silence. "What?"

"Something has him spooked," Zeke says. "You might've

been distracted when he came in, but I was watching him. Something has disturbed him. He wasn't himself."

"What could disturb a man like him?"

"I don't know, but it's enough to drag him away from us. Whatever it is, it must be something big."

CHAPTER SIXTY-FOUR

Bram arrives at The Abattoir. Babak greets him at a side door, ushering him in. He points to the two men who have escorted Bram here and tells them to help the others. "Did you happen to pass anything or anyone on your way here?" he asks Bram.

Bram shakes his head. "No," he says. "The area is quiet. But there's nowhere else for him to go. He must be coming here."

"And it was just one man? You're sure of that?"

"I know what I saw," Bram says, eyes coldly drilling into Babak's. "And I've already told you. There may have been others. He may have gone to collect them. But when he attacked us, it was just the one." Bram breathes deeply, nostrils flaring. "I lost my men. I lost my *haul*."

"Khan will replace it," Babak says. "I'll talk to him."

"It's beside the point." Bram is seething. Babak is glad to see it. "If he comes here, I will end him."

"I need him alive."

Bram stares at him.

"But you can help me hurt him," Babak says.

"That will suffice."

"There's a woman, too."

Bram frowns. "And does she need to be taken alive, also?"

"It would be for the best."

"Very well. But I witnessed this man fight. He was brutal. Cold-blooded. If it comes down to me or him, I will not hesitate."

"Do what you have to."

Bram looks around, at the corridor, at the ceiling. "The Americans will know about this place by now. You are aware of that, yes?"

"Yes. And when the American makes his move, we'll be out of here. I can't run the risk of him following. Speaking of, did you see which of the Americans it was?"

Bram nods stonily. "I saw. Rollins."

"Rollins?" Babak repeats, surprised. "From what Mohammed was able to find out, Rollins was the youngest member of the team, and the newest. You're sure?"

Bram leans closer. "I watched him kill five of my men," he says, his breath hot on Babak's face. "I know who it was." He pulls away, looking around again. "I need weapons. I lost mine in the crash."

Babak leads Bram to the armory. On the way, one of Babak's men hurries up to him. "Sir, the Taliban have been in touch. They found their men. All dead. No sign of Mohammed."

Babak dismisses him, unsurprised.

Bram demands a translation from Babak. He listens with a raised eyebrow. "For the youngest and newest, it seems that Rollins was very busy last night. He's come far."

"And this will be as far as he comes," Babak says. "He's so desperate to rescue his comrades? He can join them in my torture room. Wherever I have to settle next, he will join me there, and I will take much pleasure in flaying them all. He should have fled with the others when he had the chance."

Bram turns to enter the armory, but he pauses and turns, head cocked. "What's that? What's happening?"

Babak listens. He can hear raised voices crying out in alarm. They sound like they're coming from the front of the building. From outside, but the panic is spreading, getting inside.

"I don't know," Babak says. "I'll find out."

He steps away from Bram, but he doesn't get far.

There's an explosion.

The building is rocked.

The cries of alarm turn to screams.

CHAPTER SIXTY-FIVE

At the truck, Tom tore the sleeve off the dead Dutchman's sweater, the clothes stashed under the seats after he'd changed back into his own. He drove the truck back to the outcrop, but paused at the side of it, where the dip led down to The Abattoir. He killed the engine while he worked.

With the sleeve, he went to the gas tank. He forced the sleeve down the tube until he was sure it must have reached the fuel. Pulling it back out, he found it dripping. He squeezed the excess back down the tube and then spun the sleeve around, forcing the opposite end down into the tank until only the soaked end protruded. While he did this, he sent Maryam into the bushes, to find a long branch they could wedge against the accelerator.

The truck, luckily, was an older model with a cigarette lighter. Tom pressed it in while he waited for Maryam to return. It didn't take her long. She returned with a dead branch over her shoulder, almost six feet long and sturdy. Tom took it from her and put it into position, making sure it was long enough to do what they needed. Wedged against the chair and the headrest, and the other end against the accelerator, it was perfect.

"Start heading that way," Tom said, pointing east. "I'll catch you up."

Maryam turned and trotted off, staying away from the edge of the dip. The cigarette lighter ejected, hot. Tom started the truck's engine, then took the lighter to the soaked sleeve. He pressed it to the end until the fuel caught the flame. He had to work fast. He went to the front of the truck and wedged the branch into place. The engine roared. The door still open, Tom prepared to jump back. He pushed the stick into drive, then leapt clear.

The truck took off. It trundled over the lip of the dip and picked up speed as it descended. Tom started following Maryam, pulling the AK47 from his back, swapping it out for the MP5. He needed the range.

Through the trees and bushes, as he passed, he saw the truck heading straight for the building, still picking up speed. He saw the gas tank flaming. The guards had spotted it. They were panicking.

Tom catches up to Maryam. They see the truck make contact with the front of the building. It explodes, bursting into flame. The men there dive and duck for cover. Tom sees the men on the roof distracted, looking back. One of them has gotten to his feet to investigate what's happened. Tom drops to a knee, levels the AK47, and shoots him first.

He deals with the rest of the men on the roof, firing tight bursts and picking them off one by one before they realize what's happening. He deals with the man standing guard at the east side, too. The others have been distracted by the explosion. The sound of the burning truck disguises Tom's gunshots.

Maryam stays low. She stays behind him, like he told her to. She carries his magazines. Tom reaches back and she places one into his hand. He quickly reloads and they descend toward the building, Tom keeping the rifle raised and scanning the area. This side is clear. They're covering the front, expecting a follow-up attack. Tom won't have long before they realize there isn't one coming.

Tom goes to the body of the east-side guard and quickly looks him over, plucking the grenades from him as he does so. The bullets of his Masaf-2 are not compatible with either of Tom's rifles. Tom leaves the rifle for now. He figures if he's going to need an extra rifle than the two he's already carrying, there'll be plenty of opportunity to pick one up. He motions for Maryam to press herself against the wall and get low.

The guard at the rear of the building has kept his position. He watches the area, as he's supposed to. Tom pulls the pins on the two grenades and rolls them under a couple of the vehicles parked nearby. They explode. One of them flips a car. Tom runs toward the rear of the building. The guard is coming to investigate. Tom cuts him off, tackling him to the ground and cracking him across the jaw with the stock of the AK47. It subdues him enough. This guard also has two grenades. Tom takes them. He scans the back of the building. There's a rear door. He points to it and tells Maryam to check it.

Tom returns to the corner and rolls another grenade under one of the parked trucks. It touches off the gas tank and it erupts into a fireball. Tom takes the remaining grenade and tosses it around the west side of the building. With luck, he's created the illusion that they're being attacked from all sides. This was the plan; the only option he had. To be brazen. To be so brazen that they couldn't believe this could possibly be the work of just one man. He can hear men shouting. He hears gunfire, though none of it is coming his way. They're panicking. He's spooked them.

"It's locked," Maryam says.

Tom looks down at the guard. He disarms him and then pats him down. He doesn't have a key. Tom hauls him to his feet and forces him against the wall. He's still dazed from the earlier blow. Tom presses the barrel of the rifle into his throat. This wakes him up fully.

"Where are Zeke and Aalem?" Tom asks, talking quickly.

Maryam translates. Her eyes go wide when the guard responds. "He says they're in the torture room."

"Where is it?" Tom says.

"Down the corridor on the east side of the building, fourth door from the front, on the right. He says it's marked 'Interrogation'."

Tom taps on the wall directly behind the man. "This side? Down this way?"

Maryam translates and the man does his best to nod frantically with a rifle in his throat.

Tom shoots him. Blood blows out the back of his head, extra red against the sun-bleached wall. He doesn't have the time, or the inclination, to keep prisoners, especially not when they're complicit with what has been occurring within this building.

Tom goes to the locked door. He levels the AK47, aiming it at the lock. He fires into it until the magazine is empty, then switches it for the MP5. He kicks the door open. Makes sure it's clear beyond. It is. They head in.

CHAPTER SIXTY-SIX

Zeke and Aalem hear the explosion. They feel it shake the building. They look at each other.

Soon after, they hear the other explosions. They hear the gunfire, too. They can hear men running past the door outside, shouting loudly.

"Your team?" Aalem asks, sounding hopeful.

"Maybe," Zeke says, but he has no way of knowing. He hears more people run past the door. He looks toward the camera. To its blinking red light.

"This must be what alarmed him," Aalem says. "What scared Babak."

Zeke stares at the camera. Another opportunity. A final opportunity, perhaps. The men watching them, the men on the other side of the camera, they have to be distracted by the sounds of battle, too. They may even have been drawn into it, the fight more important than watching the prisoners.

Zeke pushes himself away from the cage door. He lies flat and reaches up, linking his fingers through the roof of the cage, bracing himself. He starts kicking at the door, kicking at it as hard as he can, throwing all of his weight into it.

Aalem sees him. He understands. He kicks at his own door, though he's only able to use his left foot and he's not as effective.

Zeke lifts his weight from the ground and he throws both boots at the door. He does it again and again. The bars are beginning to bend.

CHAPTER SIXTY-SEVEN

Tom ducks back behind a corner, an arm pressed against Maryam's chest to hold her in place. Gunfire from a couple of Masaf-2s comes their way, biting into the wall and floor where he previously stood.

From the directions the guard gave them outside, they don't have far to go. It's going to be a bloody battle to get there, however. Tom looks to his left, down the corridor toward the west face of the building. Opposite to where they want to go. He sees a man emerge. Tom drops to a knee and fires at him, putting him down. He turns back and fires the MP5 one-handed, blindly around the corner at the two men down there, then grabs Maryam and heads to the left.

"We might have to take the long way round," he says.

He checks the fallen man, but he's not carrying any grenades. He figures maybe only the guards outside were equipped with grenades. He checks the corridor. Sees a couple of men rushing in the other direction, toward the front of the building. Tom starts to move but he pauses and pulls back when he sees a door open and a couple more men emerge. They're each heavily armed. They run in the same direction as the other two.

Tom heads toward the room they've come out of, MP5 raised. Maryam stays close. She watches his back, looking back down the corridor from the direction they've just come. Tom gets to the door and kicks it open, sweeping the room. It's clear.

The room is the armory. He sees where the Masaf-2s should be, but most of them are missing. There are handguns, too – PC-9 ZOAF; the Iranian version of a Sig Sauer P226. There are crates of ammunition. There are grenades. And also, what catches Tom's eyes, there are RPG-7s. There should be five. Three of them are missing, no doubt taken to the front of the building for defensive purposes.

Tom grabs a couple of the grenades, handing them to Maryam, then takes down one of the RPG-7s. "We're gonna make a lot of noise," he says.

She says nothing. She's never been in a battle like this before. Tom reckons that as far as she's concerned they've *already* made a lot of noise.

They leave the armory. The corridor is clear, for now. Tom leaves the RPG with Maryam, then jogs back to the corner from where they came. He sees the two men he held at bay cautiously making their way forward. He fires upon them with the MP5. They scatter. Tom manages to drop one of them. He puts another grouping into him when he's down to make sure he stays that way. The other man gets around the corner, to safety. Tom looses off a few more rounds to pin him into place, then hurries back and picks up the RPG. He heads down the corridor, in the direction the men he saw running from the armory were going. Things outside must have calmed by now, he thinks. By now they must be realizing that the outside of the building is not under attack, that the assault at this point has moved *inside* the building. They'll soon be doubling back. Come searching for him and Maryam. Overwhelm them with their numbers. Tom needs to keep them on their toes.

He gets to the front of the building and sees where the burning truck has burst through the front entrance, destroying the doors. Tom doesn't see any casualties from it. He sees a few men standing around it on the inside of the building, and he can see a couple more outside, through the gaps between the building and the truck. One of the men inside is spraying it with a fire extinguisher.

Tom can hear gunshots coming from further back in the building. Automatic fire. He doesn't know who's shooting, or at what. Part of him wonders if his assault has confused them to the point that they're shooting at each other. He hopes so. He could never rely on a quiet, stealthy approach for this attack. There are too many men. He needed chaos.

And now, he needs to add to that.

"Hey," he says, getting the attention of the men at the front of the truck.

They spin at the sound of his voice, already raising their rifles, alarmed at hearing English and knowing nothing good can come from it.

Tom already has the RPG shouldered. He fires it toward the front of the truck; a solid target for it to detonate against. Before it can, he's already dropped the RPG, grabbed Maryam, and is running back down the corridor.

They hear the explosion behind them. Hear men screaming. Not for the first time, the building is shaken. Tom takes one of the grenades from Maryam. He pulls the pin. As they pass the armory, he throws it inside, toward the other grenades. They keep running. When they reach the end of the corridor, Tom takes point again, MP5 raised and ready. The corridor is clear.

The armory explodes.

CHAPTER SIXTY-EIGHT

Babak stays close to the ground in his quarters, PC-9 ZOAF held tight and pointing toward the door. He's on the radio, contacting Farhad Gorji.

"We're under attack!" he barks when Farhad responds. "We need reinforcements, right now!"

"Attack from whom?" Farhad asks. Babak doesn't appreciate his calm tone. This is an emergency. It calls for some speed. For some alarm. Some panic.

"We haven't spotted them yet, but it has to be the Americans."

"How many?" Farhad asks.

Babak thinks quickly on what Bram said. One man. One American, along with Aalem Hussain's daughter.

But that can't be right. Babak can hear explosions, gunfire from all directions. How could one man storm The Abattoir? It's inconceivable. There has to be a team of them. An army, maybe. And besides that, Babak could never tell Farhad that they're being besieged by one man and a woman. Farhad would laugh in his face. He would never send help.

"I don't know – a dozen, at the least," Babak says. "We need men, and we need them fast."

"Wait," Farhad says. He's silent a moment. Babak thinks he can hear him talking off the radio. He comes back on. "I'm sending men to your location. They're under instructions to eliminate any Americans they find. They'll escort you and your men out of there after."

"Good, that's good."

"I've called on men close to your location. It won't take them long to arrive."

Babak is nodding as if Farhad can see him. "Good. We'll be bringing the captives with us."

"They haven't talked yet?"

"Not yet. But Zeke was always going to take time."

"I'm surprised at you, Babak. Are you losing your stomach?"

Babak grits his teeth. "Nothing could be further from the truth. You'll be able to see for yourself soon enough. I'll see you in Tehran." Babak puts down the radio. He listens to the explosions. Plaster falls from the ceiling. The whole building feels as if it's about to collapse in on itself.

His door swings open and Babak raises his handgun, but he quickly lowers it as Bram enters. He's armed with a Masaf-2. He holds it across his chest. When he sees Babak lowering the gun, he frowns.

"You should have knocked," Babak says. "I could have shot you!"

Bram snorts. "Things are wild out there. I cannot find the American. Too many explosions. Too much gunfire."

"There has to be more than one of them," Babak says.

"I haven't seen any."

"What are my men shooting at? *Each other?*"

"They're scared," Bram says. "This American has scared them. They can't see him. He's like a phantom. It's making them jumpy. I wouldn't be surprised if some of your men have killed each other by mistake. That's why I came here." Bram looks around the room. "What are you doing? Hiding?"

"I've called in reinforcements."

"We don't need them," Bram says. "I can deal with this problem myself. You need to get your men under control. Rally them. Tell them to follow me, and to do as I say."

"That's easier said than done," Babak says. "And the reinforcements are coming whether you think we need them or not. They're going to get us out of here. This location has been compromised."

"They're not going to arrive in the next five minutes," Bram says. "There is still plenty of fighting to be done before then. Fighting and killing."

"If it's Rollins, I said I wanted him alive."

"That may not be an option."

"Fine – then can you get Zeke and Aalem for me? Bring them back here."

"Very well. Where are they?"

"They're in my torture room." Babak gives him directions.

"And what are you going to do? Remain here in hiding?"

Babak grits his teeth. He doesn't like what Bram is implying. Like he's calling him a coward. "No," he says. "I will corral my men. Get them under control. Coordinate our fight back against the Americans – whether it's just one of them, or a whole damn group."

"Try not to get shot," Bram says, making for the door.

"Same to you."

"I was talking about your own men."

Babak says nothing to this.

"I will see you back here," Bram says. "When I have the captives." He heads back out to the battle.

CHAPTER SIXTY-NINE

Zeke's boots burst through the cage door. No one has come to stop him yet. He quickly scrambles free and goes to Babak's tool table, taking down a couple of instruments to pick the padlock. Before he can start, the door to the room begins to open.

A recognizable guard enters, Masaf-2 raised, but Zeke charges him, closing the distance between them and slamming the guard against the wall, wrestling the rifle sideways where it can't do any harm if it goes off. Zeke headbutts him, the guard's nose crunching under the hard bone of his forehead. Pressing both hands to the rifle, he forces it up and presses it to the guard's throat, choking him.

Out the corner of his eye, through the slowly closing door, Zeke hears gunfire. He sees a man run by, but he doesn't come into the room. Zeke sees the look on his face. He's scared. Despite being posted in this butcher's shop, and all of the things he must have heard and borne witness to, he looks scared to be heading into battle.

The door closes. The guard struggles against Zeke, trying

to push the rifle back, get it away from his neck. Zeke drives a knee into his ribs and pushes harder, hearing something crack in the man's throat. Zeke holds the rifle there, almost pushing it all the way through the man's neck, his throat giving way beneath it. The guard's face turns bright red. The blood vessels in his eyes burst, the whites turning red. When Zeke is certain he's no longer breathing, he lets go of the rifle, and the man falls with it.

As Zeke turns, to return to Aalem and get him out of the cage, he feels something strike him in the side of the head. It sends him reeling until he stumbles into his cage, managing to catch himself on it and remain upright. He looks back, thinking he's been struck with a sledgehammer.

Instead, while the blond, granite face is new to him, he spots a familiar figure. From the ambush. The man who knocked him unconscious and captured him.

The man is smiling. "Hello again," he says. He has a Dutch accent.

Zeke realizes the man didn't hit him with anything other than his fist, and his brain is still swimming. And, despite his size, the Dutchman was able to creep into the room through the shut door without Zeke noticing. He was preoccupied with the guard, sure, but that's no excuse, especially not for a man of this size.

The Dutchman glances at the guard Zeke has killed. He has a Masaf-2 of his own, held low. He doesn't point it at Zeke. His smile broadens and he suddenly tosses the rifle to the side. "I know that you are Zeke," the Dutchman says. "My name is Bram. If you have not realized yet, I was the man who beat you into unconsciousness not so long ago. I am also the man who is going to kill the stupid American who has come here today in a vainglorious effort to rescue *you*."

Zeke frowns. All the shooting he's heard, all the explosions, and it's just one man? "Who?" he asks, unable to stop himself.

"Rollins," Bram says, his smile souring. "I saw him. I saw him while he killed my team. Babak wants you alive, but I want *my team* alive. Some things do not work out the way that we want them to. I am going to kill Rollins, and I am going to kill you, for you are *his* team, and he has come all this way for you. You obviously mean something to him." He glances idly at Aalem in the cage. He waves a dismissive hand. "You I don't care about."

Zeke cuts his eyes toward the rifle Bram discarded. "You're gonna kill me, huh? Why'd you drop the gun?"

Bram pops his knuckles. "Because I don't need it," he says. "Because what I am seeking here is satisfaction for Dirk, Hennie, Egon, Jacco, and Johan. I *will* have my satisfaction, and it shall come at your expense, and at Rollins'."

Zeke readies himself. He shakes his head, clearing the cobwebs and the resounding effects of Bram's initial blow. He raises his fists and bounces on the balls of his feet, loosening up, getting ready. Bram hits hard. Zeke is going to have to be fast. He can't withstand too many more of those punches.

Bram's smile returns. He raises his own fists into a boxing pose. "Round two," he says. "This won't take long."

"Second verse ain't gonna be the same as the first," Zeke says.

Zeke moves in, goading Bram into throwing the first punch. The Dutchman doesn't need much encouragement. Zeke, knowing that they're coming, is able to duck the first swing and side-step the second, but Bram is surprisingly fast, and he jabs at Zeke's ribs.

Despite the force of the blow, Zeke is able to keep from doubling over. He stays light on his feet. He manages to pepper in a couple of strikes of his own, to Bram's face and to his body. Bram shrugs them off, like they're the disturbances of an insect. He throws a punch of his own and this time Zeke is too close, and he isn't fast enough, and the fist connects with his chest.

It drives Zeke back and he stumbles against Babak's tool table, falling over the top of it, scattering the instruments. Zeke rolls back, getting back up to his feet in a crouching position. A scalpel gleams nearby. Zeke grabs it.

Bram clucks his tongue, shaking his head. Disappointed. He waves Zeke on, encouraging him to attack with the knife.

Now, as Zeke jabs and strikes with the scalpel, Bram shows off his speed. He moves with the grace of a dancer. And, worse, he doesn't seem to be tiring. After so long locked in the cage, with only a little water and no food, Zeke is struggling. He's breathing hard. His limbs are heavy. And, so far, he hasn't done any damage to Bram. His punches were practically laughed off.

He strikes with a kick, catching Bram on the hamstring. This, at least, elicits a response. Bram cries out and drops a little, his leg almost buckling. Zeke slashes with the scalpel, but Bram ducks it, and he looks angry now. He catches Zeke's arm. He pulls on it, bending it backward. Zeke can feel the joint and bones of his elbow grinding against each other. Can feel them trying not to snap, but knowing they're fighting a losing battle. He feels the scalpel fall from his fingers as pain shoots up and down his arm.

Zeke throws a left into Bram's jaw. Bram absorbs it with gritted teeth, but Zeke notices how some of the pressure in his right arm eases. Just a little, but enough to give him hope.

Zeke strikes him again, and again, and Bram begins to lose focus on the arm. Zeke quickly hooks his head with his left, searching out his throat and putting pressure on it, pulling upward and squeezing.

Bram lets go of his right arm. Zeke grabs a lock with both hands under his chin and is able to squeeze harder now.

With a roar, Bram lifts him and slams him down onto the top of the cage. His cage. Zeke's hold is broken. He coughs with the impact. He looks up in time to see Bram coming at him with both fists in a clubbing blow. Zeke manages to roll aside. Bram's fists bounce off the cage bars. Zeke sees that the sides of them are bloodied. He kicks at Bram's left knee, buckling it. Bram goes down.

Zeke doesn't have long to catch his breath. Bram grabs for him, pushing himself back up, wincing at the pain in his knee. Zeke kicks at his face, across his mouth, bloodying it. He lashes out again and buries his boot into Bram's face, breaking his nose.

Bram falls back, landing at the front of the cage, close to the mangled door Zeke kicked through. The bars of the door are bent out and jagged in places where some of them have broken. Zeke falls on Bram and grabs at his face. Bram, once again, takes advantage of Zeke's weakened state. He rolls onto his side, flipping Zeke onto his back. He grabs at his face and starts pushing it toward the protruding bars. Zeke sees one coming closer to his eye.

In the other cage, he can hear Aalem trying to get free, to come and help. Trying to kick through with his unharmed foot, but he isn't having much luck. Zeke is on his own, and the bar is getting closer to his eye.

Zeke manages to work a leg loose from under Bram and brings it up, driving his knee between his legs. Bram's movements stop at the sharp jolt of pain, and Zeke is able to get an arm free. He jabs a thumb into Bram's left eye. He pushes it in deep, close to the tear duct, forcing it behind the eyeball.

Bram screams and grabs at his arm, but Zeke keeps pushing. He scoops. The eyeball pops out of its socket. It remains in his face, but it bulges. Bram falls back, covering it. Zeke gets his legs up and kicks Bram across the room. He hits the wall and crumples to the ground, cradling his face around his swelling eye. Zeke hears him whimper.

Zeke gets to his feet. Pressing his back against the wall, Bram does the same. He pushes his eyeball back into place, blinking against it. The skin around the eye has blackened. The eye itself is bloodshot, especially where Zeke forced his thumb in. Bram's face twists. He snarls. His shoulders heave. He looks like he's about to charge.

Zeke balls his fists. "Bring it, you big Dutch bitch."

Bram attacks.

He's still fast, and big, and dangerous, but he's damaged now. The fight has taken something out of him, and it's made him sloppy. He's enraged that he's been hurt at all, and it's made him careless. All he can see is red. He almost lost an eye, and this infuriates him.

Zeke stays calm and braces himself as Bram gets closer and closer, arms spread, ready to grab for him. If Bram catches him, it could be game over. He's going to throttle. He's going to beat. He's going to bite down. He looks ready to tear Zeke limb from limb.

As Bram gets close, waiting until the last moment, Zeke ducks down, beneath his closing arms, and braces himself against Bram's legs, sweeping them out from under him.

Bram falls, his momentum carrying him forward. He lands on the damaged cage door. The broken and bent bars drive through his face. Zeke hears him roar in pain. Looks down to see him holding himself up on his hands, but his face is held in place by the bars that have punctured him.

Zeke stomps down on the back of his head, driving the spikes deeper. Bram's body spasms. His hands, his propping arms, go limp. Blood pools beneath his head. He lies still.

CHAPTER SEVENTY

The explosion of the armory felt like it might bring the building down around them, but it remains standing. Tom peers back around the corner and sees that it's blown out the wall opposite the room and the ceiling above. Sunlight streams in through the falling dust and debris.

He wishes he'd been able to watch the building for longer, to know how many men were inside. To know how many are left. He hates heading into a situation blind, but he's deep in the thick of it now. He'll just have to stay the course and remain alert.

He and Maryam press on, back to the end of the corridor where they were earlier pinned down; the corridor with Zeke and Aalem. A shooter earlier took cover here. Tom expects him to still be near. He readies their remaining grenade, pulls the pin and rolls it down the corridor. He hears a panicked cry. The grenade explodes. Tom spins around the corner and sees the man fleeing. Tom shoots him in the back, putting him down. He motions for Maryam to follow.

They make their way down the corridor. Tom counts off the doors. It isn't far now. Almost there.

He spots movement at the end. A familiar face, glancing back at them as he flees. One he hasn't seen in person, but was shown pictures of prior to the mission.

Babak Rashidi. He flees around the corner.

"This is it," Maryam says, pointing at a door. "This is the room."

"That was Babak," Tom says. "I can't let him get away."

Tom starts running. Maryam follows. From around the corner, he can hear shouts in Persian. Tom presses his back to the wall and looks round. A gunshot comes his way and he ducks back into cover, but he saw enough. Babak was gathering men to him. His remaining men, perhaps. They were pushing through the rubble at the front of the building where the truck crashed and the RPG exploded. Tom counted four other men.

He checks the magazine of his MP5, swaps it for a full one. He motions for Maryam to stay behind cover, then he sucks down deep breaths, psyching himself up. He dives from the cover of the corner, rolling through, coming up firing.

Much like this entire siege, the men weren't expecting something so brazen. He catches them unprepared, putting one of them down with his wild gunfire and quickly following up by picking off the remaining three.

Babak isn't with them. He's gotten out of the building and he's running. Tom checks that the outside is clear, and then he chases him down. Tom is faster than him. He tackles him to the ground and they roll through the dirt together. Tom comes up on top. Babak is babbling at him. Tom punches him across the jaw.

There's a gunshot. Tom's head snaps to attention, searching it out. He sees one of Babak's men at the corner of the building, bleeding from a wound to the side of his temple, covered in dirt and dust, looking dazed. He holds a Masaf-2, but he hasn't fired it. He looks down. Blood blooms from the center of his chest. Tom looks to the right, toward the wreckage of the truck. Maryam is there. She holds the Glock two-handed. She keeps it raised until the man falls forward onto his face.

Tom disarms Babak, tossing his PC-9 aside, then hauls him up to his feet. He isn't unconscious. Tom pushes him ahead, the MP5 pressed into his back. Babak walks with his hands raised in surrender. He stares at Maryam as they pass her, but Tom strikes him in the back of the head with the barrel, then sticks it into his back to push him ahead, back into the building.

"How many men did you have in this building?" Tom asks him.

"A couple dozen," Babak says.

As Tom suspected. "Any of them left alive?"

"It doesn't look that way to me. How about you?"

Tom ignores him and pushes him ahead, back toward the torture room. "Are Zeke and Aalem still alive?"

"Last time I checked. Where's the rest of your team?"

Tom says nothing.

Babak turns slightly, eyes narrowed, looking at Tom and Maryam. "It really is just you, isn't it?" He shakes his head like he can't believe this.

They get to the door. "Open it," Tom says.

Babak does. It isn't locked.

"Freeze, motherfucker!"

The voice comes from inside the room. Tom recognizes it. It's Zeke.

"It's us," Tom calls through. "Don't shoot."

"*Rollins?*" Zeke says.

Tom pushes Babak into the room, out of the way, so Zeke can see him. Zeke wields a Masaf-2, lowering it when he sees Tom. Tom quickly looks the room over. There are a couple of dead bodies. A couple of cages. He recognizes one of the corpses as belonging to Bram de Groot. Zeke has been proactive during the battle.

And he sees Aalem, seated on one of the cages. Aalem's eyes go wide when he sees his daughter. She rushes to him, running into his arms. Tom notices how he winces as she makes contact with him. He keeps his right leg outstretched, away from her. Tom can see that his right foot is bare, and bloody.

Before he can investigate further, Zeke asks, "It really is you. What the hell are you doing here?"

"I'm here for you," Tom says.

Zeke grins. "Are you insane?"

"Only if I didn't make it."

Zeke slaps him on the arm, laughing. "Where's everyone else? They still out there?"

"It's just us," Tom says. "The others are on their way."

Zeke blinks, struggling to process. "This was all you?"

Tom nods.

"Who's left outside? How many men?"

"Unsure, but we didn't see any. They could all be dead, but they might not. We'll have to be careful."

"Jesus Christ, Rollins. It sounded like an army was attacking."

"Good. That was the point."

"Your foot!" he hears Maryam exclaim.

Tom turns and gets a good look at Aalem's foot. He can see now why it's bloody. It's been flayed. Strips of skin are absent, exposing what's underneath.

"This bastard's been at him," Zeke says, tilting his head toward Babak.

Maryam slaps him. Babak grunts, unfazed. "Do you expect me to apologize?" he says.

"No," Zeke says, and punches him across the face. Babak falls. "We just want you to hurt."

CHAPTER SEVENTY-ONE

They dress Aalem's foot as well as they're able using the First Aid supplies in Tom's tactical vest and then they leave the torture room together. Zeke straps himself with the Masaf-2 he's taken, then carries Aalem on his back. They take up the rear. Tom has point. Maryam is in the middle of them.

Tom holds tight to Babak, dragging him along one-handed while in his other he wields the MP5. He sweeps the corridor before they exit the room. It's clear. Other than the fires burning and the sound of the building crumbling, Tom can't hear anything else. No men. No gunfire. No further explosions. No one crying out or groaning. No one attacking.

He remains on high alert, scanning every pile of rubble and watching every corner in case anyone is lying in wait. He observes each dead body closely, making sure they're not faking.

They get outside the building, squeezing past the crashed truck. "A couple of the vehicles are undamaged at the side," Tom says. "I'll go and hotwire one."

Zeke lowers Aalem so he can lean against the wall with his weight off his foot. Maryam goes to her father, her hands on one of his shoulders. Aalem clutches them and smiles at her gratefully, trying to put on a brave face. "I'll watch him," Zeke says about Babak.

Tom nods and starts to turn. Zeke stops him.

"Rollins," he says. Tom looks at him. "I won't forget this," he says. "I owe you one. Big time."

"You don't need to worry about it," he says. "And call me Tom."

Tom hurries to the vehicles on the east side of the building. He goes to a Toyota parked furthest away from the others, away from the damage that was done by the grenades he earlier rolled under them. The car is locked. Tom smashes the window on the driver's side and reaches in to unlock it. He brushes the shattered glass off the seat and then lies across it on his side to reach under the steering column and hotwire it. He strips a couple of wires using his knife, presses the exposed fibers together. There's a spark and he hears the engine come to life.

The car has half a tank of gas. It's enough to get them to the border. Enough to get them over it. The real question is *how* they're going to cross the border. If anyone inside was able to radio out during the assault, then the border guards are going to be on high alert. No one in and no one out. There'll be other places to cross, though. The whole border can't be heavily guarded.

The other option is to get clear of The Abattoir and then sit tight. Robert said they were coming for them. They might be another hour or two, or they might have picked up the pace after Tom said he was moving in without waiting. If they can get somewhere and lie low, they can contact Robert and let him know where they are. Tom can discuss their options with the others when he gets back to them.

He reverses the car, but pauses before he can drive down to the front of the building. Something in the mirrors catches his eye. Movement, at the top of the dip. He watches it. Sees the glint of a scope. There's someone up there. Someone is watching him.

Tom puts the Toyota into drive and heads casually to the front of the building. He sees the sun-reflecting scope following his movements, and then it disappears as he stops the car next to the others.

Tom gets out. "Everyone needs to stay calm," he says, "and get into the car as quick as they can."

"What is it?" Zeke asks.

"There's someone up on the ridge," Tom says. He watches Babak while he speaks. "Watching us. Could be reinforcements."

Babak grins. "You're not going to get far."

"You knew they were coming," Maryam says.

Babak smirks at her. "Do you really think you can make the border? And even if you do, so what? You think we won't follow? Just make things easier on yourselves. Give up now."

"We'll make the border," Tom says. "And I hope your people do follow us, because our people are waiting on the other side for them. Zeke, put him in the car."

Zeke does. Tom steps aside, pulling out his radio. Out the corner of his eye, he watches the ridge. The scope is gone, but no one has appeared yet. It won't be long, he's sure. If they're still watching, the important thing is not to let them know he's seen them. Not to act spooked. That will bring them running, and he doesn't know how many there are.

Likely the only reason they haven't attacked yet is because they've spotted Babak is still alive.

Tom gets through to Robert.

"The choppers are starting up," Robert says. "We're gonna be en route to you within five minutes."

Tom is glad to hear this. "I have Zeke and Aalem," he says. "We have Babak Rashidi, too."

Robert whistles. "Rollins, you're something else."

"But listen – there's reinforcements here. They're lying in wait right now, but any minute they're gonna come at us. I don't know what their numbers are or what kind of vehicles they've got. We might not be able to outrun them."

"I'll send you the co-ordinates for where we're crossing," Robert says. "Head there. We'll intercept them."

"You think you can make it fast enough?"

"We're gonna have to."

Tom gets off the radio. Maryam is looking back at him. Her father is in the car, in the back with Zeke and Babak. Babak is squeezed between them.

"The co-ordinates are coming through," Tom says. "You ready to be my navigator?"

"Of course," she says.

Tom hands her his map. "Your father will be all right, Maryam. He looks a little worse for wear right now, but he'll heal."

"He'll need a skin graft."

"For what he's done and what he's gone through, I'm sure our doctors will be happy to help. It's the least we could do. Now we've gotta get out of here."

Maryam gets into the front passenger seat. Tom gets behind the wheel. Zeke is looking back. "Here they come," he says.

Tom glances at the mirror. He sees dust rising beyond the crest of the dip. A moment later, open-topped Jeeps begin their descent. He counts five of them, each of them packed with armed soldiers.

Tom puts the car into drive and slams his foot on the accelerator. They take off. The Jeeps pursue.

CHAPTER SEVENTY-TWO

Tom pushes the Toyota hard up the embankment, back over the lip and onto flat land. It hits the ground hard, throwing them all around inside the vehicle, the back wheels skidding to the side, but he keeps a tight grip on the steering wheel and his foot flat to the floor, straightens it out and pushes on.

To his left, he sees a couple more Jeeps. They held back from the others, racing across the top to cut them off. They're close. Tom yanks on the handbrake and spins the wheel and manages to avoid being sideswiped by the lead Jeep. He spins the wheel the other way and kicks dust and dirt up into the windshield of the second Jeep. He releases the handbrake and straightens the wheel and drives toward the road, momentarily buying some time.

Seven Jeeps total. Five heavily armed soldiers in each. Tom needs to keep ahead of them. Needs to take the lead until they can catch up to Robert and the others. Problem is, he doesn't know how long that might take. And, truthfully, he doesn't know if their rescuers are going to be able to cross the border.

He can't think about that now. He has to keep them all alive.

"You can't outrun them!" Babak calls from the rear. He laughs. "They're going to run you down, and once they do, you're all mine!"

"Shut up!" Aalem says, and silences him with an elbow to the mouth.

They hit the road and the journey smooths out. Tom is able to pick up speed. They won't be able to stay on the road for long, he knows, but they have to make the most of it while they can.

"Two more miles, and then right," Maryam says. "It's going to be rough terrain the rest of the way after that. The Jeeps will have the advantage over us."

Tom can't get his foot any further to the floor. The Toyota is going all-out. He sees the Jeeps regrouping, and the others that descended the dip have ascended now and are joining the others in the pursuit. They spread across the road. Tom can see some of the standing passengers in the rear of the Jeeps taking potshots at them. The rear window shatters. They all duck. Zeke fires the Masaf-2 out of the back window at them, managing to push the Jeeps back a little, give them second thoughts about getting too close. Tom sees one of the soldiers fall from the back of a Jeep and be driven over by one of the followers in the rear.

"The turn is coming," Maryam says.

Tom has to slow the Toyota to keep from tipping and rolling, but he tries to leave it until the last second. He pulls off the road, onto the wild ground, and pushes on for the border.

"It's straight all the way," Maryam says. "Just keep going."

Zeke fires at the Jeeps out the back, firing through the dust that's being kicked up.

Tom drives straight, again pushing the Toyota for all it's worth. They bounce across the ground. He avoids bushes and rocks and dips as best he's able, but it's not always possible. He hears things scraping and grinding against the underside of the car. He grits his teeth tight together, clenching his jaw to keep them from rattling together in his skull. His hands ache on the wheel. He's battling to keep control. The muscles in his arms are tensed and tight.

"RPG!" Zeke warns.

Tom sees it. He swerves hard to the left as it fires and manages to avoid being wiped out as the rocket explodes not far from their rear.

"It seems they don't care too much that you're here," Aalem says to Babak.

Babak has no response for this. He ducks low in the seat, shoulders hunched, trying to avoid being shot in the back of the head.

The Jeeps are getting closer. They travel better over the bumpy ground. The Toyota is struggling. Tom can feel the wheels and the engine clogging with dirt and dust, with small rocks and greenery, the assorted debris that scatters the land.

"They're nearly on us!" Zeke says.

Tom knows. "Then they should be easier to shoot!"

Zeke fires into the lead Jeep, aiming for the driver. The bullets smash through the windshield and the driver bounces in his seat. The passenger tries to grab the wheel, to keep them from veering, but Zeke shoots him, too. The Jeep turns sharply, throwing the men in the back out, and the front of the Jeep plows into the front of the Jeep beside it. It knocks it off-course and the driver struggles to regain control. It tumbles and rolls, wiping out the men inside.

Two down, Tom thinks. But the others promptly take their place. Two might not be enough. Tom can see another RPG being readied.

Tom tries to turn, to avoid it, but the steering is full of grit and sluggish. He can't move fast enough. The rocket explodes on their tail. It flips them.

The Toyota rolls. Tom's body is thrown around. His brain bounces in his skull. He feels Maryam hitting his side as she's tossed around. The Toyota eventually comes to a stop on its roof. It takes a moment for Tom's senses to clear. For his vision to settle.

Beside him, he can hear Maryam whimper. Looking at her, he sees that her left arm is broken. Tom looks back. The Jeeps have stopped. They're holding their position. Tom gets Maryam free and then, holding onto her, crawls out of the car with her, spitting dirt. He's careful not to knock her broken arm against anything.

"We came so far," she says, looking up at him. "We did our best."

"It's not over yet," Tom says.

She doesn't look so sure. She looks back at the Jeeps.

"That's nothing," Tom says, grinning down at her. "We've dealt with worse."

"I'm not so sure."

"You've trusted me this far."

She manages a small smile. "Then I'll trust you all the way."

Zeke and Aalem have gotten out of the car. They come round to the side with Tom and Maryam. Zeke has the Masaf-2. He reaches in and drags Babak out. Babak has banged his head and blood is running down the side of his face. Despite this, he's laughing. "All of this effort, and for what?" he says, looking at Tom. "I told you to give up. This little run was futile. You're all going to die."

Tom looks at the Jeeps. Five of them, filled with men wielding their rifles, just waiting to see what they do next, no doubt expecting them to give themselves up. And they should. There's no other way out. Tom and the others have the MP5, the AK47, the Masaf-2, their handguns, and what few bullets are left for each of them. If they fight, they'll be killed. They can't survive this situation.

Zeke looks at Tom. He's had the same thoughts. "How do you wanna play this?"

Tom looks at Maryam's broken arm. She nurses it in her lap, her back pressed to the rolled car. He looks at Aalem, trying to keep his flayed foot off the ground and failing, grimacing as he does so.

Tom looks at Zeke. He thinks of Zeke's wife, and his son, and his unborn daughter. He thinks of how far they've all come, to still be alive right now, and so close to the border.

"We fight," Tom says. "It's a better choice than the alternative."

Babak has been listening. He snorts. "Then you'll all die."

Tom pulls out his knife. "But not before you."

Before Babak can understand what's happening, Tom grabs a handful of his hair in his left hand and drags him closer, pinning his back against Tom's chest. Babak struggles, but Tom is stronger than him. Tom presses the blade to Babak's hairline. He cuts into it. He scalps him.

Babak screams.

"You like to torture people?" Tom says, though it's

doubtful Babak can hear him over his own screams. "You like to flay them? How do you like it?"

Babak doesn't like it at all. Tom tears the scalp from his skull and dumps it on the ground. He lets go of Babak. The torturer falls to his knees, still screaming, staring at the bloodied matting of his skin and hair in the dirt.

Tom pulls out his Glock. He offers it to Aalem.

Aalem looks tempted, but he shakes his head. "Despite what he did to me, I am not a killer. I don't intend to start with the likes of him."

Tom rolls Babak over. He wants Babak to see him. Babak whimpers at the sight of the gun. Tom shoots him through the face.

Zeke looks back at the Jeeps. "I think they're all a little shocked at what they've seen," he says. "But now they don't look happy about it."

Tom readies the AK47. "Let's give them something else to be unhappy about."

"Look," Maryam says, pointing behind them with her good arm.

They turn, but Tom realizes he can hear it before he sees it. Three Apache attack helicopters approaching in formation, coming in low, followed by a Chinook. The lead chopper fires a rocket toward the Jeeps. The Iranians see it coming. They dive from their vehicles and scatter, fleeing from the explosion and the potential follow-up of more missiles.

The Chinook sets down, covered by the Apaches, which open fire on the soldiers with their 30mm automatic cannons. A couple of teams dismount from the Chinook. Captain Dale, Simon Collins, and Nathan Sapolsky are among them. They hurry toward the upturned Toyota.

Tom reaches down for Maryam, scooping her up from the ground. Zeke grabs her father, wrapping an arm around his shoulders, Aalem leaning into his side to take the weight off his foot.

The team are firing into the remaining soldiers, driving them back. The Iranians return fire, but loosely, sloppily. They're trying to escape. They're not interested in an engagement, especially not against superior forces, and especially not now that *they're* the ones outnumbered.

Robert grins as Tom approaches, Maryam in his arms. "Get to the Chinook, you crazy bastard."

"Gladly, sir."

CHAPTER SEVENTY-THREE

It's a couple of days before Tom is able to visit Maryam and Aalem in the sick bay.

As soon as the Chinook touched down at the base, Maryam and Aalem were whisked away in one direction, and Tom and Zeke were taken in another. Both men were checked over, and both were found, other than for some superficial bumps and scrapes, to be healthy. Then, they needed to be debriefed. And finally, Bill Irving wanted to speak to them both.

They went through their debriefings individually. Tom told them about Khan, the Taliban, and the ex-KCT Dutch drug runners. He told them all about The Abattoir, and what he saw there, and what happened. Tom sits in his temporary quarters and waits for Bill Irving to visit. He plays with the Santa Muerte pendant through his shirt, squeezing it between his thumb and index finger. If he were a praying man, he'd be offering her thanks. As it was, perhaps wearing her had been more than enough.

When Bill finally arrives, he knocks briefly and enters

before Tom can answer. He nods at Tom, then helps himself to a seat. In silence, he looks Tom over, appraising him.

"That was quite a stunt you pulled, Rollins," he says.

"I acknowledge that, sir," Tom says. "But I couldn't leave Greene behind."

"And he's very grateful for that."

"He's told me."

"I'm sure his family is, too."

"I'm not sure they'll ever know about it."

"That's up to Zeke," Bill says. He looks down at his hands, and brushes something from his trousers. "It's a shame you couldn't bring Babak back to us."

"He would have liked to have met you, sir," Tom says.

Bill grunts. "I've heard."

"At the time, I thought we were all as good as dead. I didn't want to give Babak the satisfaction of outliving us. Not after everything he's done."

Bill nods. He understands. "I heard about how you killed him..."

Tom says nothing.

Bill grunts. "Zeke wouldn't say anything about it, either. Other than that, and I quote, *the bastard got what he deserved*. The men who extracted you all, they saw what you'd done. Of course, they didn't know it was you who'd killed him. Aalem told us that."

"The bastard got what he deserved," Tom says.

Bill looks amused. "He's also very grateful to you, by the way. Aalem. He and his daughter both. You've made quite the impression. This is your first operation with the CIA, that's correct?"

"Yes, sir."

Bill grins. "I assume you were told you'll never know what to expect."

"I was told that in the Army, too, sir. How are Aalem and Maryam doing, sir?"

"They're healing. Aalem has had some skin grafted back onto his foot, but it'll take a while before he's able to walk on it again. I offered them both a move to America in return for their service. They turned it down."

"Why?"

"You'll have to ask them yourselves."

When Tom is able to visit them, he does just that. But first, he shakes Aalem's hand, and embraces Maryam. Aalem is confined to a bed. His right foot is in a cast. Maryam shows him her own cast on her arm.

"The doctors said it was a major break," she says. "But it was clean, luckily. I'll be in the cast for a few months, but they say I shouldn't have any issues with it once it's healed. They were able to repair it early enough."

"How does it feel?" Tom asks.

She laughs. "It itches."

Tom takes a seat with them.

"My daughter has told me what you have done for us both," Aalem says. "And she told me…about Mohammed…"

Tom says nothing. Maryam strokes her father's arm.

"I'm sorry that my friend was able to deceive me," Aalem says.

"He deceived a lot of people," Tom says. He asks them about America. About why they didn't take Bill Irving up on his offer.

They don't answer straight away. Tom watches them both. He sees that it was a joint decision.

Maryam speaks first. "Because Afghanistan is our home," she says.

Her father nods. "Things may not be perfect, but it is our home, our country, and we must fight for it. We must fight to make it a better place, the same as everyone else must, no matter where they are."

Tom can understand that. "That's very noble," he says. "Then in that case, I should say goodbye. I don't know how long I'll remain on the base for. I could get shipped back any day now. I might not get another chance to say goodbye."

Maryam looks disappointed, Tom notices. Aalem doesn't pick up on it. "I'm glad we could meet you," he says. He reaches out and holds Tom's hand. "Thank you for saving Maryam from Mohammed. Thank you for keeping her alive."

"She repaid the favor," Tom says. "Neither of you needs to thank me for anything."

He says his goodbyes and makes to leave. Maryam says she'll accompany him out. "I'll be right back, Papa," she says to Aalem.

She leaves the sick bay with Tom. They pause outside of the door, stepping to the side, behind a wall where they can't be seen. Maryam pulls him close to her and they kiss.

"Will you ever come back here?" she asks him when they break.

"It's always possible," Tom says. "And if I am, I'll call by."

"I would like that." She kisses him again. "Until then." She leaves him, returning to the sick bay and her father.

Tom watches her go. He hears a low whistle nearby. He turns to the sound. Robert leans against a wall. He's seen everything.

"I take it the two of you got close while you were out there," he says, a gleam in his eye.

Tom says nothing.

Robert pushes himself off the wall. "Don't look so uptight, Rollins. It happens. And besides, I come bearing good news."

Tom waits to hear what that good news is.

"You and Greene are going home," Robert says. "Pack your bags. You're heading back in a couple of hours. Two weeks of R&R. Use them wisely."

"The rest of you?"

"Well, I think some space might be good between you and Nathan for now. Give him some time to continue cooling off."

"He'll get over it."

Robert laughs. "Maybe he will, maybe he won't. You don't know him very well. Still, he's a professional. We all are. We can work together."

"But the three of you are staying behind for now."

"For now. There's still a few things we need to clear up here, as I'm sure you can imagine." Robert holds out a hand to shake. Tom takes it. "It's been a pleasure to see you work, Rollins. I look forward to seeing what the future holds for us." He doesn't release his grip. He holds it a little tighter. Tom returns the pressure. They look at each other. Neither man backs off. Robert grins. "Just remember what I told you, Rollins."

"I'll remember," Tom says. "Sir."

"Attaboy." Robert lets go of his hand.

CHAPTER SEVENTY-FOUR

Tom is back in America.
 He isn't alone.
 He travels with Zeke. They're in Louisiana, heading for Shreveport. Zeke is driving. Tom is in the passenger seat, watching the scenery as they pass by. He's never been in Louisiana before.
 Zeke turns down onto a quiet street, pulling onto the driveway of a modest house. It has a porch with a sofa and a rocking chair. There's no one out on it.
 "Won't be long now," Zeke says, looking expectantly toward the front door.
 Tom follows his gaze. A moment later, the front door opens. A small boy, Tre, hurries out on unsteady legs, running across the porch toward the steps, coming carefully down them, using his hands to steady himself on the step behind him as he goes. Zeke gets out of the car. Tom follows. Tre's face lights up when he sees his father. He hurries to him. Zeke scoops him off the ground. Tre cackles delightedly.

At the front door, heavily pregnant, stands Naomi. She smiles at the scene, one hand gently stroking her belly.

Tre stares at Tom, eyes wide and curious. Tom smiles at him. Tre giggles and buries his face in Zeke's neck.

"This is daddy's friend," Zeke says, bouncing Tre so he looks up again. "You can call him Uncle Rollins, okay?" Zeke turns to Tom. "Though it might be a while before he says that. He can say mommy, he can say daddy, and he can say baby, but outside of that he's taking his time."

Zeke leads them up the porch. Naomi smiles at Tom as Zeke introduces them. They shake hands.

"So you're the man who rescued my husband," she says.

Tom glances at Zeke. "You told her what happened?"

"I thought about not," Zeke says. "But I tell Naomi everything. I wasn't gonna leave this out."

"It wasn't exactly easy to hear," Naomi says. "But I'm glad it had a happy ending."

"We all are," Tom says.

"It was a very brave thing you did, especially for a man you'd just met." Naomi looks at him. "But I'm grateful you did it." She steps aside and motions for him to enter. "Welcome to our home. Dinner's almost ready."

EPILOGUE

Robert, Simon, and Nathan wait in the cool night, concealing themselves behind a rocky outcrop, watching the distance for signs of approach. They're dressed all in black. They're armed. They're ready in case things turn south.

Bill Irving does not know they're here. No one does.

They're not far from the ambush. From where Mohammed betrayed them. From where Zeke and Aalem were taken by Babak and the Dutch. Robert knows a lot of players were involved in getting the drop on them. The aforementioned players, certainly, but also Khan. The local drug kingpin. The opium grower. The opium seller.

"Heads-up," Simon says, nodding north.

Robert looks. He sees a flashlight signal on and off, three times. Robert returns it. They wait. A couple of minutes go by, and then they hear the approach of vehicles. A couple of Jeeps, by the sounds of it.

As they get close, their headlights come on, casting some light over the area. "Watch my six," Robert says, stepping out from cover with his arms raised so the headlights can pick him out. Simon and Nathan remain concealed. They don't point their rifles, but they have them ready. Robert feels confident having them watch his back.

The two Jeeps slow in front of Robert. A couple of men get out and come to him.

"You have come alone?" one of them asks in fractured English. The other man stands silently behind him, holding an AK47, his eyes roaming across the darkness, alert. The others with them remain in the Jeeps.

"Not alone," Robert says.

The man grins. "Very wise," he says.

"Are you Khan?"

"I am not Khan."

"Where is he? He close?"

The man shakes his head. "You will not meet Khan. Not yet. You talk to me, and then I talk to Khan. If he likes what you say, if he likes what you do, eventually you meet him. Maybe."

"Sure."

"What do you want, American?"

"I want to talk about what's gone down recently," Robert says. "I know you lost a connection. An important one. The Dutchmen. Bram de Groot."

The Afghan says nothing. He watches Robert, waiting.

"He's gone, and you've lost a big-time distributor. You've lost a lot of income because of that."

"Because of an American, I hear. One of yours, perhaps?"

Robert shrugs. "Maybe. Maybe not. These things happen all the time, right? Risk of the business. Risk of the lifestyle."

"We hear that the same American killed Babak Rashidi."

Robert waves a hand. "What was Babak to you? A minor acquaintance. He wasn't even Afghan."

"I feel you know this American."

Robert grins. "Maybe. Maybe not. But I can guarantee this – if I *do* know him, I can keep him under control. And if I can't..." Robert shrugs again. With his fingers he makes a gun and presses it to his temple, mimicking a gunshot. "He'll never see it coming."

He can see the Afghan frowning. "Why should we trust you?"

"I'm not asking for trust," Robert says. "Not straight away. What we're here to discuss is an opportunity. We prove ourselves, and then we're in business. *Then* you can trust."

The Afghan is quiet for a while. He turns to the other behind him and they quietly discuss in their own language. Robert waits. He's patient.

The lead Afghan turns back. He's not frowning anymore, though he remains silent, looking Robert over, still considering. Robert thinks he's willing to give them a shot. "What exactly do you want from us?" he asks.

"A partnership, so to speak," Robert says. "You want to get rich, and we want to get rich. We're offering to take over from Bram de Groot. We're offering to open up an American market for you."

Even through the darkness, he can see the Afghan's eyes gleam hungrily at the prospect. "Does your government know you're here?"

"No one knows we're here," Robert says. "This is for us – me and my companions. We work off the books. No one knows when we're coming or going, or where."

"Why would you take this risk?" The Afghan is asking questions, but he's salivating at the prospect.

"Why do you think? Money. I already told you. To get rich. To put all this shit work behind us and ride off into the sunset."

The Afghan nods. He's trying not to be too eager, but he can't disguise it. "Very good," he says. "Khan will be most pleased with this."

"You're authorized to speak for him?"

"I am."

Robert holds out a hand. "Then what say we make this thing official?"

The Afghan takes his hand. They shake. "We are in business," he says.

Robert smiles. "We sure are, partner."

ABOUT THE AUTHOR

Did you enjoy *Kill Zone*? Please consider leaving a review on Amazon to help other readers discover the book.

Paul Heatley left school at sixteen, and since then has held a variety of jobs including mechanic, carpet fitter, and bookshop assistant, but his passion has always been for writing. He writes mostly in the genres of crime fiction and thriller, and links to his other titles can be found on his website. He lives in the north east of England.

Want to connect with Paul? Visit him at his website.

www.PaulHeatley.com

ALSO BY PAUL HEATLEY

The Tom Rollins Thriller Series
Blood Line (Book 1)
Wrong Turn (Book 2)
Hard to Kill (Book 3)
Snow Burn (Book 4)
Road Kill (Book 5)
No Quarter (Book 6)
Hard Target (Book 7)
Last Stand (Book 8)
Blood Feud (Book 9)
Search and Destroy (Book 10)
Ghost Team (Book 11)
Full Throttle (Book 12)
Sudden Impact (Book 13)
Kill Switch (Book 14)
Choke Hold (Book 15)
Trigger Point (Book 16)
Deep Water (Book 17)
Kill Zone (Book 18)

The Tom Rollins Box Set (Books 1 - 4)

Printed in Dunstable, United Kingdom